# BEYOND AURORA —DREAMSHIP

## A Tale of the Blind Witch

*Frank Tymon*

Writers Club Press

San Jose  New York  Lincoln  Shanghai

*Beyond Aurora—Dreamship*
*A Tale of the Blind Witch*

Published by Writers Club Press
an imprint of iUniverse.com, Inc.

For information address:
iUniverse.com, Inc.
620 North 48th Street
Suite 201
Lincoln, NE 68504-3467
www.iuniverse.com

ISBN: 0-595-09946-7

Printed in the United States of America

*T*o the Program Managers, who get the job done in spite of the problems and the politics

# Epigraph

When I was young—too many years ago—I saw, or now think I saw, a picture of a placid sea. Early morning it was, the sun still slept. The moon, near full, rode low upon the horizon. Fog rose, drifted, spread, lightened by the moon's gentle beams. The ocean waters, blue, then black, oft times white from the reflection of the moon's rays, seemed empty and forlorn.

But then…

Half seen amidst the fog, now limned by the setting moon; now hidden by the whitish mist; an object loomed—a sailing ship of ancient design. The gently swirling fog obscured its proud lines. The moon slipped quietly beneath the ocean deeps, and only morning star—oft' fading—remained to light the scene.

In my mind I heard the gentle lapping of water on the bow, the creak of wooden planking, the moan of strained sailing rig.

Now seen, now unseen.

Now real, now unreal.

A tall ship? mighty, three-masted man-of-war?

Or…,

Dreamship?

# Contents

# Above an Ancient Land

A gusting wind herded groups of bounding tumbleweeds across the desert sand. Watching silently, two gray, gaunt coyotes sniffed the desert air, searched nervously for danger. The larger, a male, turned, trotted quickly across the open dirt road. As the coyote neared the road's edge a startled roadrunner dashed from the shadow of the bank, almost into the jaws of the waiting mate. At the last moment the roadrunner hesitated, awkwardly leaped aside and disappeared in the sparse shadow of an ancient Joshua tree.

Perched on the Joshua tree, head perked to one side, a raven watched the activity below, then scanned the desert for other signs of movement, signs of food. Black and somber it waited patiently.

For a moment the smaller female coyote hesitated, then followed her mate across the now empty road. Both soon blended into the brownish-gray background.

The setting sun lit the lonely reach of flat sands. Now lifeless save for the raven's silent form, the monotonous spread of sand was emphasized by the bleak and desolate Joshua trees, the white beauty of the desert candles, and the wind-driven tumbleweeds. Far off, the yip-yipping of the two coyotes marked day's end. The raven slowly raised its head skyward, searched for an unseen object.

In the evening sky brooded that object of stark black, contrasting with the natural world below. So distant was it from the blue gray Mojave Desert floor that its passage went unheard.

Only the raven uneasily sensed its presence. Unnoted by the desert's sidewinders, coyotes, and roadrunners Dreamship One roared high above. Driving at mach 8 on the thin edge of the atmosphere, 200,000 feet above the earth the huge delta shape pursued the setting sun. Slowly it turned in a shallow bank, vectoring jets bringing the reluctant mass in line with the runway at Edwards Air Force Base, far below.

---

The Antelope Valley is a region of windswept wasteland, forming the western extent of the Mojave Desert. A few cities have grown in its dusty confines. Most of the Joshua tree-studded landscape lies open to the constant winds. The winds that sing in mournful tribute to bygone days.

The Indian populace had largely disappeared before the coming of the white man. Records of their culture were few. Professor Wilcoxson had made what was, perhaps, the definitive study of their culture and mythology.

His lecture this night emphasized the latter. His deep voice reflected strong emotion as it boomed out over the audience. With subtle change of tone, appropriate gestures, and flashing eyes he captivated his listeners.

"There was a time, or so went the legends, when the valley was green and verdant. Two thousand years ago the dry lakes of today were deep with water. Geese and ducks swam, and waterplants lined their banks. Throughout the valley floor the juniper, the mesquite, and the Joshua trees grew in wide abundance." He smiled as he voiced the words.

"The peoples of the valley were gentle folk. Their history remains but by word of mouth, the legends, epics, and myths of a bygone race. It is said the Indians lived in peace here in the valley, raised simple crops, killed the wild antelope for meat. Roots and nuts, and waterfowl were their bounty." His voice was almost lulling, as he described the pastoral scene.

He stood silent for a moment. His eyes roamed over the attentive audience. Medium height, his deep voice seemed out of character with his slender frame. A professional, each intonation of voice, each gesture of hand, each carefully planned pause added to his presentation.

"The ancient ones dwelt here long before the arrival of the Tataviam, long before the coming of the Kitanemuk. Their peaceful existence was protected, each by his personal Dream Helper. And more powerful than any of these by far, protected by one other. The giant!"

"In those days a giant ruled the valley. No enemy dared enter the valley from the desert on the east, nor from the mountains north, west, and south. The ravens flew, and returned, and all they saw they related to the giant. For enemies of the valley people there were no secret places, no hiding spots, not known to the giant's eyes."

His voice was strong, warlike in its intonation. The audience leaned forward, like children enraptured by a fairy tale.

"But the people, in time, became arrogant. They believed their good fortune came of their skill, their intelligence, their courage. Around the campfires they danced and sang of the great deeds they had done. The giant maintained his guard. His ravens, ever watchful, patrolled the skies."

He started with an angry voice, ended with a solemn one.

"The giant sent this message to his people. Change your ways, be not proud, be thankful."

"The people, who had long worshiped the giant, liked not the tone. Too long had they enjoyed the largess of the Valley. Too long had they lived a life of ease and pleasure. They resented even this gentle reprimand.

"Their chiefs and wisemen held counsel. The giant's rule was becoming intolerable. He called for obedience to his harsh laws, laws that were now flaunted by all. No, he was no longer needed! And so they searched for other gods—gods who would countenance their ribald dances, their arrogant brags, their self-proclaimed importance. Led by a Shaman and his Dream Helper, they searched for another, more tolerant, God.

"And a God they found."

Here he raised his arms, paused, looked as though gazing back to ancient times, then shook his head.

"To the south a string of lakes stretched east and west. They lay in the midst of a green valley, one blessed with frequent showers and wet winds from the western sea. Beautiful, surrounded by greenery, the lakes displayed a placid calmness. Save one.

"In one such lake dwelt a creature of the night. The waters, smelling of burning brimstone, were dark and foul. Devil's Lake!

"Here lived a demon who looked on their pride and lasciviousness with amused tolerance. To him they turned, and offered to him their worship. And so they camped along the shores, and held pagan rituals, and turned their back on the giant."

"They sought out the night-blooming plant with beautiful white flowers, the Jimson weed. Its bell-shaped blossoms fold into a purple hue. From its root made they then toloache. Then drank they the toloache, the juice of the jimson weed, the datura root.

His voice was low, almost a whisper. The audience leaned forward tensely, listening to every word.

"They slept. They dreamed strange dreams. And in those dreams met they their Dream Helper. The Shaman, too, drank, slept. His Dream Helper, the demon of the lake!"

His voice grew brisk. "In time they gave up completely their labors to pleasure, their fields turned brown. The antelope left to graze in greener lands—and the giant wandered afar to the east, lay down to rest."

Now solemnly he spoke again. "They who had worshiped him spied him as he slept, and brought the news to their new master. Though this one dare not attack even the sleeping giant the cunning demon called forth the great winds that blow unto this day. Gusting torrents, the winds drove the tumbleweed before them. In their arms they carried the grains of desert sand. Carried the grains of desert sand—and buried, for all time, the giant in its massive drifts.

"There he lies, even now, his head resting on its earthy pillow. But even as the winds blew and entombed him in his desert grave he placed a curse upon this land. A curse that no more would the grass grow green, no more would the harvest come, and in this land none should prosper or find happiness." Mr. Wilcoxson ended with a slow, measured beat, as though he himself were imposing the curse.

"He called to him the ravens, and bade them a last farewell. And from their midst he chose one to live and watch that the curse would hold, and that the land would remain waste."

"And that one was the blind witch!" His voice was sharp and crisp.

"As evening settles on the wasteland still gather the ravens at his side, waiting, quietly waiting. And always perches one alone, a white raven, ancient, with eyes unseeing, silent, brooding."

Here he voiced his words slowly, solemnly, letting his voice drop in intensity.

"The peoples of the valley in time diminished, wandered away, and the valley, once verdant and bright, lay desolate. The demon, sullen and angry, waited in the depth of Devil's Lake for new worshipers who never came." Briskness had returned to his speech, and subtle anger reflected in his tone.

"In time the Kitanemuk came to the Valley. But warned by their Shaman they quickly departed to the Tehachipis, venturing into the Valley rarely and with fear. Sear and dry the Valley became but the home of rattlesnake and roadrunner, lizard and coyote."

"Still the story is told among the old ones, that one day the giant will awaken. He will rise from his bed, the ravens shall once more do his bidding, and the valley will bloom again."

"And the legends say that Devil's Lake shall open, and he who dwells therein shall likewise rise and a great battle will be joined."

The above was voiced at a normal pace, calmly.

"Seldom spoken, and then in tremulous voice and with wide-eyed vigilance, there are other tales."

He spoke with lowered tone, looking carefully out over the audience as though he could see her now, and ended with sibilant emphasis on the final word.

"Tales of the blind witch."

# Technology and Dream Helpers

Dream Ship One's progress was followed with both concern and pleasure from the Flight Mission Center. Jim Braddock, the on-site Program Manager, supported by his team of experts, monitored the TV displays, the telemetry feedback, and the oral inputs from the pilot.

Jim smiled slightly, thinking how the flashing lights of the displays, the quiet operation of the many machines, contrasted with the legends presented so eloquently by Ned Wilcoxson. Nevertheless, he had enjoyed the lecture. At first he had not planned to attend. Linda convinced him to take time off, relax with her.

Linda's interest in the unknown, in myths and legends, amused him. She peppered her conversation with tidbits of ancient wisdom. At times he felt she almost believed such stories as related by Ned.

Before they fell asleep she had asked him, half serious, "Is there really a blind witch?"

Jim paced behind the team of psychologists/physiologists. Their eyes searching the cathode ray tubes, tracing each change in the alpha-beam, they ignored him except for direct questions. The display on the cathode ray tubes, or CRTs, flickered, changed continuously. His queries were answered with guarded optimism.

"Fred, is the pattern normal? This all looks like so much gibberish to me!", he asked, a touch of petulance in his voice. He did not like to depend on others, but he knew too well that here he was out of his domain.

"Sure, Jim.", Fred smiled, slightly tight-lipped. He understood the concern. This was the critical mission. The proof of concept would be here, or not at all.

"Andy's a little tense, but that's expected. He's maintaining complete control of all functions, and…"

He paused, noting the erratic wavering of the tracking pens on his stripchart. The digital readouts, also, rapidly switched readings. A dull, repeated beep issued from the speaker adjacent to the cathode ray tubes used for display. The nearest CRT flashed an intermittent red circle around the pip representing the aircraft.

"My God, what is he doing!"

Jim seized the mike, "Dreamship one, come in. Dreamship one, this is program control. Do you read me." The silence was ominous.

Jim's eyes were on the pilot's view monitor. It displayed the view as seen from Dreamship one's cameras. The screen showed the earth's surface, rotating with ever-increasing rapidity. A surface that was growing ever larger on the screen. Dreamship one was spinning, diving…

"Take over. Initiate emergency procedures. You've got 'er, Tom." He addressed Tom Jacobs, the remote vehicle pilot.

"Doc, what th' hell is wrong with Andy!"

"He isn't unconscious, Jim. But his vital signs indicate he's in a state of shock."

"Engineering, any anomalies with the ship's readings?"

"Negative. All readings within tolerance."

Silently, without hesitation, Tom had flicked the ground control override switch to active. He watched on his screen as the whirling desert rushed to meet him. Quickly he cut power. Methodically he applied full left vector and aileron to break the spin, readied to level the vehicle and apply power.

He angrily rechecked the settings of his controls, the instrument readings, and the ominous display on his scope.

White-faced, a trickle of sweat on his forehead, he turned to Jim Braddock. "Jim, the bastard's got me locked out!" he whispered.

"Fred...?" Jim's voice held a question, perhaps a prayer.

"It's as though he were in a catatonic state. Every channel is vectored through him. We can't override!"

"Keep trying. Fred, what else we got?"

"That's all she wrote from here. Doc, can you kick his nervous system with a jolt from your rig?"

Doc Thompson gazed at them blankly for a moment. Then, in sudden recognition of what was required, he adjusted the alpha-box, turned power full up. In the tense silence of the room the hum of the amplifiers sounded loud. The monitor reflected the square wave pulse racing through the system to the transmitting antennas.

For a moment Dreamship One lurched.

Quickly Tom hit the override switch, gained control. The panel lights blinked green. The bird was his!

Again he cut power, fed full left pedal, left aileron. The vehicle slowed, the rate of spin decreased, ...

"Pull it out, Tom! Now! You've only got 50,000 left, and she's coming in fast!"

Sweating, Tom eased the stick back. With the rate of descent, the spin, and the proximity of the ground he knew how poor the odds were. But the nose was starting up! The spin was now a lazy spiral. He gunned the throttle, rammed it full—and watched in despair.

The override light had switched to red. He punched the button repeatedly, angrily. "Damn it! What in hell is wrong!"

It was to no avail. Control had returned to the vehicle.

"I've lost her! Doc, zap him again!"

Doc started to reply, paused in mid-sentence. His words were not heard as a dull rumble encompassed the building. The screen was blank. The telemetry system no longer reflected incoming signals.

For a moment there was only the sound of the air conditioners, the slight hum from the power supplies.

"Who's flying chase?", Jim's voice was low.

Even as he spoke a message sounded from the squawk box. "Colonel Phelton here. She's gone! Dug a trench near Mirage Lake. Seems like she was starting to recover a couple of times. Then she went into that final damn dive. No parachute. I'm afraid the old boy has bought the farm. I'll hang in here until the 'copters come through."

Jim Braddock stared at the blank display. He took a white handkerchief from his trouser pocket, wiped his forehead. For a moment longer he stood looking at the display, twisting the handkerchief in his hands. With a deep breath he stuffed it once more into his pocket, turned toward the door.

"I'll be at the hospital. Tom, wrap things up here for me. We'll need copies of all transmissions, and a visual record of the displays. Make sure backups are made of all the databases."

"Doc, make backup copies of vital signs up to the crash. I'll want a report by morning."

Jim Braddock walked stiffly toward the door. Too often flight tests had ended thus. Too often the desert was marred by mangled metal and torn flesh. Yet the work must go on. Could Andy have survived?

----

The same thought ran through the mind of the firemen, and of the rescue group, as they raced for the ship.

At the aircraft burning fuel heated the exotic metals. Even in the extreme heat they held their shape. Only exploding fuel finally tore the ship apart. Blown away as a unit the cabin portion held strong, carrying Andy within.

The firemen arrived first. Climbing out of the emergency vehicle in their awkward but heat resistant gear they applied chemical spray to the fire cautiously. Uncertainty prevailed as to the fuel constituents, the aircraft materials, and how they would react to the fire suppressants.

With introduction of strange composites of uncertain composition each fire had to be treated as a new and different problem. Carbon filaments, borides, and other as yet undetermined structural and fuel compounds provided potential dangers at every accident.

The cockpit and Andy were discovered within half minute of their arrival. At almost the same time the emergency personnel reached the scene.

"Get the capsule open! Watch yourself, that metal is plenty hot!"

"Cap, the damn hatch is jammed. Don, the long-handled bar! Move, man!"

He pulled on the release handle. Pried the edges of the hatch. With a metallic screech the cover partially opened. He moved the bar. Placing his back against the cover, he muscled it full open. Grim-faced he looked inside, waved his crew forward.

They transferred Andy to the ambulance. His skin was charred in spots. The odor of burned flesh permeated the air. Blood from open wounds dried in brownish clots on Andy's clothing. He moaned in unconscious pain as they moved his leg. A gaping cut along his inner thigh displayed a mixture of charred yellow fat, red blood, and torn flesh.

They moved quickly, providing oxygen, staunching blood flow. Working hurriedly, even as the vehicle sped toward the hospital. Suddenly Andy attempted to sit up, wrenched the oxygen mask from his face.

"Damn you," he cried. "Damn…"

His voice fell. His breath came in quick pants. He spoke a last time, so low as to be hardly heard. "Damn…witch!"

His voice ended in a sob. A few gasping breathes followed. He fell back. Both sound and motion quickly ceased.

"Don, CPR. Get that damn heart beating! Move this thing, damn it. We've got to get 'im to the hospital."

They worked desperately. The ambulance raced down the dirt road. A cloud of sand and dust marked their progress. Cardiac-Pulmonary Resuscitation continued, as they tried to restart the heart's beat, the lungs' functions. Their skill was in vain. Andy did not respond.

Above, smoothly, quietly, floating on rising updrafts, a raven flew. Lazily it circled, then soared northward to an unknown destination.

They wrote in their report one strange line. "His eyes expressed extreme anger, hate. Not fear, not pain. Anger and hate as he voiced those odd final words."

From the day he received the assignment Jim had felt a dim foreboding about the Dreamship program. It was nothing he could identify, yet he had not been able to shake the feeling. Although any program may have problems, he expected more than a normal share on this one.

He wasn't to be disappointed.

Jim stepped out into the warmth of the early evening, drove to the hospital emergency room. There he waited for the answer he already knew. He listened to the approaching sirens.

---

...In the evening sky brooded an object of stark black, contrasting with the natural world below. So distant was it from the blue gray Mojave Desert floor that its passage went unheard. Unnoted by the desert's sidewinders, coyotes, and roadrunners Dream Ship Two roared high above...

# A New Helping Hand

"You're Mr. Braddock."

It wasn't a question. Rather a flat statement.

"I'm Colonel Goetler. I'm the new liaison between Washington and the program. You will be working for me from this time forward."

Colonel Goetler wore dress blues. The ribbons on his jacket, topped by senior pilot wings, were more impressive than the man. He stood five and half feet tall, his light brown hair thinning. His eyes were greenish blue, and looked unwinkingly at the other man.

Jim Braddock rose slowly, extended his right hand. It was ignored. He pursed his lips slightly. "Well, Colonel, we were informed that you would be here today. In fact I've arranged for a briefing at thirteen hundred. Perhaps you would care to join me for lunch prior to the briefing?"

"What are the lunch hours, Mr. Braddock?"

"We generally break around eleven thirty, and hit it again at twelve thirty."

"Starting tomorrow there will be half an hour for lunch. It is my policy that no alcoholic beverages will be consumed at lunch. No, I think I'll not join you today. Conduct me to my office, Mr. Braddock."

"Colonel, I'm afraid we have a slight problem. Your predecessor shared this office with me. I had expected that arrangement to continue."

Colonel Goetler frowned, glanced carefully around the office.

"I see. It is large enough for one person. I'll use it until I can get a better one. Please have your desk and property removed by tomorrow morning. Don't let me interfere with your lunch, Mr. Braddock. And do return and conduct me to the briefing. That will be all for now."

Jim Braddock dropped his extended hand. Slowly he sat down, then grinned.

"Well, I think I'll just snack today. Make yourself to home, Colonel. I'll finish up some paper work, then we'll go to the briefing room. That desk over there is yours. As you say, until you can get a better one."

Jim hummed quietly as he glanced through two routine reports. In his late fifties, or early sixties, he projected the accepted picture of a civil servant. Slightly balding, hair graying but darkened by Grecian Formula, and wrinkles becoming ever more prominent. When he concentrated on a problem he tended to grind his teeth. At the moment they were grinding remarkably well.

He rose, walked out to the hall, dropped coins in the snack machine, frowned when it hungrily ate his change but returned nothing. Reluctantly he inserted some more coins, selected Ritz crackers with cheese. This time the package fell down with a slight thud. He continued to hum, a quizzical look on his face. With a grimace he returned to the office.

He picked up the paper from his desk, glanced at the headlines. The usual politics. A small entry in the lower left corner of the front page caught his eye. The Republic of Azerbaijan had merged with its neighbor, Iran.

He frowned. Baku, the Caspian Sea oil port came to mind, and the Baku oil fields. The Russian Commonwealth would suffer from that loss. Of course, Azerbaijan had long had a strong Shiite Muslim faction.

Strange how much the world had changed in recent years. Breakdown of powers, realignment of powers, International politics in a dynamic mode.

With a shrug he tossed the newspaper into the round file, the olive drab trash can beside his desk.

Colonel Goetler, emptying his briefcase, had merely glanced up on Jim's return. Without comment or recognition he continued his methodical transfer from briefcase to desk. Jim watched him momentarily, breathed deeply, and returned to reviewing reports. Perhaps, he thought, he'll mellow with time. Sure he will!

They walked quietly down the hall to the briefing room. The Colonel marched in the lead, to Jim's right. Jim nodded to a couple of engineers as they entered.

"Ladies, Gentlemen, this is Colonel Goetler. Colonel Goetler is the new liaison from headquarters. At the conclusion of our briefing he will have a few words for us. At present he can be reached at my office."

He paused, looked around the room.

"Susan, will you read the minutes of our last meeting. That will put Colonel Goetler in the ball park as to what has transpired to date."

The briefing started badly and then deteriorated. The projector bulb had burned out, the replacement was the wrong size. It took 15 minutes to correct the problem.

"The following charts provide an overview of the program. The engineers will provide greater detail in their pitch." Jim introduced the proceedings. Colonel Goetler received these comments with ill-concealed boredom.

As they began to discuss the finances and schedules his eyes brightened, and he wrote extensively in his notebook. His attention was also caught when they discussed the charts showing the logistic problems of the program. "How many parts are on backorder at this time? Does the program have priority? Who's following up on these items?"

The questions were reasonable. "Actually, we don't have a consistent approach to the backorder problem, Colonel. Logistics is developing procedures, and they should be in place within the week."

Jim's response was accepted with a skeptical grunt.

The section on the test program didn't pique his interest, although some of his questions stabbed at a few open wounds. When Captain Millan made a minor mistake in the security coverage the Colonel seemed to take great delight in prolonging his agony.

"You allow both black and red phones in the same room? How do you insure against crosstalk when both are in operation. Do you really know what Tempest means? Is the room shielded?"

Finally Jim stood up, motioned for the Captain to take his seat. "We're running a tad late. We'll get you additional information on that problem, Colonel."

Colonel Goetler started to speak, but though better of it, and nodded with a smile. His glance at Captain Millan was less than cordial.

Within a few minutes the projector bulb again burned out. "Damn, Colonel, I apologize. With your permission I'll close this thing down. If you'd like to say a few words…?" Jim terminated the presentation.

Colonel Goetler stood up, looked silently around the room, then began. "We have an important program to complete. I have been requested to give my personal attention to its progress. My impression at this point is that we have a loosely managed, disorganized, and incompetent aggregation of individuals working at cross purposes."

He looked at each individual, let his eyes linger on Jim.

"This briefing, to speak kindly, was a catastrophe. I will not sit through another of equal calibre. Starting tomorrow we will restrict lunch to half an hour. No alcoholic beverages will be used at lunch."

Turning to Susan he nodded, "See that those statements are in the minutes, and copied to our operating procedures."

He continued.

"I will be making a walkthrough of the area tomorrow. I expect to find everything in good military order." He paused, glancing at his audience.

"I do not accept failure. I do not accept excuses. I expect each individual to complete his job on a timely basis, and in a cost effective manner. When I come around tomorrow I will expect each of you to have a plan of action laid out, with tasks and completion dates identified such that the program schedule is met. Thereafter your performance will be measured in terms of how well you adhere to that schedule. Unless Mr. Braddock has something to add, this meeting is adjourned."

The team members glanced at each other. "Is he for real?" John Holms grinned.

On the way back to the office the Colonel stopped. "Mr. Braddock, that was as poor a presentation as I have sat through. I will not countenance such an exhibition again. Do we understand each other?"

"Al, I don't believe in sweeping problems under the rug, so I think you and I better talk. I would prefer to do so in our office, because some of the things I have to say are not pleasant."

The Colonel's immediate reply was unexpected. "Mr. Braddock, kindly address me as Colonel Goetler."

"Well, certainly, Colonel. We generally tend to be a little informal around here, but that's your privilege." He half-smiled. Does he ever have a chip on his shoulder, he thought.

Colonel Goetler was somewhat surprised by Jim's desire to discuss problems, but agreed to hold off discussion until they reached the office.

Jim Braddock sat down, took out his pipe, and tamped down the tobacco to half fill the bowl. Colonel Goetler waited, looking on with ill-concealed displeasure. "You know, smoking is an unhealthy habit! Tobacco is known to cause cancer."

Jim laughed. "Hell, according to California law, so does everything else." He lit his pipe, slowly blew out the match, leaned back in his chair. "Colonel, I've always made it a practice to level with my superiors. I intend to continue that practice. Colonel, you have a good team here. Your pitch this afternoon was uncalled for. It will not result in a tighter organization, but will contribute to problems being hidden, not surfaced. I've found that you solve problems only when they are surfaced and attacked. If a man can't lay a problem out on the table and talk to it with his boss, both he and his boss suffer."

"Very well, Mr. Braddock. I shall lay my position out on the table also. I was sent here with the expectation that I would not be able to save this program. There are people in Washington who would be pleased to see it—and me—fail. Mr. Braddock, I am not going to fail. I am going to see that this program succeeds, and I am going to pull down a star as a result. At that point, unless otherwise directed, I shall gracefully retire."

"Plainly, Mr. Braddock, we differ in our interpretations of the situation here. I find your team to be, at best, average. And, as I said, I neither accept failure nor excuses. If your men cannot perform their jobs, we will have to replace them with those who can."

"I see. Well, if this is to be your approach I don't think my services will be of advantage. I'll be transferring back to ASD as soon as I can make the arrangements, Colonel. I am sorry we have started off this way, but I wouldn't lie to you. I wish you luck with your assignment."

Colonel Goetler frowned. It was not the response he had expected. "Very well, Mr. Braddock. I must confess, I had intended to request a replacement, but this will make that request a little more palatable, I'm sure. In my opinion we need a stronger hand here. I shall wield that hand. Thank you for your thoughts, Mr. Braddock." The Colonel returned to reading from the notes he had made at the briefing.

Colonel Alfred Goetler's brusk manner hid a feeling of uncertainty. The need to take command had, in part, triggered his comments. He recognized, nevertheless, that departure of the on-site program manager could threaten progress. At the moment he considered it more of an irritant than a major problem.

A sequence of average officer efficiency reports, mediocre assignments, and bleak expectations had Colonel Goetler, as he would admit only to himself, running scared. He had cajoled assignment to the present slot, recognizing the potential if the program succeeded. And, always in the back of his mind, the recognition of the impact of failure.

Adding to his semi-desperation was pressure from a less than enthused wife. Jean Goetler had seen her acquaintances, one by one, move into the "Mrs. General" rank. The failure of her husband to rapidly make that transition, leaving her as a subordinate to her recent peers, weighed heavily on her mind.

"Oh, Jean, I really enjoyed the lunch. But I've got to go—you know, General Stacy's wife is holding a tea for the General's wives. I wouldn't miss it for the world. And I'll be so glad when you're able to attend. Has your husband heard anything, dear?"

Of course it was a putdown, and one she'd rather be handing out than receiving. But she smiled. "Not yet. But I'm sure he'll be on the next list."

"Of course he will, darling. Well, I really must go. It amazes me how many activities a General's wife must attend. You really should sympathize with me, Jean, dear. Bye now."

She frequently explained to her husband the misery she faced, the cruel barbs and needles from her erstwhile friends.

"I cannot continue to suffer like this! Do you have any idea how it feels? I'm even embarrassed to enter the club! How can you do this to me?" She would burst into tears, retreat to the bedroom, slamming the door.

What was he to do? She had no suggestions. She only knew that he must be promoted. Nor was he sure of a quick fix to insure promotion. Successful completion of a major program would help. Friends in high places wouldn't hurt.

In their earlier visits to the high desert she had commented on the sand, the dust, the heat, and the wind. "I cannot believe people live in such a God-forsaken wilderness. That horrible wind! It never dies! It seems to be whispering to me, to be moaning...! There must be snakes. I know there are snakes! And you know how much I loathe them!"

With their move into a home on base she also found herself suddenly faced with an infestation of scorpions. The base, of course, sent out exterminators. Nevertheless the experience provided her with additional ammunition for verbal assaults on her hapless husband.

She would wake him at night. "Listen! Hear them! Do you hear that rustling! I'm sure there are more of them. I want you to get the exterminators back! Don't just lie there! But you don't care, do you?" Once more she began to sob.

He sympathized with her. He, too, yearned for that first star. And he worked the problem methodically, evaluating his own actions and their results, and looking for opportunities.

Amazingly, his native resilience prevented him from falling prey to despondency. On the other hand the pressures did little to improve his contact with the program team.

His initial introduction to Jim Braddock was a normal pattern. He was, in many ways, a loner. It had been brought forcibly to his attention.

"Al, you got this promotion because of your record, flying airplanes. But you're going to be dealing with men, not machines. So loosen up, talk to people. You've got to get cooperation, you've got to motivate your troops. Work on it!" General Randolph handed him the orders, grinned, shook hands.

To overcome that tendency to work alone he had developed a brash, pushy approach to the people around him. It often did not set well with his associates. On the other hand, he generally prevailed, and had his way, got the job done.

"Mr. Braddock, I would like a brief run-down on the projects leading up to the Dreamship series."

"Certainly, Colonel. Many of the basic ideas extend back to the B-1 bomber, the original version before they bastardized it. The primary consideration was a small radar cross section. Use of ultra-light, strong structure. And provision for continuous upgrading of avionics without substantial change in the basic platform."

Jim sipped at his coffee, stared thoughtfully at the ceiling as he leaned back in his chair.

"Then there was more extensive use of computers, particularly to support stable flight under extreme conditions. You probably recall the forward-swept wing activity that contributed to that development."

"Extension of the fiber optics capability was folded in. And much of the radar cross section minimization that came with the B-2 before it was dumped."

"We've provided some significant advances in use of the carbon and boron filament techniques, as well as use of pseudo-ceramic materials for the engines. With those materials the engine temperature can be maintained at extreme values for indefinite periods."

"Actually, the Dreamship series is a logical extension of state-of-the-art development of the early '90s. Over time aircraft speeds have increased, sometimes slowly, at times in quantum leaps. New and more advanced engines have emerged and more powerful fuels have been concocted. Flight altitudes have moved closer and closer to the limits of the atmosphere. Airbreathing engines have been supplemented by jets more suited to the new environment."

"Heat resistant materials of unprecedented quality are coming out of the labs. They are essential if the aircraft is to survive the temperatures introduced in the engines, even on the craft's surfaces as it races through the atmosphere."

"As you well know, in the military world speed and altitude are important. But of even more significance, the ability to fly undetected."

"In this domain greater strides still have been made. Where early efforts had concentrated on passive means, emphasizing curves rather than sharp angles, and absorbent materials, now an alternative approach is being taken."

"Dynamic methods of generating signals, signals essentially 180 degrees out of phase with incoming waves, are now being applied. Appropriate sensors, high speed computers, and algorithms which were once thought impossible to apply support this technology. Sound, sight, infra-red, and radar waves are being detected and neutralized."

Jim stopped to relight his pipe.

"If I bore you, just sound off, Colonel."

"Be assured, I will."

With a grunt Jim continued.

"The approach had major importance. Use of Absorbent materials could be countered by the enemy, using subtractive processes. A constant signal between a transmitter and a receiver would be perturbed if an absorbent vehicle passed through. With the dynamic approach compensated signals could be passed on to the receiver. No perturbations would seem to exist."

"Concurrent with these advances have come advances in control approaches. For years the pilot has sat vertically, viewing the world from a cockpit whose very presence interfered with the flowing air. Tortured by unbearable G-forces, he reached the point when he was no longer functional. This has changed, the pilot now lying horizontal, viewing the world through instruments. Now he controls the ship with arms and legs, as though swimming through the atmosphere. G-forces are more bearable, and with extremities supported the pilot can exert more controlled force on rudder pedals and on the stick."

"The Dreamship series proposed a new quantum leap. Man's response time was becoming ever more of a constraint. Response time would be improved."

Of course, any weapon of this nature is subject to counter actions on the part of the enemy. Some such actions may result in damage to the dreamship. So the systems are, for those that are essential, redundant. Additionally, the computers are programmed to take control under extreme circumstances, implement graceful degradation. In the old computer world these type of capabilities were designated as wizards. They led the user through the right procedures. The artificial intelligence incorporated in our computers goes a step further. They don't just guide the users actions. Instead they take over and implement corrective actions.

It's an old concept. On the old B-1 the CITS was initially devised to perform in this manner under appropriate circumstances. Pilot objection resulted in that capability not being implemented. At least, not completely. Anyway, where wizards ran the old computers we call this capability the Witch. And you know, as sophisticated as we are in this day and age, there's a superstitious objection to that title.

"As always, with every major advance in knowledge, there exist major risks."

"These risks, naturally, are faced by the Dreamships."

He did not say it, but in the back of his a mind a thought flashed, "And one additional risk."

"But the real advances we've made have been in the three areas of upper-atmosphere engine design, dynamic rather than passive visibility control, and in pilot-aircraft interface. I'll not touch on details here. You'll find the details well spelled out in the classified material you'll have access to."

Colonel Goetler nodded, once more returned to the material on his desk, then glanced up.

"That's a good pitch, but it sounds like pure PR, public relations. I'll talk to each of your project engineers for specifics."

"Yes, sir." He rose, "I'm going over to engineering now, if you'd like to come along?"

"No. I'll have them come here and brief me."

"How are we looking. Gonna' keep the Colonel happy tomorrow?"

"Hell, there's no way we'll keep that joker happy. But we're putting together schedules. Damn if I know whether they can be met. What's bugging the old boy, Jim?"

"He's new, not sure of himself. He'll settle down." Jim said it, but he knew his voice lacked conviction.

Jim regretted the impression made by Colonel Goetler. A program needed, above all other forms of organization, a team approach. He himself tried to nurture such an approach, working closely with his people. Colonel Goetler's inputs had undercut his success, might make day-to-day interface much more difficult.

While returning to the office he reviewed the events of the day. He mused over the Colonel's actions and attitude. Finally he shook his head and thought, Well, I tried! I wonder if they have a manager for the Permaflite System. I'll check it out tomorrow. It could be a winner.

At home Jim ate quietly, listening to Linda's vivacious description of the day's events. Though taciturn himself, he loved to watch the excitement in her eyes, her hands moving to illustrate every idea even as she talked.

"We played Mahjongg until two. The salad bar was so fresh! Sally brought her baby, and she won two hands. Not the baby, I mean Sally. The baby doesn't play yet. Everyone hissed and booed. I lost 35 cents!" She threw her hands into the air, as if in disbelief. "Oh, and the chocolate cake! I do like chocolate cake."

He smiled at the disconnected comments and arranged them within his mind.

"Young lady, that chicken is good. And those mashed potatoes and gravy were out of this world. No wonder you have one B . i . g...husband."

She said nothing but her smile showed her pleasure.

After dinner she poured him a glass of Hungarian Green. He stepped to her side, and kissed her softly on the neck.

For a moment she was silent, looking at him and returning his smile. "My little sparrow," he whispered, hugging her close to him.

She had aged gracefully. There was a touch of gray to her hair, and slight wrinkling of her brow. But her smile still lit her face and eyes, and her voice had never lost the happy tone he loved.

Not that they hadn't had problems. God, how close she came to divorcing him. He had brought that on himself.

Teddy was very attractive, she plainly found him desirable, and he still had a roving eye. He had danced with her at a new year's party, kissed her at the end of the dance.

Linda said nothing when they returned to the table, but the fire in her eyes was sufficient. She was silent on the way home. When they entered the house she turned to him. "Jim, sit down. We must talk."

Reluctantly he had sat down and she very quietly asked, "Is she what you want, Jim? If she is, I'll leave. I know she will take you. You have to decide. I wont share you with her." She didn't raise her voice, and there was a slight sob as she finished. Still she looked at him bravely and waited for his answer.

"I'm a fool, Linda. Yes, she's attractive. But your the best thing in my life. I'm sorry. I almost made a mistake. Thank God I'm married to you."

She had cried in his arms that night. He didn't tell her, but tears flowed from his eyelids too. They never talked about Teddy again. When they met her the conversation was reserved, and Teddy realized there would be no affair.

How many years ago? Hmmm, too many! But good years!

"I saw the most beautiful bird."

"What...", she had interrupted his reveries. "Ah, a bird? What kind? Where?" He smiled.

"In the backyard. On the very top of our Joshua tree. A great white bird. This morning. It was a raven. The others were on the ground. But she sat all alone in the tree. She looked so alone. Would you like some more wine?"

She refilled his glass.

"Are there white ravens? I'm sure there are. She looked like the others—just white. Well, maybe..., different. Kind of majestic. I've never seen a white raven before. I wonder if they are worth something. I bet Professor Linden would be interested. Don't you think?"

"Eh, yes, I think I've heard of an occasional albino crow or raven. I don't really recall. Why don't you call the Professor at lunch tomorrow? Or go by the school and talk to him. Why do you say she?"

For a moment Linda was uncharacteristically silent. "Well, I think because she looked like a queen with the black ravens all around her. Oh, I don't know? Just she is a she."

He laughed. "Come here."

She wrinkled her nose at him, hesitated, then walked over and took his hand. He pulled her down on his lap. Arms tightening around her, he pressed his cheek to hers. "Damn, I love you," he growled.

"Jim, I feel nervous. I wish we hadn't gone to Professor Wilcoxson's presentation. When I saw the white bird I thought…Well, I thought of Professor Wilcoxson's blind witch. I…"

She paused, pressed her cheek against his chest. He could feel the tenseness, the occasional uncontrolled quiver.

"Damn, Linda! Those are old wives' tales. Every country, every culture, has them. It's nothing to be nervous about."

"I know… And yet I feel, well, apprehension. As though there were a storm brewing, beyond the horizon. Isn't it silly, though!"

She got to her feet, smiled slightly. But her eyes didn't reflect the smile. Instead they showed a fear she could not escape. In her mind was a vision of the white raven. She didn't say so, but he knew. He drained his glass quickly.

She wore a baby-doll negligee, teased him with both look and action.

"Come here, woman." He growled, reached for her caveman style.

With a laugh she danced away, but he caught her hand, pulled her close. He kissed her softly at first. The softness of her lips, the sudden catch in her breath excited him. He breathed in the fragrance of her, the perfume of her skin. His hands moved quickly. The negligee slipped off, fell unheeded to the floor.

How soft, so fragile. His moods fluctuated, one moment a feeling of tenderness, followed by one of desire. She smiled, took his hand, pressed it to her breast. She pressed against him, her lips hard on his.

"You devil!"

She nodded.

Afterward he held her close to him. He treasured those few moments, pressed closed together, their bodies relaxed as he held her in his arms. Her face was like that of a child. He kissed her cheek softly, and she smiled, snuggled closer still.

He didn't sleep too well. Sleep came less easily each night, now. Perhaps the pressure of the job. He wasn't sure. It was not that the entrance of Colonel Goetler bothered him. No, it was a recurrent dream (or nightmare, he wasn't really sure which).

He was in the midst of the desert, on a dark night, with only the stars shining down. The wind was blowing, but softly, not even gusting. Occasionally he heard a coyote pack, their calls dampened by the distance. The Joshua trees, their arms extended in weird patterns, formed looming hobgoblins around him. And out of the darkness a huge black shape, one he knew too well, was pursuing him. A Dream Ship, and at the controls, a dead man.

He ran! The desert sand shifted treacherously under his feet. He fell. Scrambled to his feet to fall once more.

Rose again, dodged, ran, fell!

The ship drew closer.

The engines roared louder.

He fell again, rolled over!

The ship was upon him!

It's huge mass was coming down, down!

And then it was gone!

The desert sky was clear. The only object—how strange! Always, above, a lone raven flew.

The dreams were unpleasant. Their recurrence concerned him even more. He awoke with sweat on his forehead. Upon awakening he felt drained of energy, wilted, irritable. At times he would get up, drink a coffee in morose silence. Eventually his better nature would resurface.

Stupid dream, stupid nightmare! he mused. A dreamship, and a dead man at the controls!

And he wondered, "Before we are done, how many dead men will fly?"

# General Tiller's Pitch

The technical interface meeting was held at ASD this month. Preparation, as usual, was a hassle.

"They've changed the agenda again. Didn't Knox say we'd slip the laser project. Well, he's got it right here at the top of the list!"

"I can't pitch the active stealth generator. The engineers have everything on scratch paper. We won't have drawings until next month!"

The same pattern prevailed for item after item. Make-do's and alternatives were quickly rushed into place.

He sent his engineers ahead by commercial flight. They would talk to their peers, hopefully resolve any concerns before the formal start of the session.

"I'll be taking the SAT back. You are free to ride with me if you wish."

Jim was taken aback. Colonel Goetler rarely responded to a request. Now he was offering to be of assistance. "Sure, Colonel, I appreciate that."

"Mr. Braddock, I merely prefer having someone ride right seat. Just in case problems surface."

They flew to Wright-Patterson together, with Jim monitoring radio transmissions. Colonel Goetler piloted the two-place jet trainer with a skill that Jim envied. The supersonic advanced trainer, better known as SAT, cut across the continent in unprecedented time. With a jet stream assist they were ready for letdown in less than three hours.

"Hell, Colonel, it takes me that long just to drive to LAX," Jim grinned.

The technical presentation to ASD's General Tiller and his senior staff was well received. After comments and discussion the General dismissed the audience.

"And the working relationship between you, colonel, and you, Mr. Braddock? I'm not receiving the kind of feedback I'd prefer!"

Colonel Goetler hesitated, and Jim replied.

"We differ rather significantly in our management approach, General. So much so that I have requested reassignment. I believe my services could be better used on the PermaFlite system. No offense to the Colonel, but I think the task will progress more efficiently if there is a single position at the top level. We really don't share such a common view."

"Colonel, what are you thoughts?"

"General, I agree with Mr. Braddock. I think he is a competent manager, but would best serve on the PermaFlite effort. I've coordinated on his request for transfer."

General Tiller was silent for a moment, then nodded. "Thank you, gentlemen. "Jim, you know where the exercise room is in the other building. You both are welcome to use it if you care to. I believe the club has a special tonight, steak and lobster. The wife dearly loves that combination. Would you join me there at seven thirty."

It wasn't a question.

The evening meal was well prepared. General Tiller's wife enjoyed the food, and seemed to enjoy their company. General Tiller ate quietly, let his wife carry the conversation.

"We'll be having a formal ball on the 19th. You should arrange a Technical Interface Meeting, or TIM as you seem to prefer to call it—or some other such event so that you can attend. I love formals. All the girls do. It gives us a rare chance to put on the dog. My, that cliché really dates me, doesn't it?" She laughed.

"That would be pleasant. I fear the workload will preclude it, however. Thank you for the suggestion." Jim smiled.

She's a lot like Linda, he thought to himself. Women seem to have greater facility with conversation than the men I know.

"You run the Dreamship program, don't you? The one everyone whispers about, and my husband won't even use the word." She glanced at General Tiller in mock anger.

"They say it's like nothing that has ever flown before. Flies faster, higher, and invisibly—oh, I know. Everything is secret. But couldn't you give me just a tidbit of information, so I can impress the other wives?"

General Tiller took a deep breath. "Louise, would you go talk to some of the ladies here tonight. Say, oh, for fifteen minutes?"

"Ah, business. Of course, dear. Do be nice. I like these gentlemen." She smiled while rising, and quickly joined another party at a nearby table.

"I'm not going to accept your transfer at this time, Mr. Braddock. The corporate memory you represent on this program is a priceless commodity, one too often undervalued, I fear. I've talked to Headquarters, and they concur in my decision. I've requested that you talk to the System's Command honchos at the quarterly presentation. You'll probably have to talk to Mathis. Damn shame for piddling problems to be dropped in his lap, but it happens all the time. If you can convince him I'll abide by his decision, of course. Now, gentlemen, let's enjoy our meal."

The flight home was uneventful, though they met a headwind and traveled more slowly. They neared Colorado and Colonel Goetler decided to refuel at New Field, in olden times called Lowry Air Force Base, as weather in the Los Angeles area was bad and they might be diverted to an alternate destination.

They spent about an hour at New Field, time for a coffee and a quick snack. "I served a hitch here. Used to enjoy KP. The work was hard, but they sure fed us well." Jim grinned, thinking back.

"Getting bad here for flying. Too much smog build up. I've been grounded here a few times, waiting for it to lift. Luckily, with the gear we have on board, visibility is no real concern." The Colonel was more talkative than usual.

They downed their coffee, returned to the aircraft. Colonel Goetler did a careful walk-around, nodded.

They rolled to the run-up area, completed the checklist, and were once more airborne.

By the time they reached Edwards the weather had lifted and they completed their letdown and landing without incident.

"Thank you, Colonel. You're a good jet jockey."

Colonel Goetler grinned like the proverbial kid with a new toy.

Well, he does have feeling at that, Jim thought to himself.

# General Mathis World View

The meeting at Systems Command was inevitable. Since ASD had rejected Jim's request for transfer, had rejected Colonel Goetler's request for a replacement—the problem had moved up the hierarchy.

Key members of the program flew commercially to Washington. Much of the material presented duplicated that given to ASD, but here the emphasis was heavily on the financial aspects. Again, the presentations were well received, both moral and practical support tendered.

Their audience with General Mathis had been pre-arranged. The General's concern was evident on his face, as he invited them to be seated.

"Gentlemen, I am not interested in your management philosophy, your personal preferences, nor your ambitions. I am interested in bringing the Dreamship program to a successful conclusion."

General Mathis paused, smiled. At least, his lips curled in the semblance of a smile. But his eyes expressed little humor. Nor did his voice.

"You are two adults who have excellent track records. You have successfully brought in program after program in spite of the politics, rampant stupidity, and back-biting that makes your positions, at best, endangered."

"Now, children," his smiled was replaced with a grim frown. "Now let's get down to business. You two are responsible for the program, you will devise whatever modus operandi is necessary to work together and get the job done, and you will resolve your personal antagonisms such that the program is not threatened."

"I don't have time for baby sitting!"

"Colonel Goetler, Mr. Braddock has been managing programs for nearly 20 years. The corporate knowledge he has gained in those 20 years is indispensable. Take advantage of it."

"Mr. Braddock, Colonel Goetler knows well the intricacies of the Air Force. He has the ears of key military personnel, and of congressional committees with whom you will be dealing. You need those skills in this program."

"Too put it bluntly, gentlemen, don't come crying to me with your hurt feelings. There is a job to be done, and you will get it done!" He spoke the last sentence through gritted teeth, his face reflecting determination.

"I will be checking the progress reports with great interest."

The General looked at them, waited for a reply which didn't come. He rose, walked to the door and spoke to his secretary. "We're not to be disturbed for the next half hour. A classified discussion will be in progress."

"Perhaps you don't realize the importance of your program. Let me enlighten you."

He pressed a switch on the side of his desk and a panel opened at the top, a small computer rose into position.

"If you will watch the display on the far wall I think you'll begin to understand my concern."

He pressed a key on the computer and a world map came into view. At the base of the map were such terms as population, area, rank, military, and other entries. General Mathis spoke quietly, "Military".

The computer responded by displaying a set of bar graphs, reflecting the military might of the world's major coalitions.

"With the dismemberment of the old Soviet Union the world reacted in a typical pattern. The Pollyannas quickly opted to eliminate military power as we knew it, and the armed forces of our country were decimated. That, of itself, might not have been a major problem.

"However, in conjunction with the emasculation of our military, congress elected to destroy the industrial base on which military defense rests. Our ability to regroup, should conditions warrant, was eliminated.

"To make the situation even more difficult, the accumulated corporate memory of our key personnel has been dispersed. To reunite the key players is no longer within our power. Such critical organizations as the Skunk Works disappeared. DARPA was relegated to the level of a hobby shop, its funds almost non-existent.

"Peace, it's wonderful was the theme of the day."

He frowned, sipped at a glass of water.

"It's human nature to dream. And it's human nature to want peace. But we forgot one thing the founders of our country knew well.

He opened the right hand drawer of his desk, pulled out a short cat-of-nine tails, and a pair of handcuffs.

"Peace is easy. Just bow to the oppressor, give him your women as mistresses, your children as slaves, your property as tribute . He'll give you peace.

"It wasn't the kind of peace our forebears would settle for!

"Unfortunately, it is that type of peace-at-any-price thinking that encourages aggressor nations to exploit the situation. When this is combined with blatantly visible military weakness in a nation, it eventually leads to some hard decisions—accept the domination of the aggressor—or attempt, too late, defensive measures.

He paced the floor for a moment, then returned to his chair.

"Our leaders flunked history in their academic careers. They fail to recognize that bullies do not attack the strong, and rarely fail to attack the weak. War after war has been triggered because of that simple fact.

He moved the mouse to Red China, pressed the button. A detailed breakout of the Chinese Military was graphically displayed.

"The Chinese rather quickly brought many of the more extreme elements from the old USSR to their fold, including the most brilliant of their engineers and scientists. They concurrently obtained, while the new Russian Commonwealth was being espoused, at least one of each of the major weapons of the old Soviet Union.

"Hydrogen bombs, advanced intercontinental rockets, advanced bombers, advanced submarines—the majority of the latter now sail from Chinese ports.

"They have used these as models, prototypes, and have expanded on them in quantity and in features.

"At the same time they have expanded their army to the point that it now exceeds the combined military might of the original USSR, the United States, and the European Community.

"The mere existence of that huge military capability has allowed them to subvert the whole of Asia to respond to their demands."

"How well do you know your history, gentlemen?" The question was purely rhetorical. He continued, quietly. "And national cultures? In the Orient there has long been a major element of the culture that has influenced decisions."

He paused, looked down for a moment. "Have you read of the first flight of World War III? I think not. Never reached the papers."

He laughed. It was not a pleasant laugh. "History. My God, how much of it is pure propaganda. Freedom of the Press? Not one journalist in a hundred can pull off a thorough investigation. And fewer than that ever get the results published."

He clicked on a menu item and the display, enlarged, showed the coast of China, the outlying islands. Various colored markers reflected the number and makeup of the military forces on mainland.

"Back in the '50's. Quemoy? Matsu? Ring a bell? No, I think not. Loss of face. Being publicly embarrassed. In the Orient that is one form of hell. And memories are long."

He stood up, walked to the window and looked out.

"I was there. Had a heavy date that night." He smiled, a real smile as his thoughts wandered. "Lovely girl. Should have married her. Well, well, that's beside the point. Sorry to ramble."

He returned to the desk, sipped his coffee. "Restricted to base. No specifics. Rumored that a mission would fly that night. The briefing was short and to the point. Several participants were excused while the mission was discussed. Top Secret. There were some scared sons-of-bitches left that briefing room, I'll tell you. Two damn little islands could cause the world to go up in flames!"

He took a deep breath, let it out slowly. "Preflight was routine. Nukes on board. Rolled out and did our runup. Airborne and on the way. First flight, World War III. No news coverage, no pictures, no alerting of the populace!"

"Sorry, gentlemen. It's important that you understand. You may well shape destiny as you shape your aircraft. Well, the mission, in fact, was not a secret. The Chinese knew, even before we were airborne. The comm' wires were hot that night. US to USSR. USSR to China. China to USSR. USSR to US. And time was running out."

He sipped his coffee, contemplating the displayed map.

"We were just short of the IP when the message came in to hold when we reached it. Moments later, we got the word. Mission aborted. Return to base."

He clicked on another menu, and the varied objects on the China Mainland rapidly dispersed away from the coast. "Was said to be one of the fastest retreats in modern history. And it's stuck in their craw up to this day."

He stood up, walked to the washroom.

"Colonel, you familiar with this?"

"Well, there are incidents that get reported, and incidents that don't get reported. I've heard rumors. Never saw an official report. By the way, Jim, I wouldn't discuss this at all after we leave this office. Besides, no one would ever confirm it."

The General returned, clicked on the menu again, and reran the dispersion sequence.

"Years later, threat to take Taiwan. Our leaders discounted it. Not worth the negative impact on the Chinese economy, so they reasoned. They ignored the key factor, loss of face. Strange, emotions over reason. Loss of face… Ah, gentlemen, be very careful how you put down anyone. Resentment triggers some weird responses."

He clicked the menu once more, and a display reflected China's current leader. "He was there. He suffered the indignity of a forced withdrawal, a frightened retreat. Loss of face. He remembers Quemoy, Matsu very well. And it influences his every decision.

"Our leaders reason. They examine facts, and they evaluate national policies based on those facts. Unfortunately, the facts are meaningless. Loss of face is the underlying fact. And its ignored. Well, enough of history. Keep in mind, culture, emotions, loss of face, resentment. These, rather than facts, shape policy!

"They lull the United States into apathy by endorsing capitalism as an economic mode. We forget, it seems, that one of our fiercest enemies, Nazi Germany, had also a capitalist economy."

He moved the mouse on the map to the United States.

"The military might, present and potential, of the United States is negligible compared to Red China. Even so, the congress continues to demand further cutbacks.

"Gentlemen, the one area in which we hold a potential winning card is the Dreamship program. Admittedly, it could not win a war against odds reflected there." He nodded toward the screen.

"But it is one weapon Red China could not detect, could not intercept. They know that, and they aren't even attempting a military countermeasure. They are throwing billions of dollars into propaganda, using the American media as their tools. They are paying off key congressmen, they are paying off those who shape the mind of America in order to block further funding of the Dreamship program. Even the grade schools are being bombarded by literature purchased through their largess.

"With the dreamship program eliminated they will be able to bully us into additional concessions. As you know, we have, to put it bluntly, been forced to withdraw from the Pacific west of the Hawaiian Islands. The transfer of Guam to Red China, as well as transfer of the other Pacific Islands, temporarily appeased them.

"Last week the White House received an ultimatum. Transfer of the Hawaiian Islands must be negotiated by the end of this year, or they will take, as they phrase it, 'unilateral measures to bring about that transfer'.

"They have succeeded in neutralizing the European Community and other potential allies we might have had. The current assessment of their long term goals include, initially, picking up Alaska, followed by Canada. Already their supporters have so undermined the governments of Central and South America that those governments could be quickly overturned. The Shining Light is glowing brilliantly in that region." There was bitterness in his voice. "And we stood by and did nothing."

He was silent for a moment, rose from his chair.

"We gave them the Panama Canal, hoping to convince them of our friendly disposition. We've allowed them footholds throughout our nation, military footholds, disguised as trading posts. Remember your American history? Trading Posts in Indian territory? We have exactly the same pattern here. And our leaders, amply paid largess by the communists, ignore the pattern, even support it."

Ignoring them he paced behind his desk, his eyes on the map display. Finally he paused, looked at them with apparent embarrassment. "I'm sorry, gentlemen, I am truly concerned. Please bear with me."

He waved toward the map.

"All this, gentlemen, without a shot being fired. A world at peace!"

He picked up the cat-of-nine tails, brought it down across his desk top.

"We have to have the Dreamships. "I'll level with you. We've lied, cheated, transferred funds illegally. Whatever it required, we have kept funds flowing for that program. I, and probably most of the System

Command and ASD managers, will undoubtedly eventually be court-martialled for our actions.

"They hold the aces. They've brainwashed our nation into the belief that we want 'Peace at any price'. A few of us think the price is too high.

"Gentlemen, that's my pitch. Listen to TV, radio, read your newspapers. I think you'll see the pattern I've talked about. Follow the negotiations for Hawaii. The conclusion is fore-ordained, but they like these little parodies.

"Press on with your task, and good luck. If I can help, call me."

"Now get the hell out of my hair, I got work to do!" He turned his attention once more to his desk, returned the computer to storage. He picked up a classified folder, then glanced at them as they rose from their seats.

"And, children, I don't scream and yell. But you make it happen—or by God, Daddy will spank!"

They knew full well what he meant.

As they left the office Jim looked at Colonel Goetler. "Colonel, is the old boy paranoiac? I know the world situation is fluid, but he makes it sound like Armageddon is around the corner. Did you know any of this?"

"Not in its entirety. Of course, we get intelligence briefings, and the build-up in Chinese military capability has been pretty evident. The fact that she is already throwing her weight around has been down-played by the diplomats."

"You know," Jim shook his head. "I actually thought those negotiations were in good faith. But what did we really receive in return for that territory. Some trade rights. And that's it!"

"Intelligence has maintained fairly good coverage of the situation. The media knows full well what is happening, but spouting the party line is money in the bank. They aren't going to say anything to cut their flow of funds. And, hell, the politicians are still taking care of number one. What's new!" The Colonel took a deep breath, started to speak again, but closed his mouth, words unsaid.

"Is one weapon system enough to thwart them. We could only field a few birds, even when we get into production."

"That will depend on the President. It's a poker game, and he's stuck with the cards he has. If he can bluff with them, great. If they call his bluff, a lot of us will have to fly a one-way mission, our last one."

"Well, I knew the pressure was on. I never realized why, 'til now. Scary situation. Anyway, business as usual."

Jim shrugged. He had known, once his request for transfer was rejected, that he and the Colonel were teamed for the duration. It was senseless to buck against the bit. Unfortunately the modus operandi might well be at best mutual tolerance, with little cooperation.

Thinking about the situation he almost laughed. Calling on a General to solve the problem of two feuding schoolboys! General Mathis had recognized it as that typical situation. *I wonder how many other children he has had to chastise. It is ridiculous, really.*

They drove silently to National, returned the rental car, and sat quietly on the tram carrying them to the terminal. Finally Colonel Goetler turned toward him, nodded, and commented slowly. "Well, Mr. Braddock, a divorce no longer seems possible. I suggest that we allocate the chores ahead so that we minimally interfere with each other. I have my way of doing things, you have yours, and there seems to be little common ground. Would you give me your suggestions as to how we assign those chores?"

"Of course, Colonel. That will be my priority project when we get back to Edwards."

A touch of surprise was in his voice. The request for suggestions had actually been worded as a request, not an order. And the tone of voice had supported that interpretation. *Would miracles never cease!*

Far below the Blue Ridge Mountains reached skyward. The haze that gave them their name appeared more gray than blue from the aircraft's altitude. *It's been a while,* he thought.

Though protected from much of the dynamic world outside the mountains, still changes occurred.

At his last visit to the backwoods he found the old one room school and church had burned down. The spring was no longer maintained, and had filled with sand, although the clear water still welled up and flowed into the neighboring stream. Oddly enough there were few new dwellings. The Smith place had disappeared, perhaps burned down, perhaps gradually dismantled. The still on the ridge was gone, and only rusty metal to mark its place.

But the old dirt road still meandered along the valley floor, climbed reluctantly up toward the ridge and disappeared among the trees at the mouth of the hollow. The papaw tree stood by the spring, and across the valley the huge walnut loomed.

He could almost see his mother, wearing the gray bonnet she had sewed, waiting for him. The bottom lay between home and the school. She had stood at the other side of the log crossing the creek. He was returning from the little school, and a thunderstorm had filled the creek to its brim and above. Below the log the water whirled and splashed in a deep churning pool. How frightened he had been!

"Jim! Don't look down! Just look at me, and walk straight to me." Her voice did not show the fear and concern she felt. But somehow he knew.

Yet, when she held out her hand he crossed the log. "All right, Ma. I'm coming. Don't worry. I can make it."

Unquestionably, if he had slipped, she would have gone into the water after him. But, of course, he didn't slip and she hugged him close, then tried to keep up with him as they climbed the hill to home.

He laughed, and Colonel Goetler glanced at him. Strange, the things we remember, he thought.

He recalled the night he had seen the will-of-the-wisp. He had gone to bottomless pond, frog gigging. The long-legged bullfrogs lived there in abundance among the weeds and grass. That night the moon was near full, and their songs filled the air.

Suddenly, even before he drew near, their cries ceased. He stopped. Perhaps a thirsty panther had come to drink. Or a bear wandering down from the high ridge. Then he saw it.

At first a small wavering light. It had grown in brilliance, taken on a bluish tinge. It hovered just above the weeds. The air was still, and the only sound his own breath. At first he halted, tentatively turned back. A haint, he'd thought. But, shamed by his fear, he moved quietly toward the pond.

The light flickered and danced above the bamboo reeds, seemed to respond to music he could not hear. As he reached the pond's bank, it quivered, grew large and thin, and faded. The only light came from the moon.

The frogs began their mating calls once more. A light breeze rustled the weeds. For a while he stood by the pond, waiting for its return. Finally, unused gig in hand, he had walked thoughtfully home.

The backwoods bred many a superstition. The elders enjoyed, it seemed, passing on such lore to the children. When he told of his experience his grandfather frowned, lit the corncob pipe, and related story after story. They all centered on bottomless pond, and what might be found in its depths.

"Boy, you had a right smart of luck. There's them what seen it that came back addled. And stories go that some just didn't come back at all." His grandpa, glanced at him, measuring the impact of his words. "A' course, it ain't like seeing a haint. I saw one a' them, once, over Bald Knob way. My horse spooked an' almost threw me, then cut out for home. I was just as glad."

He stayed awake that night, eyes wide open.

He had gone frog gigging many times after. He never saw the dancing light again.

"Damn wine is making me a little groggy, I do believe." he mentioned to Colonel Goetler.

The response was merely a grunt.

He continued to sip his glass of blush, ruminated over the results of the trip, and let his thoughts drift over the events leading up to their present status.

How long now, this program? Three years! Actually more, if the conceptual stage, the preliminary Research & Development—good old R & D, never really complete before commitment to the next phase. Yes, these had to be considered. And, of course, the time spent bringing together the initial cadre has to be included. He shook his head. Everything moves more slowly than you plan or expect. And yet the time went by so swiftly, the calendar pages discarded, one by one.

# Tab Klooster

They had tagged Tab Klooster for the Program Management slot. Tab had brought in the Airborne Reconnaissance Probe (ARP) under cost, within schedule, and all spec requirements met. Subsequent events revealed discrepancies, but there are always discrepancies.

"Tab, we need a strong hand on this one. There's opposition from all sides, and even the engineers aren't convinced it can be done. We think you can bring it in." Everyone at the conference table clapped loudly.

Tab sat quietly for a moment. He had heard rumors, had discounted them. Now he had been offered the program. At the time all indications were that she would never fly. The known unknowns, combined with the unk unks, or unknown unknowns, made it a high risk program. Tab valued his career progress too much to take the risk.

"Your trust in me is deeply appreciated. Nevertheless, I have to turn it down. I'm running into problems with my blood pressure, and the doctor says I've got to back off for a while. Let me recommend a good man, one who will get the job done."

He opted for an administrative job, recommended Jim Braddock for program manager. "I've worked with Jim, followed his career. If it can be done, he'll do it. If not, he'll level with you and let you know the score."

Tab accepted the voiced concern with good grace, and waited for the next program to his liking.

Jim sipped the wine slowly. In many ways Tab was a likeable person. But Tab took care of Tab. Well, this hadn't worked out too badly. And Tab was still an administrator—a well paid one, no doubt.

When Jim had been selected from the alternates Tab was the first to wish him well. He did so in his typical manner.

"Congratulations, Jim. You are certainly the man for the job. But just remember who bowed out, and gave you the shot. You owe me one."

"I don't owe you a thing, Tab. If you'd thought you could handle it you'd have cut me out. I've known you too long to be conned by you, Mr."

"I don't like that kind of talk, Jim." His voice was belligerent. And, suddenly, without warning he lashed out with a jab, striking Jim's eye. He followed it immediately with an uppercut.

Jim found himself lying on the ground.

He pulled his legs under him, watching carefully to avoid a kick. Tab had a half-smile, perhaps a smirk, on his face.

Neither spoke, the only sound their labored breathing.

He figures it's over, and he's won, Jim thought.

Jim moved in quickly, took several jabs to his face.

Quickly he landed half dozen hard blows on Tab's stomach, noted his opponents rapid withdrawal.

He continued to bore in, working on Tab's stomach.

A blow to the temple once more knocked him to the floor.

For a moment he saw nothing, heard a strange ringing. Then he saw Tab smiling, saw the foot smashing toward his ribs.

He rolled, caught Tab's foot and twisted, bringing Tab down. Quickly he struck him on the jaw, landed a blow in the solar plexus.

A few more punches, a roundhouse that landed on the temple, and Tab lay still.

The fight had ended. Wearily Jim staggered to the washroom, splashed cold water in his face. He washed blood from his cheek, and from his knuckles.

He turned as he heard a sound behind him.

Tab stood in the door, his hand pressed against his cheek bone, with blood dripping from between his fingers. He looked at Jim, then walked to a sink and washed the cut.

Tab turned to him and grinned. "There was a time I could have taken you, Jim. I've let myself get out of shape."

"There never was a time, Tab. There never will be."

"I am sorry, Jim. I lost my temper. I shouldn't have started that. We're not school kids anymore. Damn, I'm sore. You do pack a wallop!"

"You landed some good ones yourself."

"Yeh, I did, didn't I. Boy, we both look like hell," he grinned wryly, looking in the mirror.

Oddly enough the fight seemed to clear the air between them. Jim became more tolerant of the faults he saw in Tab. Tab, for a period, became a strong supporter of Jim. The fight was largely forgotten.

Tab Klooster had grown up in the tenements of Cincinnati. His parents were poor, lived on the third floor of the building in a small, dingy apartment. "I thought you had fixed that leak. And you didn't take out the garbage. God, this place stinks!" His Mother's complaints, delivered in a high, nasal whine, caused him to shudder.

"I need some washers. I'll see if Danny has any." His old man carried out the bag of garbage, closed the door with a sigh of relief. His Mother stood by the kitchen window and he heard her sniff. Quickly he slipped out the door. Soon she would be crying, and he didn't want to hear.

They shared a restroom with the other tenants on that floor. Usually it was busy, or busted. No one cleaned it. Every morning he carried the chamber pot from their room and emptied it in the commode.

Tab Klooster decided he would not be a loser. Whatever it took, he would have the things denied his parents. He would have a fancy apartment, big cars, beautiful women—and a private bathroom that worked.

Tab learned to fight early, and learned to fight dirty, learned to fight to win.

He learned how to make money, how to protect himself from the gangs that roved the streets—how to survive.

Everything he learned as a child on those streets he applied as a man.

In actuality, Tab Klooster was not as mean as often portrayed. Nor was he, on the other hand, any sort of angel.

"Shine, mister?"

"Nah, kid, not now. No time."

"Please, sir. It's only a quarter. I need the money."

For a moment Tab frowned, then felt in his pocket. "Here, you owe me a shine."

The boy grinned. "Yes, sir."

When his own interests were not at stake he made level-headed, objective decisions, showed little bias.

Tab liked and respected Jim Braddock. But, where his own welfare was involved, he had no friends. It was a characteristic those around him soon recognized.

"Jim, I'm sorry. I had to recommend against signing a support contract with your group. To put it bluntly, I've got a major holding in your competitor, Dolan Corporation, and if they lose this contract they'll go under. I can't sit still for that. You mention this to anyone and, naturally, I'll deny it. I just wanted you to know it's nothing personal."

While still quite young Tab decided that school was important. Books were important. Teachers could be useful. So could preachers. He cultivated people who could be useful. He learned those things that were important.

"Professor Odile, I am repeatedly amazed at the subtle, hidden, facts you surface and illustrate so well in your lectures."

Professor Odile smile, "Why, thank you Tab. I've certainly noted your keen interest in the class."

"I understand that Mr. Wentworth, one of your more distinguished students, is here at the reception. I'd enjoy meeting him. I'm sure he has many interesting reminiscences of your lectures. I hope to be doing business with his company in the near future."

"Ah, Jamie! Yes, Jamie Wentworth is one of our prized graduates. I'm sure the two of you would work well together. And he is such a generous man. He donated a vast sum of money to the college only this year."

Tab also found that school furnished excellent opportunities to prey on those less skillful in the ways of the street. When he finished high school he had enough money to buy a car. A long, black Buick convertible.

Girls liked big cars, and convertibles.

He liked girls.

He determined that engineers often did well. He attended engineering school. Though not brilliant he was an able scholar, and graduated high in his class.

He also made money while in college.

"Say, Freddy, I'm not going to be using the car this week-end. You want to rent it, I'll let it go reasonable."

Freddy had money, liked to show it. Big, black, Buick convertibles radiated the sense of wealth. Freddy rented the car.

Rather quickly Tab found that such wealthier students were always interested in renting his convertible. He found that many were even more interested in renting his convertible with girl installed.

"Brad, that little wagon of mind is free this week-end. And Nancy would like to go on a week-end skiing trip. I can set it up, if you're interested."

"Nancy! God yes. How much you asking for the car."

Brad was taken aback by the price, but when Tab explained that the price included all peripheral gear Brad grinned broadly, considered it a bargain.

Of course, things didn't always go smoothly.

"Say, you're nothing but a high-priced pimp. Who the hell got you into the fraternity? I'm going to have you tossed out on your God-damn ear."

Randy Tolsome stared at Tab, his disgust evident on his face as well as in his words.

Randy was unprepared for the action his words triggered. Tab land two quick jabs to his stomach, followed by an uppercut that closed Randy's mouth. Blood dripped from a split lower lip.

With two teeth missing Randy lisped an apology. No one bothered to call Tab names thereafter.

Tab's rise was not meteoric, but neither was it slow. He established a network of contacts who either owed him something, or who wanted something he could provide.

Perhaps one reason he liked Jim Braddock was simply that Jim was an exception. Jim accepted Tab, knowing him to be a scoundrel, but neither asked nor gave. He ignored Tab's solicitations, and continued on, as Tab explained it, a perpetual plodding course.

Weird! was Tab's interpretation.

The aerospace engineering world is small. They repeatedly met, at seminars, at trade shows, frequently at ASD at Wright-Patterson Air Force Base. If not friends they were at least close acquaintances.

———————

Jim's first visit to the contractor's facilities had not impressed him. The huge old buildings, constructed during the Korean War, with little subsequent maintenance, were hardly precursors of an advanced new ship.

It was characteristic of the times.

The government had limited longterm planning. With the fall of Communist Russia in the early '90s defense had been relegated to the lowest priority category. There'd be no more wars. How many times had that naive refrain echoed in man's history!

"I'm the caretaker. I had heard they were going to refurbish the old place. Last year, they were talking about tearing it down. Do you know, a few years back they were rolling out three fighters a day. Seems strange, don't it?"

Regardless, defense factory after defense factory deteriorated. Some were outmoded, and their disappearance had little real impact. Others were on the leading edge of technology, but they, too, suffered the same fate. Only the wise thinking of a few contractors resulted in mothballing of jigs, fixtures, and a variety of critical machinery.

———

Red China watched.

Quietly, methodically, they built up weapon systems to supplement their huge population. Quietly, methodically, they continued to expand the world's largest military establishment. The world turned its eyes away.

Peace! It's wonderful!

The perceived military threat had dissipated. The internal squabbles of the USSR, the need for a viable economic base, had rapidly curtailed her offensive build-up. The quiet progress of Red China in the fields of nuclear weapons, space systems, and launch capability attracted little attention.

Only Senator Peters made an impassioned plea.

"We are handing her the world on a platter. When the Russian military removed two-thirds of the long range missiles to China we should have interceded. When their nuclear subs began to declare Hong Kong as home base we should have objected. When their military leaders moved wholesale into Red China we should have seen the writing on the wall. Our technology has given her huge aircraft plants, major electronics capability, and weapons' skills equal to our own. Continued cutback in defense is madness!"

The speech brought instant response from such diverse groups as Women For Peace, Environment Uber Alles, the Tinanaman-Square-Was-a-Hoax Alert Group—and even of his own party.

"Senator Peters is a war-monger of the worst type. He would end the long period of mutual friendship that has existed between our countries. As two of the world's greatest democracies we must work together for continuing betterment of the world. If Senator Peters would visit our country, I am sure we could rid him of this racial phobia that possesses him. We have some excellent facilities for helping those irrational few who oppose the world's progress."

Communist China's representative received rousing cheers as he completed his address to the Joint Houses. "We have no territorial aspirations, look only for internal growth of our economy. That is the only reason for allowing the former USSR territory of Siberia to affiliate with us. We have a need for the oil so abundant in that wasteland, and they have need of the guidance and aid that only China can provide. It is an alliance based on mutual needs, and works to the advantage of all."

He smiled at the round of applause, bowed slightly. "You may be sure that, just as we have allowed Hong Kong to maintain its identity, we shall allow Siberia to continue its own government. Of course, in the interest of close relationships and to protect the people from the reactionary elements who steadfastly resist this merger, we shall station our army at strategic locations within Siberia. This is, I would have you recognize, at the request of the people of Siberia. Long live world peace!"

At the cocktail party that evening he remarked to Senator Peters, "And are there Chinese Communist killer squads hiding under your bed, Senator?" The comment brought a laugh to the lips of those within hearing, and was repeated throughout the evening.

The attack on Senator Peters that night, in his bedroom, was an oft-commented-on coincidence. Quick action by a security guard resulted in the Senator suffering only a slight wound. One attacker was killed, and the other died of undisclosed cause while being booked. The cause of the attack was not determined.

Senator Peters read the letter from the Communist Chinese representative.

"We regret the unfortunate incident that resulted in your being wounded. You might well have been killed! Better luck next time."

"The son of a bitch," he growled. "And he's being wined and dined as though he were a hero."

The Senator soon found that his problems had just begun. Demonstrators from across the nation assembled in his state capitol.

"Recall the Warmonger!" was a favorite sign.

"Peace, Yes—Peters, No," read another.

His wife and children were dogged by members of various groups. As soon as one received a court order to cease the harassment a new group took over.

"What are they doing! There must be a hundred. I can't even sleep of a night with their screaming!"

Mrs. Peters was hospitalized for a nervous breakdown after the third week. His son, William, knocked down two of the demonstrators who had been tormenting her. His arrest was immediate.

The injunctions against the protestors were reviewed by the state supreme court, and voided. "The injunctions are plainly interference with the right of free speech," Judge Knauper stated with a smile. "It is unfortunate that the injunctions were ever issued. I am sure these people mean no harm, and it is a sad, but irrelevant fact that Mrs. Peters has had a nervous breakdown. Perhaps she would recover more quickly if she divorced this warmonger."

# The Contractor

NLR, as a single entity, had never worked on a defense contract. But they had maintained a joint capability that gave them the potential. The union of three once powerful contractors had survived through combining their skills in aircraft and space systems. They worked commercial contracts, but maintained cadres of men skilled in the defense fields.

"There isn't going to be any significant defense contracting. And there is no way any of us could individually compete for what little is out there. So we combine forces, develop joint capability, and wait. History says we'll be needed." The business conference closed with agreement to that approach.

This contractor, NLR Corporation, had retained some capability, had bid on the Request for Proposal, or RFP, had been chosen. The company was composed of the fragments of three major aerospace companies. With the fall of the Russian Communist dictatorship the Pollyanna syndrome enveloped the US legislature. The cutback in defense was a kneejerk reaction, with little analysis of future needs or economic impact. Defense contractor followed defense contractor into the bankruptcy courts.

"More cutback. I want a list of engineers with program experience. Prioritize it, with the best men listed first. One way or the other, we'll keep them. Look at the papers. Someone is going to wise up. We can't continue to ignore the expansion taking place, the envelopment of country after country. We'll be needed."

Their managers were well-read in history. They knew, eventually, the world would repeat its old cycles, warlords would arise, and defense would be needed. And they watched with jaundiced eye the activity in Red China.

For major contracts of this type the System Program Office establishes a Source Selection Board. The Responses submitted by competing contractors are thoroughly reviewed by the Board. Members of the Board must be technically qualified.

The Source Selection Board was composed of an experienced crew. Of course, they only recommended. The final decision would be made up the line, in Washington. Would the best contractor win? Who could really say.

With the limited number of contractors who even qualified to respond to the RFP, competition was really minimal. One contractor had gone overboard on brochuremanship, with slick pictures of Flash Gordon vehicles. Perhaps they didn't hurt, but the contents of his proposal failed to reflect any of the futuristic characteristics.

The remaining bidders had addressed the technical, management, and financial volumes in a common manner, but each emphasizing its own strength. They responded to the requirements, methodically and thoroughly. Even the creative approaches to the technical problems had similar concepts.

The weighted results differed by only a few points.

"Well, with that kind of spread, whoever you choose is a winner," the reviewers commented. Everyone hoped it was so.

"Just evaluate 'em by the rules," Major Cortez grinned. "Let the chips fall where they will. Personally, I liked that space ship picture, but his tech team didn't follow through. Get those evaluations in by day's end. Our recommendation goes out tomorrow."

SYSTEM DESIGN REVIEW

From contract award to System Design Review the Program Office, and the contractor's facilities, were in turmoil. The requirement had to be refined, the supporting documents prepared, personnel briefed.

Hectic was the term most used by all concerned.

The System Design Review, or SDR, went well. In spite of the appearance of the plant the contractor's people were either doing an excellent snow job, or they had a handle on the task.

A major function of the SDR was, in fact, to confirm that the contractor did indeed have a thorough understanding of the job to be done.

Discussion after discussion, meeting after meeting, the grasp of the requirement was analyzed, questioned, tailored.

At times the activity was grueling slow, as key personnel discussed intricate details in technical jargon. At other times it went swiftly, with readily recognized understanding between the Air Force and the contractor personnel.

"You know," Kingston growled, "no one is sure the dynamic stealth technology is even feasible. Sure, for simple single frequencies you can feedback 180 degrees out of phase. But were dealing with complex, changing values. Not just frequency, but amplitude, phase...you name it."

Nevertheless they plodded on. The intent, at least, was understood. Whether the technology would be there was another problem, for later meetings.

Occasionally there were wide divergences between the military intent and the contractor's understanding. In a few such cases the bid was impacted, and decisions had to be made on financial adjustments. Even these discrepancies were eventually resolved.

Certainly the program management assigned by NLR wasn't lacking in credentials. The company program manager, Joseph Kingston, was Vice-President in charge of System Engineering. He had at least half a dozen major programs under his belt. "As you have undoubtedly noted,

I've worked both the space and aircraft field. By the way, it's ridiculous when your security people go overboard on their investigations. So I wet the bed when I was a kid! Only joking. They did a thorough job."

"I would like to mention a few areas I've reviewed in preparing for this assignment. I've gone back over various directly and indirectly related programs, even as far back as the Dynasoar. Interestingly enough, the concepts even then were well thought out. Dollars, technology limitations, and competition between organizations terminated that effort. These same problems have to guarded against, even today."

The Avionics System Integrator had assigned an equally able manager, Thomas Dwight, who also had been well-grounded in the avionics world. He responded to his introduction with a few words. "As some of you know, I've got a rather mixed background. Most recently I've worked the defensive electronics field, specializing in dynamic stealth technology. But I've also worked both electronic countermeasures and electronic counter-countermeasures systems. I believe this task is going to be the most interesting one of my career. I hope it is."

The only immediate concern was software. Although the Software Group seemed competent, they were younger, lacked some of the methodical image projected by the other engineering groups. Nevertheless, they talked a good war.

Mr. Kingston introduced the members of his team, went quickly over the agenda, then stated his philosophy.

"We encourage the members of the Air Force team to meet with their counterparts one-on-one, at any time, to discuss status, concerns, or to merely maintain rapport. If problems arise at that level, and you can't get them resolved, I am available at any time. You have access, of course, to those documents covered in the CDRLs. However, I recognize that the Contract Deliverable Requirements List items may not always provide you with the information you need. Therefore I am directing my people to provide you access to any of our documents you wish to peruse. The exception, naturally, are those documents that are proprietary to the company. And, generally, if the need is critical these can also be made available."

Jim nodded. At least it sounded like they were taking a team approach. Of course there would be problems, if only from personality differences. But, with a positive attitude, they could be resolved.

The program people participated well, asked significant questions, and provided accurate and detailed responses to the questions asked of them.

"Your flight test envelope has the ship flying at 150 knots at max altitude," Major Algordo smiled. "Isn't that unrealistic?"

The test envelope was revised.

"It appears that, when you are running ground tests, all the aircraft stabilization systems will be activated. Are they needed at all times for those tests? And if not, will we be burning them up rapidly?" Jim Frazier queried.

"Good point," Mr. Kingston examined the diagram. "We'll change that."

Fine tuning. It would continue until the airplane became operational. Over all, the SDR went well.

But it was during the evening social get-togethers that Jim began to identify those on whom one could depend, and those who were shaky. The daytime organization, and the real network that tended to show through after hours, were not too divergent. Often, in other organizations, they were. The result under such circumstance was almost always unpleasant. Here the contractor teams were pulled over, as an established group, from earlier programs. The longtime rapport between the members was evident.

"If you logistics jokers were on the ball we'd have the ship half completed by now."

"If you'd design realistic parts and materials, instead of pipe dreams, we'd already have the stock rooms full."

The friendly banter, with just a touch of barb included, was taken in good grace. It was evident that team members were well-acquainted, would work well together.

Even the rapport between the lead contractor and the associates was, at least superficially, good.

Of course, there were always some exceptions. Again, the Software Group seemed aloof. He wasn't sure whether it was choice, divergent background, or some yet unrevealed peculiarity.

"Advanced Realtime Ada is fine for the individual subsystems. But it is just too slow for the embedded gear. Like it or not we have to go to assembly language. And whoever chose that damn computer has never done realtime programming."

The software group talked shop in their own arena, occasionally mixing into the mainstream conversation. Based on his limited exposure they seemed to be knowledgeable.

Regardless, it was something to keep an eye on.

"Mr. Kingston, I hope your work is as successful as this party has been. I admit, I had some reluctance about attending. But I've learned more about you and your people than a month of work would have told me."

"Jim, were not really the sots we appear. I've found that, when people relax and socialize, they often solve a lot of problems they didn't even know they had. For example, I've been worried about Davidson. Turns out his wife is ill, and I didn't know until tonight. I'll try to lift the pressure off him some, and we'll still get the work done. Actually, I've got a damn good crew here. They'll give you your money's worth—and more!"

While at the plant he arranged to have an office assigned for the liaison officer, himself, his secretary, and an in-plant representative. He figured he'd be spending a good deal of time on-site. "Mr. Kingston, I'd like the offices in close vicinity of your own. I figure we'll be arm-wrestling a good deal of the time."

"I hope not Jim. We have the same goals, the same problems. I think we'll work well together."

He had walked by the facility where the original prototype had been assembled. It was here the plant director had lost his arm, leading to his subsequent death.

Little things can be deadly. A small piece of metal pipe, the size of a .22 shell. Matt Taylor had stopped by to observe mating between two reluctant body parts. After extended last minute adjustments they had prepared to insert the pins in place. The large nitrogen tank was uncovered, the pins immersed. The extreme cold would shrink them, allow them to be fitted into the close tolerance holes.

At that point Matt stepped on the pipe. It rolled and he awkwardly tried to catch his balance. "Hey...," slipped from his lips. He struck the floor with a thud. His left arm hit the deck, partially supported him. He reached out with his right arm. Tried to grab the railing for support. He missed the rail. His arm fell awkwardly through the guard fence—plunged into the frigid hell of the nitrogen bath.

In shock he lay still for an instant. Wide-eyed, rolled away. He pulled the now frozen arm out of the liquid.

His arm fell, striking the metal railing, then the floor. Shattered pieces of brittlely frozen skin and flesh scattered. Matt rolled his head, looked wide-eyed in disbelief at the fracturing extremity. "God, no? God...!"

Mercifully, he fainted.

Matt Taylor, following operation on his arm, died in the hospital from the complication of pneumonia. The story of his accident and subsequent death laid a cover of gloom over the workforce. It also introduced stories and rumors more frequently found in backward communities than in modern factories.

A seed such as the bean, once planted, may remain long dormant. Then, when conditions are right, it begins to grow. A bean, swelling with moisture, soon breaks the surrounding seed coat. A root tip extends and anchors in the nourishing earth. Soon the stem reaches upward, the cotyledons open, and the plant flourishes.

An idea, once planted, may likewise remain dormant. But when conditions are right, it too may grow and flourish. Matt Taylor's accident planted a seed of fear and superstition. Stories of another people and of ancient times circulated. Stories of a land cursed. Stories of a blind witch.

"Man, watch yourself. There's bad vibes here. This ain't no way for a job to kick off. And I've heard stories about this valley. Spooky ones, I mean. Hey, let's have a drink at the Cove after. Did you see Matt's arm. Shattered like a damn glass vase!"

With the fertilizer of coincidence and implied causation the seed began to grow. Every accident, each problem, became an indicator of bad luck—or of something worse.

Jim shrugged. It wasn't a subject he wanted to concentrate on. With an effort he turned his thoughts back to the SDR.

Matt Taylor's death occurred the same day the Treaty of Mutual Aid was signed between Iran and Red China. The Treaty provided China with the totality of oil from Iran's wells, and provided Iran with a source of weaponry of defense.

"Ever work in that area, Mr. Kingston?"

"Never did. Started to go over toward the Middle East, years ago. Wife didn't care for the idea, and I'm just as glad. Look's like China has her fuel situation well in hand. Wish we could say the same."

The annexation of southern Iraq by Iran had raised fears of an imminent war, and Iran had moved quickly to find a powerful supporter.

Strange how unrelated events and incidents associate with each other in one's mind.

The minutes of the SDR, along with hardcopies of the various presentations would be hand carried to him as soon as they were completed. The logistics of the SDR had been carried out smoothly. This may be the rare exception, but maybe things will go well, he thought to himself. "You gotta be kidding," a little voice whispered. He nodded in agreement.

Jim and the Colonel worked out a semblance of logically allocated chores. They left enough flexibility in the assignment to cover eventualities.

Colonel Goetler had been strangely quiet since the meeting with General Mathis. He had introduced the team at the SDR, but let the members carry on without interference. He reviewed incoming reports, redmarked areas of concern, then passed them on to Jim Braddock. The Colonel was spending more and more of his time in Washington, fighting the political battles and hitting the cocktail circuit.

It seemed to pay off. The Congressional teams no longer dogged the program, and funding was essentially automatic. The Colonel's picture hit the newspapers from time to time, associated with "A major hush-hush program." It was a split of responsibilities that suited Jim, as he continued to perform the on-site program manager function.

"Oh, Colonel Goetler, how are you? How is Jim doing?" Tab Klooster stood beside him. "Lois, this is the co-manager of one of our most important programs. Colonel, Lois Donnor. She just starred in a remake of 'The Jungle'. Are you a movie fan, Colonel?

"I haven't been, but if Miss Donnor is in it, I could change my mind."

"Well, how gallant, Colonel. Thank you."

"Exciting world, Washington. Did you hear that the President and China have signed a Treaty of Perpetual Friendship? We are indeed in an era of universal peace!"

"By the way, tell Jim that he'd better tighten his ship. With the continued progress in development of world wide peace treaties there is strong pressure to drop all the military contracts. The Joint Defense Committee will be out next month looking for some basis to close down the Dreamship effort. They've heard of some of the blatant discrepancies that have occurred."

"I am afraid they have the advantage on us, Mr. Klooster. I'm familiar with no blatant discrepancies."

"No? Well, Colonel, perhaps you should be. Ah, I see General Mathis. Excuse us, Colonel."

After returning to the program site the Colonel was overly quiet throughout the day. At quitting time he stopped at Jim's desk. "Have you time to stop at the bar and have a drink, Jim?"

For a moment Jim pursed his lips. The Colonel wasn't one to issue such an invitation. Something plainly was on his mind. "Sure, Colonel. Let me lock up the desk here. Oh, hell, I have a few more chores to clean up. Tell you what, I'll meet you at the club in half an hour."

Colonel Goetler had chosen a small table in an out of the way corner. "Saw you come in, and went ahead and ordered. She'll have a round here in a moment." He leaned forward.

"Tab Klooster is poisoning you at headquarters."

"Hmmm, Tab and I have crossed paths on occasion. He's right ambitious. But I haven't really given him reason for a vendetta against me. Exactly what's happening?"

"I don't have a lot of details, but the old whispering campaign is in full swing. They are slinging mud without regard to the facts. I slip in some common sense occasionally, but no one cares for that. Common sense just isn't juicy enough."

"Jim, I figured to tell you. You and I haven't always got along together. But I have nothing to do with what's happening there. I know of no one I'd rather have working this program."

"Colonel, I appreciate that. Sounds like neither of us is likely to be calling the shots on that problem, though."

"Regardless of how it goes, I'll throw all my support to you. You know, I came in here with a chip on my shoulder. I'm a little wiser now. I've had a lot of pressure on me, from the military, my family, and from my own ambition. Anyway, I think we've been a good team, and if I have my way we'll work the problems together."

"Well, thank you. I reckon this next round is mine."

They didn't talk much after that. They didn't have to. The rapport had been established.

# Manufacturing

The plant covered acres of buildings, open areas, sheds—a hodge-podge that supported aircraft production. The newest building housed administration offices, engineering labs, and drafting centers. In addition, well equipped conference rooms supported the frequent meetings associated with a research and development program.

Bill Davidson glanced around one such conference room, conference room E. His face was grim, but a slight smile gradually formed on his lips. A good crew. Men he had worked with over the years, with a few exceptions. They were dependable!

"Gentlemen, I...Excuse me, Ladies and Gentlemen—I didn't see you over there, Ruth, Sally. Glad you are here with us, though."

He looked at the notes on the lectern. "Most of you sat through the System Design Review, so I'll only touch briefly on that activity. By the way, minutes of that SDR will be in the classified library. I'd advise each of you to review those sections relating to your discipline."

One of the new men raised a hand. "Do we need special authorization to get into the classified library?"

"Yes! However, when you show your badge at the entrance a check is made of your clearance status. Talk to your group leader, he'll walk you through the procedure. Good question."

"I'll knock off here in a second. When I do we'll break down into working groups, one for each discipline. Get yourselves organized, let me know what you need to get rolling, and start putting together a rough management network for your activity. I've done mine already, and it's posted on the board here at the front of the room. Pull your requirement dates from my network."

They stretched to glance at the board.

He covered administrative details, requirements imposed by the bureaucracy, and other material appropriate to initializing a task.

"Now's a good time for a break. You'll note that I'm right general with my drawing. I expect you to flesh it out. If you identify any dates that you can't meet, let me know. And, of course, let me know why. We'll meet here every day at 8:00 until further notice. Any questions?"

They were reluctant to raise any questions until they had a chance to examine his rough management network. He stepped down, walked to the rear of the room and filled a styrofoam cup with coffee.

"Hey, Chief, when will we get a valid requirement spec?"

"Hell, if this goes like most programs, sometimes after first flight!"

Everyone laughed, though perhaps with some bitterness.

"By the way, go through the contract, identify the contract deliverables you owe the Air Force. And while you're at it, check the DOD and Mil Standards that apply. Tomorrow I'll expect each lead to give a short briefing on his network, problems, and plan of action. Have fun."

A mock groan escaped the group, and Denny started "For he's a jolly good fellow," only to be quickly squashed by a crescendo of boos.

Bill Davidson grinned. "You think it's bad now, do you? Just wait!" He wasn't being entirely facetious.

Organization change followed organization change. Groups shuffled from office to office as they grew or shrank. Old leaders were displaced, news ones crowned.

The typical hectic process of getting started on a new program was underway.

Kingston grinned at the furor throughout his organization. He had fought this type of battle often enough to realize that things would settle down. He applied band aids to hurt feelings, joshed with his men when morale was low, kept everyone looking at—if not attaining—the immediate goal of getting properly organized.

"Mike, you didn't get the big office because it's the only area big enough for the CAD group. They've got to have their computers to do the drawings, and plotters to kick them out. So I've put you in the converted warehouse for now. I know. It's cold. We'll get that squared away."

Procedures were written. Procedures were discarded. Computer programs were installed, used, rejected. Others better met the needs and were retained.

People transferred from unit to unit as skills were recognized, and lack of skill removed.

It was a time of bustle, hustle, and confusion. It could roil your guts, or drive you to your best performance. Mr. Kingston performed well under the pressure. He was a rare manager who enjoyed bringing order from chaos.

On the other hand, he had continual battles with the typical politicians who thrive under these conditions. What they lacked in ability they made up for in their skill in manipulation. Mr. Kingston had found that, properly directed, even their skills could be useful. Over years of experience he had learned to direct them.

"Thomas, there is no way I can put you in charge of that group. I recognize that you want the position, but you're the only man I have who can bring everyone together and get action. You've got to continue as my facilitator. I know it isn't an official position, but God knows you are the expert at it. I can't do without that expertise."

Perhaps he laid it on a little thick. But Thomas could manipulate people, bring them together, and obtain consensus where others might fail.

———

It was in this time frame that he Treaty of Mutual Respect was signed between Iran and Kuwait following the summoning of Kuwait's leaders to a meeting in Tehran. In addition to recognition of that mutual respect, the treaty transferred responsibility for marketing Kuwait's oil to the Iranian Oil Ministry.

"We find that, through cooperation with the Oil Ministry, that we can insure more equitable income from these resources. Iran's kindness in providing this support is greatly appreciated." Kuwait's ambassador smiled, would answer no additional questions.

He was escorted from the news room by Iranian security personnel.

"Colonel, I'm putting more and more faith in General Mathis' position. I had him figured as a pure paranoiac, at the start. But there sure seems to be a pattern showing up."

"Jim, a lot of people are scared. They think we're in a too little too late situation. But I don't see anything coming out of the White House. I don't know whether it's him, or his staff."

———————

Assembly foreman Joe Walsh examined the drawings in perplexity. They were well done, meticulous. With the exception of a single missing refdes, or reference designator, they seemed perfect. He shook his head, picked up the phone.

"Ruth, get Bill Davidson for me."

He waited impatiently. Bill Davidson was lead design engineer. He should have an answer.

Davidson's deep voice boomed over the talk box. "Davidson, what's up?"

"Bill, I got the drawings for the prototype on the new bird. They look good—except, well, you've left off a few things."

"Damn? Did they forget the wings again?" He knew Davidson was grinning.

"Almost, almost. Look, I'm sure there's an explanation. But you don't have an instrument panel, you don't have a yoke, nor rudders—hell, you don't even have cockpit windshields. Is this the result of Johnson's cost saving kick? What's going on, Bill?"

At the other end there was a moment of silence.

"Joe, just build it like it reads."

"Build it like it reads."

"Yep."

"Hmph!—See ya, Bill."

He hung up the phone, reexamined the drawings. With a shrug he called in his team leaders. Hell, he thought, the damn government is crazy—build it like it is?

Build it they did.

---

Jim followed the world news with interest. He had always been a prolific reader, and the changing world provided an always exciting story. He felt that his view was jaundiced by the Mathis' pitch. Yet he wasn't sure. Today's news related to the Middle East.

Major progress had been made for further stabilizing the world, another step to permanent peace. This was the amicable merger of Iran and Iraq. It came as a surprise to many. Previous wars, antipathy between the factions in the two countries, the annexation of southern Iraq by Iran—No one would ever have suggested this event. Neither would the recent statements by Iraq's dictator, suggesting instead an on-going struggle.

But Iraq's leader had resigned, retired to a villa in southern France. His successor moved quickly to convene a meeting with the Shiite leaders of his nation, then with the leader of Iran.

The merger had come in a matter of weeks. Throughout the world the arrangement received applause. China immediately recognized the new nation, which retained its title of Iran.

Oil shipments from the previous state of Iraq was now being rapidly diverted to China. "A happy result of earlier treaties with Iran," the Chinese Ambassador to the United States explained.

With the disbanding of the Iraq army placement of the military, particularly the officers, constituted a problem. China graciously acquiesced to accept the officer contingent to work in the interior of their nation, under a comprehensive contract. A few recalcitrant officers refused the offer, and were being pursued by Iran and Chinese security personnel.

"It is a delightful opportunity which I would not think of resisting," General Hashim smiled, shaking hands with the Chinese representative and his security guards.

---

Dream Ship One had been a manufacturer's nightmare. The physical shape of the bird was unorthodox, the materials used resisted all ordinary means of assembly, and the schedule was man-killing.

Nevertheless the jigs had been developed, the fixtures put in place. Machines were jerry-rigged to mold and shape reluctant metal. Welders learned techniques directly from the laboratories, and PhDs mingled with assemblers to resolve the problems that continuously surfaced.

Kingston smiled. "Jim, we've managed to advance aircraft manufacturing technology by an order of nagnitude. I'll tell you, this program has had me worried. We're moving materials from a lab situation to factory floor overnight. I've had to have machinists specially trained to work some of this stuff. But it's falling into place."

"I reckon the program has paid for itself if only because of those advances. Let's just hope Congress doesn't cut off our water."

The mock-up was built from more amenable materials. It quickly became an all-purpose vehicle. Form and fit were checked and rechecked, wire runs were measured. Displays were installed and removed, modified, and re-installed.

Major problems surfaced with the multi-mode engines. Although operation in any given mode was resolved, the transition between modes introduced pressures and vibrations the materials could not tolerate. Transition to the scramjet mode resulted in shifting forces that on two occasions destroyed the engine module. The final solution included a wire-wrapped unit, which flexed under pressure and then returned to shape.

When Bill Davidson first saw the final engine module he shook his head. "I always thought barbed wire and scotch tape was a figure of speech! Oh, well! Whatever works."

Security made the test phase extremely difficult. Rollout and initial run-up were conducted at night, with minimal participation. Trial runs on the long runway were similarly night exercises. The decision was made to lift off first flight during the early morning hours, and to terminate the flight at the Navy's China Lake facility if necessary. Risks were increased, but security was paramount.

"Bill, have you coordinated with the Navy? They'll have to provide equivalent coverage. Maybe you better take a trip to China Lake, have a look around. Get with the chief of security there and feel him out."

"Actually, Jim, I was up there last week. Stayed overnight at the huge metropolis of Ridgecrest. They are growing, you know. Anyway, I'll keep close with China Lake's security people. At the moment I don't see any problems."

Overall the activities had proceeded with only limited difficulty. The oxygen system had malfunctioned on one occasion, resulting in a hasty descent. Buss lines had carried unexplained noise until terminators of the right impedance had been incorporated. Vector jets had failed to swivel over the needed range.

For the early flights they weren't required. But once the ship flew at altitude the air became so tenuous that surface controls no longer functioned. The vector jets, based on Newton's action/reaction law, took their place.

Each problem had been worked. Each glitch removed. Each success had resulted in a glow of satisfaction. As problems were resolved time after time a feeling of euphoria developed. Until that final flight!

Actually, the Outstanding Item Status Report, 3 months prior to rollout, encompassed 500 single line computer pages. In theory each line item had to be cleared before rollout would be authorized.

In practice the military always maintained a hardnosed attitude until the last minute. "Every item will be completed and signed off on by Quality." AFPRO personnel maintained constant vigilance to insure nothing slipped through the cracks. SPO personnel supplemented them to keep the visibility high. When it became evident that time would not permit completion of all identified outstanding items everyone worked closely together to isolate alternatives. "We could substitute an aluminum fitting there for the early flights, replace it prior to flight three."

They attempted to identify entries that potentially could be delayed until after rollout—in other words, they worked together to insure a timely rollout. "We won't fly at altitude until at least the 6th flight. That vector jet problem can be worked. It just doesn't have to be solved by rollout."

Rollout had been almost a non-event. Air Force personnel were on hand. Not the bigwigs, but members of hush-hush groups rarely seen in public. DARPA and NASA members from seldom mentioned organizations. The CIA was represented. There was no publicity.

Jim found himself, more and more, defending the program rather than running it. Query after query was generating from Congress. "Colonel, you know I can't pass that information out in the clear. If necessary I'll address a closed session of Congress, but even that is risky. Get those people out of my hair, will you!"

"They are looking for a basis to attack the program, Jim. Political hay to be made. And a few are truly concerned. I'll do what I can, but I suspect you'll have to give a pitch to at least some of the committees."

To add to his troubles the press was beginning its normal anti-defense smear, and the Dreamship series was being alluded to.

The allusions were typical. High risk. Over cost. Behind schedule. Unable to meet the specification. Jim wondered. Had any defense program not faced those very charges? He knew of none.

"Mr. Braddock, there is a great deal of concern that the people aren't being informed of major problems with your program. Rumors have it that the engines are underpowered, the maneuvering units don't operate properly, that your behind schedule, and running well over cost." Duane Castle glanced at his notebook.

Jim thought, "He's got that memorized, he didn't read it."

"Every program has problems. That's why they hire managers, to solve those problems. I'd say we have no more, perhaps even fewer, than for other programs of this complexity. As for the specific items you cited, I expect each to be operational in the time frame when it will be needed. Cost and schedule are continuously reviewed, adjusted for changed circumstances. Overall, we are doing remarkably well."

"Well, what significant problems do you have?"

"Come on, you know I'm not going to play that game. My most significant problem right now is a nosy news correspondent." Jim grinned.

---

The Congressional Committee investigating the Executive Office had just completed its third session. The Executive Office had sent diplomatic messages to Iran, Saudi Arabia, and China. China, though not a party to the negotiations, was acting as broker between the Mid-East nations.

The messages had condemned the political merger of the two states, implying that military pressure from Iran and China forced acquiescence on the Saudi nation.

Congress strongly favored the merger, was investigating the Executive Branch to locate the writer of the diplomatic messages. Already several witnesses had been found in contempt of Congress.

Secretary of State Jodan and his Saudi counterpart discussed the matter on public tv. "This merger will place the preponderance of all Middle East oil supplies under the control of one entity. There is no question that it will lead to higher fuel prices throughout the world."

"My dear Secretary, not at all. As our Chinese counterparts have noted, with this merger we can introduce efficiencies because of the comprehensive approach to drilling, pumping, shipping, and marketing. These savings, I assure you, will be passed on to our customers." The Saudi Arabian glanced at his Chinese advisors, who nodded in assent.

---

Jim had unloaded as much of the Congressional interface as possible on Colonel Goetler. Nevertheless, he was finding little time to monitor the progress of the program, participate in the critical decisions that had to be made. Even worse, he felt that his judgment was flawed by emotion.

He was finding himself responding to those around him in angry voice, even when he was only inconvenienced.

"Linda, damn it, where is my wine!"

She looked at him, startled. "Why, Jim, you just drank it. Do you want another glass?"

"Honey, I'm sorry. I guess I was thinking about work. I don't even remember drinking it."

She sobbed, turned to leave the room.

He touched her shoulder. "I...Look, I'm sorry. I love you."

He held her close. She looked up at his face, and he noted the concern in her eyes.

"It's okey, baby. It's all right."

It wasn't.

He hadn't been thinking of work. He'd been reliving the nightmare. With an effort he put it from his mind.

Adding to his problems was the recurrence of those odd dreams. They were almost always the same, yet always with some new and minor twist. At times he felt as though a worm were threading its way through his brain, triggering weird and irreconcilable visions.

He made up his mind. Tomorrow I'll talk to Wilcoxson. Damned old wives' tales. But he might know something.

"I met you, oh, about a year ago, Jim. Doctor Harty's promotion at the college. Anyway, I'm glad to see you. What can I do for you?"

Jim hesitated. He could feel his face reddening.

He took a deep breath. "Professor Wilcoxson, you had a lecture several months ago. One about the history of the valley—and about the myths and legends. My wife and I attended. We found your presentation very interesting."

"Well, thank you. I'm flattered you still remember. Actually it's been quite a bit longer than that. Yes, it is an interesting subject. Unfortunately, there is little material available on the subject. Much of it has come down by word of mouth."

Professor Wilcoxson smiled, evidently well pleased.

"Have there been events, either real or imagined, that contributed to some of these legends? Or anything that would imply there is some factual basis for such superstitions?"

"Jim, that's an odd question from an engineering type." Professor Wilcoxson frowned, glanced out the window. A bird fluttered from the ground, disappeared skyward.

"See that? That's a raven. They are interesting birds, birds around which numerous superstitions have arisen. Did you ever read Poe's work, 'The Raven'?"

He didn't wait for a reply.

"There are always events which the superstitious associate with the supernatural. The moon and its effects. The witches of New England, believed in by even the wisest of their leaders. Coincidence can be a scary thing."

"I've been subject to some odd dreams, dreams that started well before your lecture. And ravens seem to be a key part of each dream."

"That is strange. Do you know, the Indians are said to have had weird dreams. Not just those from the Jimson weed, but others. Often, quite often, with the raven as a theme. Of course, we have many of the ravens here in the valley, so it's not unreasonable."

He stood up, sat on the edge of his desk.

"But as for any real connection between the ravens and real world events—no! I would hardly think so! Jim, don't take this wrong, but you may want to talk to your doctor about those dreams."

As Jim left he walked over to his bookcase, removed a worn notebook. Opening it, he flipped through the pages. "Damn it, coincidence! I know these are coincidence!"

# Dreamship Two

The loss of Dream Ship One resulted in increased pressure on the production line. Dream Ship Two was needed yesterday. A third shift was added, additional trouble shooters brought in. Parts Pushers scooted throughout the plant on their errands. Several logistics expediters were added to the team. The result was the typical pandemonium resulting from too little too late actions.

And there were other problems.

"Joe, I'm having a little trouble with my third shift people."

"Yeh, what gives?"

"You know Sandy—Sandy Bellevue?"

"Sure. She quit last week, right? Damn good worker. Nice looker, too. Is she getting married, or what?"

"No, she's not getting married. She quit cause she was scared as hell. She swears old Matt Taylor is out here at the airplane every night. And she is one scared woman!"

"Hey, you better can that talk quick. Stories like that can mess up the schedule in a hurry. You better be out and around during the shift. And if you hear anyone spreading that kind of tale, lean on 'em."

Subassemblies arrived, were installed. Fiberglass optical lines were strung. Form and fit problems surfaced. Form and fit problems were resolved.

People problems remained.

"Stan, walk out to the plane with me."

"Sure, Julia. Something wrong?"

"No, not really. I just don't like working around it at night. You know they say Matt Taylor walks, right there above us on the platform, at night. Sandy quit last Thursday. She swears he was up there on the platform, his arm gone, just standing looking at her. Sure, I know, it sounds silly. Anyway, it makes me nervous."

Superstition breeds in the backwoods—and on the assembly line.

Rags! They had accumulated, and the metal can was full. Rather than empty it someone decided to drop them into the wooden crate.

Spontaneous Combustion? Perhaps.

Perhaps someone had discarded a cigarette, rather than be caught smoking in the area.

Smoke and fire were reported at 10:30. Van Estes had gone to pick up parts. On his way back he smelled something hot, something like oil. "Sid, you smell that?"

"Yeh, yeh, I do. Smells like a transformer getting hot. Or maybe something burning. Better let Brown know."

Fred Brown was the line supervisor. He started a walk around when informed of the odor. He noted the odor was stronger near the rear of the aircraft. Unfortunately, as he approached the wooden crate he was interrupted.

"Hey, Fred! You got a phone call in the office."

He climbed the stairs to the office, located on the upper deck looking out over the assembly area. Picking up the phone he sat on the edge of the desk. "Hello, Brown here."

There was only silence. The line was open, but no one spoke.

"Hello, is anyone there? Hello…"

Finally he hung up, lit a cigarette, and waited. If it's important they'll call again, he thought. He finished the cigarette. Still no call. With a grunt he snuffed out the butt, started to read a report, then recalled the problem with an odor.

"Damn!" He looked out of the cubicle toward the rear of the ship. Flames were already enveloping the wooden crate, licking against the building walls. "Oh, Hell!"

Quickly he turned in the fire alarm.

"Simpson, Randolph—grab some fire extinguishers," he yelled to the floor below. "That crate behind the aircraft. It's burning."

The building side was warped from the heat, the paint burned off and the metal blackened. The platform at the rear of the ship was damaged. There was no identifiable damage to the Aircraft.

Lucy Severn had a strange report. "It was him. I've seen him before, standing there, his arm missing. And a cigarette in his mouth. He's the one."

Of course, she meant Matt Taylor.

Strange, how easily superstition spreads.

Sabotage came to mind. But the combination of facts didn't support that conclusion. A saboteur would have managed to do more damage, and in a more intelligent way.

Fighting the fire was a routine process. The truck arrived quickly, braked to a screeching halt. The firefighters leaped into action. "Hanson, get through those panels. Bradley, get that foam ready. You two, around the other side. Move it!" The firefighters had used axes to break through the metal panels of the building. In a few moments they had their chemicals feeding in, and the fire died from lack of oxygen and lowered temperature.

At times you could almost believe the weird tales passed around on the line. But, overall, the program had gone well. No, Matt Taylor hadn't triggered this one.

And, in spite of such incidents, the day did arrive and Dreamship Two rolled out of the plant.

There had been minor publicity in the papers. Actually, the event had only been mentioned in the inside pages. The papers headlines had been saved for the meeting between the President and Iran's leader.

The occasion was the signing of the Treaty of Mutual Consent, in which the United States acknowledged the new state of Greater Iran, now incorporating the prior Saudi Arabian domain.

"This merger, one always encouraged by the United States, eliminates a source of irritation in the Middle East, and provides a basis for an integrated development of the petroleum resources of that region. Additionally, by uniting the marketing task under Iran's Oil Ministry, it insures stability in the pricing structure."

China's ambassador, invited to be present with the two leaders, smiled at the President's words.

# First Flight for Two

The Dreamship article did not mention the craft by name, merely noted that rollout of an R & D aircraft was imminent.

"Klooster plans to be here for first flight. He's standing in for the General. He is one mean son-of-a-bitch. Did you know the program manager on the Ground-Follower? Klooster had him drummed out. Didn't fire him, but he made life so miserable the poor bastard resigned." Colonel Goetler watched Jim closely for reaction.

"Yeh, I heard Tab was the cause of that. But the program wasn't well run. I saw the write-ups, and I can't knock 'em. Anyway, if the old boy is after blood, I afraid he can bleed us easy. We've got more than our share of problems."

"It is interesting, though. Tab doesn't want any part of this job. And he shouldn't be after me, 'cause he helped me get this program. I can't psych out what he wants. Maybe he'll tip his hand when he gets here."

"Of course, he's a conceited, ambitious bastard. I wouldn't mind seeing him take a fall. He thinks he's so damn superior. God, I hate that bastard!"

Jim stopped suddenly. My God, what am I saying! Tab! Sure, he and I have had run-ins. But hate? Actually, I've always had a warm feeling for the scoundrel, though I don't know why.

"Colonel, ignore that. I guess I'm a little tired. Tab's all right in his own way."

Colonel Goetler nodded, was watching him from the corner of his eye.
He almost shouted, "Don't stare at me, you son-of-a-bitch," but
controlled the impulse.

"I'm going down to the hangar."

He got up, hurriedly left the office.

What is getting into me, he wondered. I don't react that way. It's not
my nature, and it's not my style. Seems like I behave like that more and
more frequently. I think I scared Linda badly the other night. And the
Colonel seemed a little surprised.

He stopped at the hangar entranceway. He hadn't really intended to
come here, but it was as good a place as another.

They were working on the fuel tanks. Tests had detected major leaks at
several points in the cells. A special caulking compound was being applied.

"I'm not going back in that tank!"

"Not going back in? Look, we gotta finish caulking that seam! Come
off it!"

"You finish that one. I'm telling you, I saw something in there. I don't
know what it was, but I don't want to see it again. No, you go ahead."

"Mr. Braddock! Didn't see you there." They looked guiltily at each other.

"He was…That is, I'm just getting ready to finish caulking this cell."

Jim waved, walked on. He didn't like what he had overheard. And he
knew the stories making the rounds. A strange problem, one he had
never met on other programs.

---

Jeremiah—Jerry to his friends—was assigned as chief pilot for Dream
Ship Two. He knew he would be. It was both an honor and a tribulation.
When informed of the choice he grinned, commented, "It figures. You
want the best, and here I am. I just hope that bird treats me nice."

It had been a long time coming. Even while in grade school he had
dreamed of flying. He odd-jobbed during high school, spent his money

on flying lessons. At eighteen he flew tail draggers from the local dirt field, built up hours and skill.

He worked for more than a year after high school, bought a wrecked biplane and rebuilt it. The money he made from flying passengers covered his college expenses. He majored, of course, in aeronautical engineering, and passed in the upper third of his class.

With his interests and training he naturally gravitated toward a flying career. With the severe cutback in active military the Air Force was not recruiting. By a lucky fluke he learned of a special program for test pilots. "Jerry, got a tip for you. West Coast needs some fliers. If you got the hours they'll run you through a training course, put you to work." The word had come from a fellow pilot, and Jerry responded immediately. He had no trouble qualifying, found himself in a crash course to become a new version of the 90-day-wonder, civilian type. As a follow-up a special military requirement resulted in direct appointment to a commissioned slot as an Air Force officer. He went through an accelerated course on military custom, protocol, bureaucracy. Upon graduation he shipped to Edwards AFB for Air Force test pilot training.

He knew flying, and knew it well. His grasp of engineering principles was excellent. His training consisted mainly of learning the Air Force way, and he picked up on that quickly. His maturity and skill gave him an edge over the other students, and his successful graduation was almost automatic. He served a one year commitment, was transferred to active reserve, and went to work for NLR as a test pilot.

He spent his days with the designers, the programmers, the assemblers. His nights he lived with the specifications, test plans, and schedules. The one focus of his life—Dream Ship Two.

"I don't understand this change, and I don't give a damn what the engineer says. You don't modify the plans unless I sign off on it. I want to know what I'm flying." Only when he felt comfortable with changes would he approve them.

He knew the avionics, the control surfaces, the multi-purpose engines, the hydraulics—there was little on the aircraft that he had not personally examined.

He identified missing rivets, bad solder joints, impedance mismatches, minor and major glitches throughout a system such as this. The workers grinned when he came near the airplane.

"He's got a sixth sense. If you left a fingerprint on his airplane he'll find it and want it wiped clean."

In spite of the simulation time, the first flight was agonizing.

Although the simulation was thorough it lacked the vibration, the unprogrammed motions, and the sense of danger that only the real flight could trigger.

Perhaps even worse, there was a decided difference in the interface. The simulator was comfortable, warm, supportive. The interface with the ship was hard, cold, antagonistic. He felt as though he had gone from the arms of a loving mistress to those of a spiteful bitch.

He felt his skin crawl. The real problem was even worse, and one that he preferred not to voice. The ship seemed to have a will of its own, a will that he had to bend to his needs. A will that was ever independent, ever fighting back. Yet, once his dominance was established, she yielded to his demands, reluctantly.

At first, when he donned the skull cap, the fires of hell etched paths through his brain. His muscles, spasmodic, twitched and flexed. With effort he suppressed a scream. Darkness, with painful flashes of terrible light, crowded his vision.

Rarely did the problem re-surface during the actual flight. This was one such exception.

He concentrated his mind on a point in his skull between and above his eyes. As he concentrated the flashing pains receded. He breathed deeply, slowly. He concentrated. Warmth, relaxed muscles, deep pleasant breathes.

The pain, still there, lessened as his mind blanked it out, His thoughts stayed on the spot between and above his eyes, on his breathing, on relaxing the muscles. He wiped away the cold sweat trickling down his cheek. A shiver ran through him. Partly nauseated, he repressed a heave.

Still the increased flow of saliva in his mouth, the taste of saltiness, reminded him of drinking bouts and their unpleasant consequences. He took slow, measured breathes, fought the malaise.

Slowly he righted the aircraft, gently sensing its response. At last it flew straight and level.

He grimaced, and tears trickled from the corners of his eyes.

How stupid, to be so afraid now. The crisis was over. Once more he had survived. Always it happened this way. But almost always, on the ground. He shivered again uncontrollably.

He could sense resentment, rebellion, each time he drove her through her paces. At times she bucked, fishtailed, threw herself violently toward the earth. But he never felt fear then.

No, only the need to regain control, reimpose his authority. And always he succeeded. It seemed she needed to show her independence, yet desired the strong rein still.

He banked her slowly, cut power, nosed downward. Raising the base he notified the field, "Clear traffic. I'm coming in hot. Not an emergency, but potential problems. Just give me room."

Soon the dark skies of space blended to the blue skies of earth. The Pacific Ocean rim stretched out, bending and twisting, to his west. On the east the mountain ranges formed an inverted V. Far ahead in distance, but minutes away in time, home base waited for his return.

The landing proved smooth and uneventful. He completed the postflight debriefing, letting the engineers pursue the problems which had surfaced.

He breathed deeply, once, twice. There was little physical exertion, but the stress of controlling her drained him of energy. Tonight he would sleep well. He would sleep well—if the dreams didn't return! But they would return.

Klooster's face was angry. Plainly there was something about the flight which disturbed him.

"Jim, I really don't like to lean on you. But the flight test people run the flight test! Your continual interference was contrary to normal procedures, and in my opinion it endangered the aircraft and the pilot. I did not interrupt during the mission, in fear of making things worse. I strongly recommend that you stay out of the flight center during future test runs."

Jim listened somberly. Of course, Tab had to find fault. And he was partially right. The program manager shouldn't be calling the shots during flight test. Nevertheless, if he had allowed to test to continue, using the existing flight cards, there would have been a major problem. The engineering data being received plainly indicated that transition to scramjet would fail. So he had canceled that portion of the flight. Tab, of course, wasn't too interested in explanations.

"Now, Jim, don't be too upset. We go back a long way, so there isn't going to be any of this in the write-up. I'm just telling you for your own protection." Tab smiled and patted Jim's shoulder.

"Ah, Jim, how long have we worked together? Twelve, no, more like fourteen years. Yes sir! And friendship counts for a lot in this dog-eat-dog world!"

"Colonel, you're real quiet. I must say I like the way you run your shop, overall. A few bad spots here and there, but nothing of consequence. I'll take back a good report to the General."

Colonel Goetler nodded, smiled slightly. Now what is he after, he thought. There are too many real problems, and he's letting them all slide.

"Jim, I need to ask a favor of you." Tab had regained some lost composure, and he smiled and sat down.

"I've a friend, Major Nestor. Fine boy. Comes from a good family, of course. And definitely a future general. And an excellent pilot. Extremely impressive combination!"

Jim nodded, looking for the bottom line.

"I'd like for you to bring him on the program. He would definitely be a strong contributor. You might consider giving him a staff position, supporting you and the Colonel. Tell you what, suppose I leave a resume' and copies of his ratings. Everything down the right hand side, you will note. I'm flying back in the morning, so give me a call tomorrow."

"Damn!", he frowned. "Still smoke that pipe, eh. Thought I told you to throw that away!"

"By the way, I told Bill—Major Nestor—to arrange to move. I'm convinced you'll recognize his qualities."

"I see, Tab. Has he been through test pilot school? I'll take a look at the paper work. But I'll tell you up front, the joker better carry his own weight. His ratings will be skewed a long way left otherwise.

"Of course, Jim. I wouldn't have it any other way. Well, I've got a date, and an early plane to catch. Exciting flight. Thank you, gentlemen."

"A date? That old reprobate! I wonder who he's conned into going out with him. Heaven help her." Jim groused in a low voice.

Jim and Colonel Goetler glanced at each other. "Well, we have a new staff officer, Colonel." Jim smelled of his pipe. "Tab never did care for this pipe."

Ilene was uncharacteristically quiet the next morning. Around noon she knock at Jim's door.

"Come on in, bring your own bottle."

The remark didn't elicit a smile. He looked at her carefully. "Bad day, Ilene?"

"I don't like him!"

"Yeh. Okey, who him?"

"Tab. He can't keep his hands off of you. He's got just one thing in mind, and every time he comes in here it's the same. And the jokes he tells. I've never heard anything so gross. I suppose he thinks they're suggestive. But they only sicken me!"

Jim took out his pipe, started to charge it, then tapped it on the desk. "He ask you for a date?"

"Yes," she stared at the floor, her face reddening a little.

"You go out with him?"

She was silent, but nodded affirmatively.

"He's a bastard. I thought we'd have a few drinks, dance a little, that's all. But that's not enough for Casanova. He was supposed to drive me home. Instead he drove me to his hotel. Rather than create a scene I agreed to go in to have a nightcap with him. Well, it sure wasn't a drink he was thinking of. I slapped him, left, and caught a taxi. I don't know what he thinks I am. Well, I guess I do know what he thinks."

She walked around his desk, looked out the window. "What kind of woman am I, Jim? What do the men say about me? Oh, but I shouldn't ask you that! You play by the rules, don't you! But they do talk about me. I know that."

He leaned back in his chair, the unlit pipe in his mouth. "Ilene, I like you. You have helped me more than you know, time after time, doing your job. I've never questioned you about your love life, 'cause I figure it's not my business. I know, naturally, that you've dated several of the men. Hell, you've told me yourself. And I reckon that's normal."

He lay the pipe down.

"Now, Tab, that's something else. I know old Tab from way back. And you're right, he's got just one thing on his mind when it comes to women. I've heard of many of his escapades from his own lips. He doesn't go along with the 'A gentleman doesn't kiss and tell' routine, you can bet on that."

He stood up, walked over to the window beside her, watched a dust devil whirl across the vacant area outside. "Next time he's here I'll tell him to back off. I think he'll listen to me. But if he still bothers you, hell, file a complaint. You don't have to put up with guff from him—or from anyone else, as far as that goes."

She looked at him for a moment, then began to sob.

He handed her his handkerchief and she wiped her eyes. Between sobs she suddenly started to laugh. With a wan smile she returned his handkerchief, suddenly put her arms around his neck and kissed his cheek.

"They're right, you know, the good ones are already married. Thank you, Jim."

He dabbed at his cheek as she walked out the door, smiled slightly. Damn, he thought, I believe I received a compliment. That damn Tab is going to get himself hung out to dry one of these days. Wish Ilene would find the right man and settle down!

Captain Millan is sure eligible. I'll sic Linda on 'em. She's a matchmaker from way back. Serve 'em both right, blast 'em.

He grinned at the thought.

# Jeremiah's Dilemma

"Sarge, you ever notice them ravens?" Airman Thomas was watching a flock wheeling high above, their wings almost motionless as they rode the thermals.

"Yeh, Thomas, why'd you ask?"

"There was a flock out at the test stand the other day. They were walking around the tarmac, and one big white one was perched on the railing. I never saw a white one before."

"Yeh, they're kind of rare. Albinos, they're called. Them ravens are nervy birds. Walk right up to you, sometimes. Smart, too. Understand you can split their tongues, teach them to talk."

"Ah, come on, Sarge! Anyway, that white one, she has something wrong with her eyes. They look different. But they all flew away when I got closer."

The hangar had been built underground for two reasons. First was cost. The size structure needed could not be cost-effectively built above ground. The second reason, security, also supported the underground approach.

The construction had proceeded without incident. The only concern was operation of the pumps. During the rainy season there would unquestionably be an influx of water. The construction was intended to be waterproof. But old hands prevailed and large sump pumps were installed all the same.

Jerry stood at the edge of the hangar. The slow spread of moisture on the floor caught his eye, and he shook his head. At the same moment he heard the sump pumps coming on. Thank God someone thought to put them in. Otherwise the old gal could be knee-deep in water.

Silently he turned, stood gazing at the monstrous craft. The huge delta-winged mass overwhelmed the senses by its size alone. The dull black lusterless finish triggered a mood entirely different from that inspired by the slick gleaming ships he had flown before. The windowless cockpit area triggered a shudder.

A blind witch!

And though he felt revulsion, it was combined with fascination. For he and she were mated, committed to a life together here on the ground and in the sky.

His feelings were strange, different from any he had felt before. Every new ship had with it the thrill of wonder and excitement. To climb aboard, rev up the powerful engines, begin the slow roll out to the runway. Then to feed the throttle, watch for any semblance of problems, to climb into the air.

It was a world of pleasure in its own way. The slight fear of the unknown, coupled with the tense readiness to react should problems occur, accompanied every flight.

And then the final return to the field, casual conversation with the ground crew, the flight debriefing. Yet, although he projected the image of calm assurance, how often long after the flight a chill enveloped him, cold sweat on his forehead.

With this plane it was different. Just looking at her he felt the chill, the sweat already forming.

Nor could he explain this touch of fear, of foreboding. Yes, the configuration was different. The size was unbelievable. Perhaps the lack of vision was a contributor. And the fact that no physical controls existed to occupy hands and feet.

"Jim, I've always liked camping. But I've never been able to sleep in mummy bag. Sure, they are compact and convenient, but I can't take that constraint. Maybe that's how this bird effects me. I feel like I'm pressed in on all sides, as though I couldn't move."

"Yeah, Andy talked about the same problem. Get with Doc Poulter and give him your feedback. He needs all the dope he can get. You're not by your lonesome. All the pilots are facing the same thing, or will be."

But inwardly he knew that these were incidentals. The ship as a whole cast the spell. Deep in his mind the thought formed. She's an evil thing. She's like nothing of this world.

Certainly he had heard the stories. The death of Matt Taylor following an accident during the prototype development. The frequency of accidents in the great domed hangar. The reluctance of the airmen to work in the hangar at night. The unexplained disappearance of Sergeant Driscol.

The investigation had been carried out carefully. That last night Sergeant Driscol had reported for duty on 3rd shift.

"God, I am tired. The baby has the colic, and she isn't letting anyone sleep. I'll get more rest here than I'm getting at home!"

"How's your wife doing? This being her first, I guess it was kind of rough?"

"It really surprised me. She was up the first day, and if I didn't stop her she'd be doing housework right now. They don't look it, and they wont admit it—but women are damn tough!"

"Not much to do tonight. We cleaned up just about everything on second shift. For which we'll hit you for a beer at the club. Anyway, unless something comes up you got it made. Just don't get caught sleeping."

When day shift arrived they didn't see Sergeant Driscol at the desk. "Hell, he's probably over at the John. See if there's anything written up."

"Sergeant, was he drinking last night?"

"Hell, I don't know! Why?"

"Look at the log!"

The first entries were routine. The three o'clock entry had caught their eye.

Damn ravens are noisy outside. The weather I suppose. That albino I've seen several times has gotten into the hangar, but I can't tell how. Probably when the hangar door was open during the day. The entry continued in a general way, then was interrupted with a dash, and a new line was started.

There's something near the plane. I can't quite make it out. It could be that raven. It sure looks huge in the shadows. Anyway, I better check it out. It is unusually cold in here tonight. And the lights are dimmer than usual. Are we on generator power? Have somebody check it out in the morning.

There were no further entries for the shift.

When Sergeant Driscol didn't report for duty that night they called his home. "George? No, I thought he was working over because of some kind of exercise. You aren't kidding me, are you? He really isn't there?" His wife's amazement was genuine.

They checked the parking lot. His car was still there, door locked.

A Board of Inquiry was formed. Everyone who had actual or potential contact with the Sergeant was interviewed. There was no indication of foul play. No additional information surfaced. With no better explanation available, they determined that he was away without leave, or AWOL.

Jerry shrugged. Don't know why he comes to mind. I wonder what really happened to Driscol. With a shudder he hurried from the hangar, to his 'vette. He drove frantically from the parking lot. Even in the heat of the day he felt a coldness enveloping him. To the west lenticular clouds were forming over the Tehachapis. A flight of ravens circled over South Base. One swept down, crossed in front of his car, then climbed swiftly upward. The reflected light gave it a whitish sheen.

It had flown so close that he had braked automatically. "Stupid bird," he growled. "I wonder how many of them get sucked up by the jets?"

Once off base he floor-boarded the accelerator. So the Security Police had radar. He hadn't been caught yet. The tachometer, the speedometer, rose steadily. He grinned.

Next to flying, he loved driving. At times he had thought of becoming a race driver. He still might. They had classes over at the Willow Springs track. At least, that's what he had been told.

The road was empty and he braked down as he entered Rosamond, turned north on Highway 14. The wind was gusting, and as his speed increased he could feel the gusts as they caused the car to wander. But it was a good feeling, and he enjoyed making the minor corrections that kept it on course.

He pulled into Mojave, rolled out on the Tehachapis highway, headed toward Bakersfield. There were more curves as he crossed over the hills and they made driving a little more of a challenge, a little more exciting.

The speedometer indicated 130 mph, and he still had play in the accelerator. But he held it at that speed, laving in the thunder of the engine, the whistling of the wind in the partially opened window. "This is traveling," he said to no one in particular.

Glancing in his rear view mirror he suddenly paled, held the wheel tightly in his hands, braked rapidly.

He shook his head, turned to look over his shoulder, behind his seat. "God! I could have sworn someone was seated there! That was weird!"

He slowed down further, brought his wheels off the highway and stopped, turned off the engine. He made a careful inspection behind the seat, of the mirror. Then he got out, walked around the car.

As he returned to the driver's side flashing lights appeared on the highway, coming from Mojave. He stepped close to the car to let the vehicle pass, but it pulled in behind him.

"Having problems?", the highway patrolman inquired.

"No, just overheated. Figured I'd let her cool off, then be on my way."

"Yeh, that grade can do it to you. Might pop your hood, it'll cool faster. Oh, would you turn on your emergencies, so you're more noticeable. I'll bet those job will move. What year is it?"

After the patrol car pulled away he started up, crossed the median and headed back to Edwards. He held his speed between 60 and 70, glanced frequently at his rear view mirror.

Whatever it had been that caught his attention, it did not recur.

He felt tired, irritable. He stopped in Rosamond, had a brew before returning to the base. An airman, the only other customer, sat at the bar, stared moodily at the mirror.

"Evening, Sarge. Can I but you a drink? You work on the Dreamship, right?"

The Sergeant looked at him sullenly, returned silently to his glass.

Jeremiah shrugged, finished his glass. Leaving a tip at the bar he walked out, taking a final glance at the morose sergeant. Jeremiah grinned. "Well," he said under his breath, "It takes all kinds!"

The Sergeant sat at the bar, downing shot glass after shot glass of straight whiskey. Finally the bartender refused him service. He stood up, picked up the shotglass, looked gravely into the emptiness. Suddenly, and without warming, he threw the glass. The bartender ducked, and the mirror behind him shattered.

"All right, buster, you just shot your wad." Shaking his head, he called the police.

They arrested Sergeant Driscol without incident. He seemed to be numb, to neither understand or care what happened. The Air Force was notified, picked him up and returned him to the base. He was duly charged with being AWOL.

They questioned him extensively.

"Sarge, quit conning us. You can't have gone off like this and not remember anything. Look, level with us, take your hit, and let's git this behind us."

"I wish to God I could. But I don't recall anything. Just the airplane, and that damn albino, and.... And that's it, damn it!"

He could not explain what had happened after the last entry in the log. He did not know how he arrived at the bar. Examination by the hospital failed to provide an explanation. The Courts Martial was delayed until more extensive tests could be made.

His commander reviewed the case, talked to Sgt. Driscoll.

"No way am I going to support a Courts Martial. Whatever happened, I'm convinced he did not intend to go AWOL. Look at his record! He's a solid, hardworking NCO!"

The newspaper had a brief article on Sgt. Driscoll's arrest. Jim read it carefully, grunted, and turned to the headlines. His eyes widened.

What was it General Mathis had said. Negotiations on Hawaii! And here was the conclusion. The Hawaiian Islands to be transferred to Chinese management, as a transition measure, as the two superpowers continued negotiations. For this transfer the United States was to receive monopoly rights to provide agricultural goods to China. A great victory for America's astute negotiators, the paper stated repeatedly.

Those Americans who choose to remain on the Islands would have 90 days to apply for Chinese citizenship. Those who elected to travel to the States would receive full value for their property left behind. On a later page a footnote mentioned that no payments in excess of $5000 would be made.

Starting immediately no material wealth would be transferred from the Islands without approval of the Chinese managers. All foreign visitors have one week to vacate the island. Gun registration records had been turned over to the Chinese, and all guns were to be confiscated by week's end. Failure to relinquish guns identified on the registration records would result in immediate incarceration with prison terms of not less than 5 years. Each member of the household would be subject to the sentence.

Colonel Goetler entered, glanced at the headline. "Major Fairson just took a month's vacation. Going to sail over there and bring back evacuees. Says he'll make a killing in two trips. All the regularly scheduled boats and planes are booked. My God, what a mess! Still think the General is paranoiac, Jim?"

Jim took a deep breath. The noose was being drawn tight, much quicker than he had realized.

# Sexual Harassment

"This is the Base Commander's secretary, Mr.Braddock. The Colonel would like to see you at thirteen hundred in his office."

"May I ask what is on the agenda?"

"It's a personal matter. He'll explain it to you when you arrive."

Personal matter! All right, whose got himself into trouble this time. The pilots are too busy, can't be them. The test team's working double shift, they don't have time to get into trouble. Ah, guess I'll know soon enough.

"Colonel, how are you? Still playing tennis?"

"Not too often, Jim. Don't have the time since I picked up this job. Sit down, light up that damn pipe if you want. You shoulda' thrown it away years ago."

They both grinned. He lit his pipe, took out a bound notebook and his pen.

"No, put that away. This is strictly between you and me."

With a raised eyebrow Jim looked him in the face. "Okey, hit me."

"It's a sexual harassment charge."

"Hell, I oughta' feel complimented, at my age."

"All right, Jim. It's not you, of course. Tab Klooster is the bastard."

"Doesn't really surprise me. Who filed it? I know at least half a dozen who could have."

"Ilene."

"Yeh, she came to mind. So why am I here."

"Headquarters wants it withdrawn."

"Eh-heh. So why don't they ask her to withdraw it."

"Don't play naive, Jim. You know full well they want you to do the dirty work. Talk to her, get her to withdraw it. If she doesn't there are some wheels at Headquarters who will make things real unpleasant. Wheels with stars! You get my slant?"

"Where do you stand, Colonel?"

"I'm up for my first star, Jim. I can't buck them. And I dare say you'd be wise not too."

"I'll talk to her, because you asked me to. But I'll not lean on her. If she decides to withdraw, fine. If not, hell, I'll testify for her. I know that old stud."

"Jim, if you want to commit suicide, a gun is quicker."

"Take care, Colonel. Good luck on the promotion."

As he returned to the office he felt his anger building. Damn Tab, damn the generals, damn Ilene. She knows better than pull a dumb trick like that. Why doesn't she think of anyone but herself! Stupid miniskirt, braless blouse, simpering around! What does she expect! I'll give her a piece of my mind!

He started to walk faster.

Then he stopped, felt a cold sweat on his brow. He wiped it off with the back of his hand.

What in the world is getting in to me!

When he reached his office he turned, went to the coffee machine. He didn't want to enter the office just yet, even though the coffee was better there.

I wonder, he thought. Maybe I should get off this program.

"Ilene, could you come in, please."

"You're awful polite. What have I done wrong this time?"

"Sit down. I understand you filed a sexual harassment charge with the base?"

She was silent. She looked at him, and he could see the anger in her eyes. "Yes—Klooster. He made another one of his caveman passes a week ago when he came through." She paused.

"You don't really know how he acts, do you. The bastard, he makes me feel cheap. He comes up behind me, puts his arms around me, cups his hands under my breasts. And he holds me like that while he tries to kiss me. He doesn't care who sees, either. If he has an audience I guess he feels more macho."

She stopped, and began to sob softly. She took the proffered handkerchief. "Why are you involved, Jim? Oh, the meeting with the Base Commander! They want you to tell me to drop it, don't they!" Her eyes widened. "Are you going to tell me to drop it?"

He laughed. "You know me better, Ilene. Yeh, that's what they asked me to do. I told them I'd talk to you, but you'd make the decision. And I told them that if you don't drop it, I'd testify for you."

"Can they hurt you, Jim?"

"Of course they can. But I'll tell you a little secret. Once they got you running they'll never quit. So to hell with them. If you got a case, we'll hang old Tab higher than a kite."

Her face was sad as she left the office. She was concerned about the impact of her charge.

Around 1600 she came back to his office. "Jim, you call Tab Klooster. You tell him I'm temporarily withdrawing the charge. And you let that son-of-a-bitch know that if he so much as speaks to me again, I'll reinstate it!"

"Ilene, wait a minute. I've told you what they wanted me to tell you. Don't you make them think we're running. If you think Tab warrants slapping down, don't chicken out. I'll support you."

"Damn it, I know you will. And that's the problem! No, you tell him what I said. He'd better not touch me again. I won't back down twice."

Reluctantly he made the call.

"Tab, Jim Braddock."

"Good to hear you, Jim. I've been expecting your call. Everything is arranged, I take it?"

"Listen, you bastard. Ilene says she's withdrawing the complaint temporarily. And she says that if you so much as speak to her again, she'll reinstate it. You understand?"

"Certainly, certainly. Sorry she feels that way. Very sensitive girl, very sensitive. I'd be careful of her, if I were you, Jim boy."

"I'll do that. Now let me tell you something personal, Tab boy." The sarcasm in his voice was heavy. "If you go near her again I'll work you over like I did years ago. You wore those marks a long time."

"Ah, yes, Jim. Didn't I. I haven't forgotten. Anyway, don't worry, she really hasn't anything I find interesting. Too highstrung, a little drab, actually. You amaze me, Jim. You'd actually work me over, wouldn't you? She's only a secretary. Don't be a sucker."

Jim hung up the phone with a grimace. Only a secretary. Only a girl. Tab might behave, but his thought processes would never change.

"Ilene, I passed on your message."

"I know Jim. I shouldn't, but I was on the other phone. And Jim, thank you. I believe you would, how did you say it, 'work him over.'"

"Hey, I'm going to hang you out to dry if you don't stay off my phone. But, yeh, I get a tad riled at Mr. Tab Klooster. He messes with me too much more and I'll have to cut loose my tiger."

"Mr. Braddock, you talk strange English."

"Hell, Miss Ilene, that ain't English. That's Tennessee hillbilly!"

# Third Time Charmed

Third flight. The earlier flights had not entirely met expectation. Many of the flight cards had been re-issued, would be completed during this flight. But that would put them back on schedule.

He pulled on his skull cap, a grin on his face. Odd, after the first two flights, how the voltage no longer signified pain. With a slight mental effort he triggered the turn-on system. The accompanying shiver, always there, was comforting. It was as though the ship was welcoming him, quivering with pleasure. He never knew, really, whether it was the ship's response, or his own. But the response, short and almost sexual in its intensity, pleased him.

The huge mass was alive now, and the sensors, located at all key points, were rapidly feeding status to him. He probed each operating unit, verifying the condition. All was well. He drove the standby signal down the multiplexed fiber optic line, and each unit accepted the signal, adjusted threshold response, and waited patiently in slave mode. He closed his eyes, blanked his mind, relaxed.

He smiled. Me, John, and Fred. Damn it, Fred had been a good man. From day 1 they had been the designated pilots. But the almost inseparable trio had suffered its first loss. Not in the air, but on the ground in the relatively safe confines of the simulator.

Fred was making the run. He was making a slow, climbing turn, checking the stall characteristics at the edge of the envelope. Voltage feedback level rose to an unprecedented high during this seemingly ordinary maneuver. Due to some unexplained phenomenon, instead of providing a negative input, Fred had sat the control console, eyes closed, and mentally excited the response, driving the system into a resonant state that built up beyond his capacity to control. The feedback currents literally cooked the control segments of his brain, including critical adjacent areas. One of the adjacent areas controlled the breathing function. With the destruction of that area, breathing ceased.

Andy had been Fred's backup. They laid a crash course on him to get him up to speed. Middle-aged, hardworking, he lived with the simulator; the psychologists; and most all, the ship—and finally he died with her.

Jerry shook his head. Breaks of the game! "Dream Ship 2, ready for line up." Almost unconsciously he had set on the apron, completed the run-up. Strange, how quickly it becomes routine.

He moved her onto the flight line, engines fully rev'd even before line-up. Seeing the runway through her sensors, moving non-existent controls with his thoughts, he maneuvered her rapidly down the field, rotated, pulled her into the air.

The flight to the test area proceeded without incident, and they worked through the flight test cards methodically. The ship's response throughout was nominal.

"Jerry, we've got another half hour of test time. I'd like to expand the vertical window. Are you game?" Jim Braddock's voice sounded in his ears.

"Eh, Roger that. You're calling the shots, Jim. I don't have a card on this one, though."

"Understand, Jerry. We'll feed it to you over the airwaves, and monitor the feedback data. Let us know if you note any anomalies. Head her west and climb out to 100,000, then level off."

The muffled thud-thud-thud replaced the low-level vibration as he climbed, shifting to scramjet mode. The thin air at this altitude made low-level operation mode worthless. Similarly the flight control surfaces were of little value. The vector jets automatically compensated, orienting the craft at his command.

"Jerry, bring her around to an easterly heading and continue climb. Level off when you hit 150,000 and 80 degrees heading. At that time begin your let-down."

"Understand, ground control. She's showing some tendency to wallow, but nothing serious. How does the data you're getting look?"

"We've noted the wallowing. It's to be expected at that altitude and speed. Open it up a little more during the climb, and let's see if it smoothes out."

Mentally he gently moved the throttle forward. He laughed to himself. Of course, there was no real throttle. But, visually in his mind it existed, and the aircraft responded. How smoothly she responded. He could fly her to the stars, he really could!

He felt strangely relaxed, perhaps too much so. But she handled so well! The flight was becoming almost dreamlike. He felt a lethargy that he didn't understand, but did not resist.

Suddenly, with a shock, he tensed. Someone, something was with him on the ship. A cold shiver ran down his spine. He was awake now. He was getting irrelevant images from the sensors. Meaningless returns. A huge object! A boulder in the desert! An animal running, a wounded coyote. Ravens! Flying close, but not too close. Waiting for the inevitable exhaustion, death.

What kind of weird garbage is this, he thought to himself. Concentrate! Get on with the job!

He tried to blank his mind. What has this to do with me? I've got an airplane to fly. My God, I've overshot by 10,000 feet!

Vaguely he noted the incoming call. "Jerry, you've overshot. You're at 160,000 and climbing. Level her off and start your let-down."

He hummed a little to himself. Odd, how that tune came to mind. His sister used to sing it to him, sitting of an evening on the porch. She sang softly, The Church in the Wildwood. She had married the preacher, a life that suited her well. Her voice blended with the night sounds that were just starting, and nighthawks could be heard chasing after low flying insects. Someday I'll fly, he had thought.

"Jerry, Jerry! Bring her down! You're approaching the limits. Jerry, do you read me!"

Nonsense! She has no limits. I can fly her to the stars!

"Jeremiah, Jeremiah"—he heard his mother's voice. He laughed. To everyone else he was Jerry. He started to answer, stopped and frowned. Five years since her death. And still he could hear her calling him. Almost as though she were there in the ship with him. Almost as though she were calling him home.

Ah, to go home again. Green, tree-covered, rolling hills. Not the brown-brown desert with its burning sun and eternal wind. The winding river beyond the backwoods, the blackberries ripe for the taking and the hum of the frightened Junc Bugs, disturbed at their meal.

At night the cool breezes and the sky dotted with stars. Weenie roasts in the meadow with schoolmates. So many wonderful memories!

—"Yes, Momma, I want to go home!"

Jim Braddock flipped through the logbook. Jerry—Jerry, the Old Master. He performed so damn well on the simulator. Never the slightest hesitation, always the right response! And the first two flights had been out of the book. Every maneuver followed an exact path, every test card successfully completed. Perhaps that was the problem.

A sense of assurance prevailed.

No one maintained a fear of the unknown, a fear that is every pilot's life insurance.

It was on the third flight that the anomaly was first noted. Jerry had just put the ship through a tight turning maneuver. As he returned to straight and level at 90,000 feet he notified ground control of a feeling of unease, not pain, but more like dread. For unexplained reasons the call was recorded on the ships electronic log, but transmission was inhibited.

Had ground control received that message they would have canceled the mission, recalled the ship, and attempted to isolate the problem. The mental condition of the pilot was the key factor in the ship's operation.

A subsequent message, also recorded but with transmission inhibited, followed shortly. "I am feeling pain in my joints, eyes, and have a severe headache," he attempted to notify Ground Control. "My muscles are flexing weakly, not under my control, and my eyesight is weakening. Also, I seem to be getting extremely lethargic. I am finding it difficult to concentrate. Why the hell aren't you bastards responding!"

The messages were not transmitted. A filter of unknown origin had effectively inhibited their transmission. Ground Control continued expanding the envelope, moving the ship toward a not yet attained altitude. Transmissions received remained nominal, reflected only successful maneuvers and standard aircraft conditions. Data on pilot condition, likewise, remained nominal.

Only when the ship passed through the 150,000 level did Ground Control realize that an anomaly existed.

When maneuvers on the flight test cards had been completed early the try for altitude had been initiated. Only when the aircraft's penetration of the safe level was noted had Ground Control attempted to activate the override system. If they had succeeded normal operation by way of ground signals would have been sufficient to bring the craft safely home. It was not to be.

The telemetry responses on the screen went rapidly from yellow to orange to red, then flashing red. There existed a variance between ground and air status reports. Override was locked out. It was not logical, as only the pilot could lock out override, and the telemetry signals showed that Jerry was unconscious.

The next transmission, again recorded on the electronic secretary, but never transmitted, was cryptic. "The damn black witch! I'll beat her yet!"

There was a pause, and the last statement, slightly incoherent and certainly a strange non-sequitur seemed to be "Yes, Momma, I want to go home."

The Transportation Board, the FAA, the Air Force, DARPA, Fred's Booze to go—well, scratch that last one. But the whole world seemed to have shown up for the post mortem.

Strange! They had believed that the anomalies were under control. Jim Braddock shook his head, thinking of the preparation for the flight.

The Accident Board examined the records, examined the parts of the craft, listened to the recorded voice transmissions, analyzed the data transmissions, listened to witnesses. No pattern evolved. The inevitable conclusion, like clockwork—pilot error.

The accident made the front page, a small entry at the foot of the sheet. No details were included, but the board review was mentioned. An editorial aside suggested the day for developing military aircraft was long past.

The headlines, as many had in the past few weeks, addressed the growing diplomatic ties between China and Greater Iran. Cultural exchange between students of the two world powers was in progress, and a picture showed the smiling students shaking hands with their counterparts.

———————

Jim finished supper, sipped slowly at his coffee. He glanced around the dining room listlessly. Dull, weary old room.

He looked at Linda, sitting quietly across the table, eyes on her plate as she ate slowly, without relish.

"You don't talk much any more, Linda. You sick? Don't sit around like a stick. I need some more coffee." He thrust the cup at her, and she jumped up, almost dumping her plate.

She took his cup, and her hand trembled slightly. There was a touch of fear on her face.

He frowned. Linda might really be sick. She was usually so talkative, so outgoing. The past few weeks she had become more taciturn, had quit going to the mahjong games, had little to say when he arrived home.

Of course, come to think of it, he had little to say to her. Except to demand another cup of coffee, or a glass of wine.

"Damn it, Linda! Will you hurry. I want my coffee! And get this garbage off the table!"

What in the world is going wrong with people. I put in my workday, I get home, and it's like a mausoleum. And the way she looks. Her hair is starting to gray, she's getting wrinkles, and she's wearing too much lipstick.

"And bring me an aspirin. Bring the bottle!"

"Jim, don't you think you should see the doctor about those headaches. You seem to having them more and more often." She stopped, licked her lips, looked at him head down, seeming to cringe.

Nightmares and headaches! And married to a nagging bitch. "Will you get off my back. I don't need a doctor. I need an aspirin."

He took three, chased them down with coffee.

"Jim, what is it? You've changed terribly since transferring to this program. And I keep hearing some strange stories—something about a blind witch. Jim, I'm scared. What is going on?"

"Get out of my sight. I'm tired of looking at you. I'm tired of listening to you. Get in the kitchen and clean up the dishes. Bring me my wine in the front room. Bring in the bottle, you hear!"

He started to stand up, and she hurried to the kitchen.

"Goddamn the blind witch. She'll not beat me, you understand! She'll not beat me…"

His voice trailed off. He sat down, stared blankly across the room.

Why do I have to tell her time after time! She knows I want my wine in the front room. Why do I put up with this!

# Georgia Bound

A manager has to handle the current fires, and still look ahead for any significant conflagrations. Joseph Kingston flipped through the study quickly, returned to the Executive Summary in front. The delta costs for the coming fiscal year were unbelievable. Even more shocking was the likelihood that resources required to meet commitments would not be available.

He picked up the phone. "Gina, get me Mr. Braddock, please."

He leaned back in his chair, casually rested his long legs on the mahogany desk. Once more he looked through the material, noting a few areas of questionable data. Overall, however, he could not fault the analysis.

"Gina, make that a 3 way conference call to Mr. Braddock, Elmer Strider, and myself."

Elmer Strider, an operations research analyst, had gathered the information, completed the study. Detailed questions would have to be addressed to him.

"Joe, how are you? Jim Braddock here. What's up?"

"Jim, hold for just a moment 'til Elmer Strider picks up. By the way, you haven't met him, but he's an ace ops research type.

He's completed a study here that we need to discuss."

"This is Elmer Strider. Is everyone on line?"

"Elmer, Joe. We have Jim Braddock, the Program Manager, on the line with us. I think the three of us need to consider the ramifications of your study."

"Certainly, Mr. Kingston. I can discuss it; or, if you prefer, answer any questions you have."

"Hang in with us, because there will undoubtedly be some questions."

He paused, took a deep breath. "Jim, I asked Elmer to forecast our situation for the coming fiscal year. He went a little deeper than I had requested, but it's just as well. His conclusions are upsetting, to say the least."

"Okey, Joe, what's the bottom line."

"There's no way we can live within budget. Even worse, with the constraints being laid on us, it is unlikely that we can meet our commitments, regardless of funding."

Jim whistled.

"What th' hell has fallen apart. All right, what's the driver for this deterioration?"

"Several factors. Primary drivers for the costs are state taxes and state mandated programs. The drivers resulting in our inability to meet commitments at all are both state and other. Electric resources are going to be limited due to historical failure to expand on the part of the Electric Industry. That's been driven largely by insurance and legal costs, which derive from environmental constraints and punitive damage awards. The latter are being applied indiscriminately to industry, whether or not industry has made the risks known to the user. As a result the insurance costs facing us are astronomical. And, as you probably know, California has laid on the possibility of additional punitive costs in these cases."

"I'm familiar with them. I recall that production of whooping cough serum was almost ended because of that situation."

"The second insurmountable problem is water. Our operation requires significant quantities of pure water. The failure of California to solve its water problems leaves us with huge penalties imposed."

"Finally, the environmental constraints preclude us from either bringing in the chemicals we need, storing them, or transporting the waste products to disposal facilities. And, of course, storing wastes at the plant again subjects us to astronomical penalties."

"You make it sound damn bleak!"

"Not me. Elmer did the study. But our other experts have reviewed it, and they endorse his conclusions. Elmer, do you have anything to add?"

"Yes, sir. At this point in time, even if the attitude in California were to change, it would not be possible to reverse the deterioration of the industrial situation here. It will take years to upgrade their energy base, years to implement a workable water system. As for the environmental maze, it is so convoluted that I doubt they will ever solve it. Legal entanglements and court cases will largely preclude California from ever again becoming a major industrial state. And, of course, the state has lost its credibility with industrial leaders. They no longer trust its leaders."

Jim laughed grimly. "Yeh, they are going to have the worlds greatest environment—and 99% unemployment! I'll tell you, though. That study sounds like it was written by someone far right of the far right."

"That's funny, in a way. Elmer hated to give this report. He's been a supporter of the Democratic Party, the Sierra Club, and just about every group this study takes issue with. But he says the facts are there, and he can't dispute them."

"All right, Joe. Where do we go from here?"

"I'd advise a get-together at AFSC to lay it out. There is only one practical alternative that I see at the moment."

"Good. I was afraid there were none! What's your thinking?"

"We pick up and relocate to a state that takes a more balanced approach. Now, the short-term impact is going to be severe, but at least we can then insure the successful completion of the program. Like

Elmer said, even if you jaw-boned the state into common sense changes, it's too late to help this program."

"How long would it take to break things down, ship 'em elsewhere and get up and running? How about personnel, would they transfer or do we have to re-hire?"

"Six months minimum, probably nine months. Our engineering types will generally transfer. As for the others, I think we can hire off the street. We're having problems here with education level, anyway. We'd get away from that in regions where the emphasis is on quality, not just keeping the kids in holding tanks."

"Well, I think you're a little hard on the state with some of your comments. Of course, you know your problems. I'll set up a meeting at Headquarters for Friday. Can you support that?"

"Yeh, we can support tomorrow if you can get it arranged."

The move to Georgia was a nightmare. Commitments had been made by the government, by the company. Contracts had to be changed. Shipping directives had to be canceled, reissued. Layoffs and hiring were being conducted simultaneously.

The local papers were blasting the Air Force, the Company, and himself for the decision to move. Larger papers were extolling the environmental advantages to be gained with the program's departure.

Quietly the politicians were trying to get the decision reversed, while not exposing their actions to voters who were being moved by media hype, not economic sense.

They were, of course, too late. Even if promises, made under economic pressure of the move, were kept, the results were many years away.

Jim decided to sell the house. The realtor told him flatly that with the continued departure of business and industry sale would be difficult at his asking price.

"Admittedly, the population is growing. But mostly lower economic level. Anyone with professional skill is heading out. Prices on housing aren't going down that much—at least, not yet. It's just that nothing is selling. The potential buyers are moving out."

After thinking the problem through, he kept it. After all, they'd still install the avionics and instruments locally, and flight test would still be at Edwards.

He couldn't escape.

They had little trouble fielding a new group of assemblers. The majority of their engineering staff moved with the company. Some bonuses had to be paid to get that kind of cooperation, but it was worth it. The engineering skill and corporate memory were precious commodities they couldn't afford to lose.

Fortunately for the program the move was largely completed within five months. Jim congratulated Mr, Kingston on his management of the crisis.

Dreamships were still go!

"All right, Mr. Kingston. Just what do we have to work with?"

"It's not bad, Jim. The facility is all that's left of a once huge manufacturing center previously owned by Lockheed. It'll require extensive renovation. Fortunately, though, the state and the local populace strongly support this development effort. Then, too, we have a well-skilled source of workers at hand from the school system. That will more than offset some of the other inconveniences."

Documentation had been maintained largely on CD ROMS, and generation of assembly drawings required merely running the associated plotting routines. Almost as quickly as the equipments were set up the workers were in place, assembling the parts to the specifications and drawings.

Georgia's governor and other dignitaries visited the facility, promised maximum support from the state. The papers carried headlines welcoming the plant to their town, and the weekend became a two-day fair.

The usual contingent of placard carriers from Environment Uber Alles and their associates turned out. The crowd rather quickly disposed of the placards, and the carriers wisely decided to picket elsewhere and at another time.

Jim located a small, reasonably priced house near the plant. He was pleasantly amazed at the cost differential, and found that those who had transferred with the company were likewise well-pleased.

A meeting was called early-on to provide information and to give the employees an opportunity to sound off. There were a variety of inputs, generally favorable.

Bill Davidson, nevertheless, growled. "It ain't bad, but when I saw that mosquito carrying off a swamp alligator it caught my attention!"

"Hey, Bill, that weren't no mosquito. That was a gnat. The mosquitoes raid the zoos and carry off elephants!"

Everybody laughed. They were getting settled in. Sure, there were mosquitoes, and the weather was humid. But the job here went much more smoothly.

"Hell, I don't have to fill out a form every time I spray oil on a bolt. Or weigh the oil can when I pick it up and return it to storage. And Lord knows we have water, and no damn penalties for using it."

"Did anybody check the local taxes. I got a substantial raise in take-home pay, just by moving. Let's build an airplane!"

Ruth Gordon tossed out a quick comment. "Did you know the schools actually teach the kids the multiplication table? You ask 'em what 12 times 12 is, and they really know? And they can read? And the teachers run the schools, not the trouble makers. They don't just pat their hand, they expel trouble makers. I'm just glad my children can feel safe in class, and going to and from class."

Plainly they were readily adapting to the local atmosphere. Hiring of additional workers proceeded well, and within weeks the production process was operating normally.

Nevertheless, problems surfaced rapidly.

"We're getting corrosion on some of the materials, apparently because of moisture. It isn't bad yet, but we need to control it."

The engineers contacted the local university. They were familiar with the problem, had arrived at a practical solution. A thin spray of plastic provided protection, yet did not interfere with mating of parts.

The contact with the university proved extremely fruitful. The faculty had worked with aerospace industries prior to nineties before that industry had largely died. Their archive of studies, and files of data solved many problems even before the problems materialized.

Key players sat quietly in the conference room. Kingston kicked things off, quickly addressing the crisis. "A major problem has surfaced with the facility. Because of disuse much of the original valuable material had been stripped, disposed of. As you all know, with testing of transmitters, radars, and other less common emitters huge shielded rooms are needed. There were once a suite of such Faraday shielded areas. These no longer exist."

"The University has done some extensive work in that area. I've read some of the studies done on systems previously developed, and they've been actively involved. Get with their engineering or physics group and see what they can do." Jim recalled facilities developed for Edwards.

The university could not provide the material, but they were instrumental in locating local sources. Copper mesh was located to form Faraday shields. Absorbent materials for radar emissions were available from local sources. Even more exotic materials were located and delivered. Time and money resolved the problem.

As with any influx of a large group into a new community there were some problems between the local populace and the newcomers. However, meetings of city residents, composed of both the newcomers and old timers, helped lessen that turmoil. As did the prospects of being hired by the plant.

At times Jim felt the move had been ill advised. Months of time had been lost because of the move. And though some of it was being made up under the new conditions, they were still well behind schedule.

And he carried problems with him. Problems of another kind, not so easily solved.

He leaned back in his chair, closed his eyes.

Had this been another ripoff, the thought came to mind. It's getting so that you can't trust anyone.

God, I'm tired. Every night, every damn night, that stupid dream. Used to, the wine helped me sleep. But no more.

And I'm drinking too much coffee. Look at that hand.

He held it in front of him. For a moment he kept it still and unmoving but only for a moment. The quivering returned and he brought his fist down on the table.

As he did so the door opened and Colonel Goetler entered.

"Damn you, Colonel. Didn't you ever hear of knocking!"

Colonel Goetler looked at him carefully.

"Jim, this job is getting to you. You don't look like you've had any sleep in days. How long since you've had a vacation?"

"Colonel, this is my program. I'll sleep when I want, I'll vacation when I want, and I'll damn well maintain the privacy of my office! When you want to come in here, knock. Do you understand!"

The colonel looked at him strangely, walked quietly from the room in deep thought.

He received a call from ASD, inquiring as to the success of the move. The conversation seemed casual.

"Jim, how are the employees taking it? Any significant problems?"

"No, General. We have a good team here. They've settled in right well. Some minor grumbling, but you'll always have that. I hold a nasty hour every morning for anyone with a gripe, and nobody has showed up for the past week."

"Okey. Different subject. I want you to attend a meeting in Washington. A Dr. Volte is going to give a pitch. We need you evaluate what he has to say. At the moment we think he may have some useful ideas, but you're the best one to judge their validity."

# Dr. Volte

The flight up was bumpy, with thunderheads rising well above their flight level. Ilene, who accompanied them, showed signs of air sickness, but managed to overcome it.

"How can you people stand to fly like this! I'll hitch-hike back to Georgia!"

"It's generally not this rough, young lady. On a hot day, and with thunderstorms around, you kind of expect rough air. But you shouldn't have too much trouble hitching a ride."

She wrinkled her nose at him, leaned back in her chair, and suffered in silence.

They took a taxi from National, driving through almost empty streets to their hotel. Though the rooms weren't adjacent, they were on the same floor. The skies were a dirty brown, and a steady drizzle lasted throughout the trip. With his personnel squared away Jim Braddock retired to his room, took a warm shower. Sleep would come easy. Or so he hoped.

The knock on the door came just as he turned down the bedcover. "Damn!" was the best response he could come up with. Grumpily he opened the door.

Ilene smiled at him. "I couldn't fine your favorite wine, Hungarian Green. I bought a bottle of Japanese Plum wine. I thought it might help you sleep well."

Although angry, he still appreciated the intent. "Well, young lady, I must admit it looks good. Will you join me in a glass?"

Plainly she expected the invitation. She glanced around the room, smiling. "I'm glad I didn't wake you. You know, I've never been to Washington before."

"We don't often need a secretary with us. But this is an exception." He located two glasses, half filled each with the plum wine. "Kampai, as they say where this was brewed."

He sipped slowly, relaxed.

She watched him curiously. "Jim, you are a strange man. You're the only one in the whole project who hasn't made a pass at me. Don't you find me attractive?"

He glanced up, startled. Plainly she was attractive. Vivacious blue eyes, blonde hair coiffured like a movie star, and a beautifully proportioned body. He grinned at her.

"Young lady, I must admit the thought has crossed my mind. But I like you. I like you as someone I can talk to and level with. And my other needs are well cared for at home. Sure, you are damn attractive. But I need you most as a confidante. Let's keep it that way."

"I was curious. I know you aren't one of those," and she waved her arm, hand hanging limply at the wrist. "You love Linda, don't you? You're the kind of person who wouldn't want to hurt her. I think that has a lot to do with it," she mused.

"Hey, its getting late. Come on, Chugalug."

She finished her drink quickly, laughed. "Goodnight Jim. I appreciate you're considering me your confidante. Maybe that's a closer relationship than just crawling into bed with a man, right?"

Next morning Jeff and Conrad grinned at him across the table. He looked at each suspiciously, then sipped his coffee.

Finally Jeff broke the silence. "Well, did Ilene put the make on you last night?"

He put his coffee cup down, looked at them quietly, then shook his head in mock alarm.

"You bastards are bad as a couple of high school kids just learning about the facts of life. Hey, you just don't worry about my virginity."

"You know, that's the high point of the trip for her," Conrad commented.

"Eh-huh! Okey, you studs! So that's how you spend your time when I send you TDY. It'll be a long time coming when I send you yokels out on a trip with Ilene again."

"By the way, you two know, this can be a wild town, and a dangerous one. Don't let her go wandering around and getting into trouble."

"We'll keep an eye on her, Jim. This is her first trip, isn't it?"

"Hey, there she is. Knock it off, understand."

He stood up, waved. "Ilene, were over here."

As she sat down he commented, "The eggs and sausage aren't too bad. And I don't know these two hanger-ons."

The meeting with Doctor Volte ended up being a working session rather than the expected show-and-tell. Doctor Volte, but Bill Volte to his friends, placed an agenda before each of them. "The Secretary of the Air Force extends his apologizes. The crisis with the recalcitrant USSR army elements has him fully occupied. Hopefully he and our other leaders will handle the crisis well, and we shall not be interrupted by the arrival of nuclear armament."

"I must tell you that I am only partially cognizant of your activity. Hmmm, in English, I don't really know what's going on. Put's me in a good position for helping you, doesn't it?"

"Hell, Doc, we've been working the problem for nearly five years, and we're still wondering what's going on," Jim growled.

"I read of the loss of Dream Ship one. Some inkling of the approach being taken was detectable. The concepts intrigued me. It became a, what shall we say, an exciting mental exercise, to examine and analyze the situation. Of course, I have my contacts, so a great deal of information has come to me. But I need confirmation on some of it, and fill-in where the gaps exist. You will note on the agenda my clearance information. The fact that I am here vouches for my need to know."

"We have been provided all the relevant security data, Doc. Why don't you walk us through your understanding of the situation. We'll sound off if we see errors, and butt in when something is missing."

Dr. Volte rehashed the history of the last flight. He spoke in a subdued voice, occasionally speaking louder to emphasize a point. At first he stood at the head of the table, but soon selected a chair beside Jim Braddock as the discussion continued.

"No, Doc. It is true that we have Jerry's comments. But none of them were broadcast over the comm system. By whatever means, the transmission was inhibited at the ship."

"Ah, that didn't come out in the press accounts. In the final moments of flight, then, he was trying to alert ground control to his problems?"

"Absolutely!"

"You knew there was a problem when the ship began to behave erratically, I believe. Ground control attempted override. But it locked out. You did, as I understand it, succeed in establishing override temporarily, but quickly lost it again."

His voice was soft, musing. "The aircraft picked up speed, continued to dive and to maneuver uncontrollably. Until finally it struck the ground and tore up a furrow in the desert floor. The aircraft was largely destroyed. The pilot lived, amazingly, long enough to reach the hospital. He never regained consciousness. That is correct?"

Jim nodded. Correct. A neutral word, no touch of emotion associated with it. "Yeh, that's it in a nutshell. Actually, Jerry died in the ambulance on the way to the hospital."

"Tell me, sir, was there substantially new equipment or software associated with this flight?"

"Negative. Some peaking of the system, but no changes from prior flights."

"And flight maneuvers as you expanded the envelope. Was there substantial change over earlier flights?"

"Again, no."

"So I surmised. I'll tell you what I told the Secretary. I am of the opinion, based on data available to this point, that man—the pilot—is the primary contributor to the failure. Not in the sense that the FAA uses pilot error, but in the sense that your training, your practice, have concentrated on the simple interfaces between man and aircraft. I believe that you have a very complex organism, man, and that he does not have sufficient control of himself to support continued development of this system."

"Give up the program? Doc, is that what you have recommended to the Secretary?"

"It is one contingency plan that must be considered. On the other hand, there still exist alternative approaches. Do you believe in the process of incubation, Mr. Braddock?"

"Well, yeh, or something similar. Why?"

"I have mulled over this situation. But, Friday, I went to a little restaurant near home—nice, quiet," he smiled. "After my meal I relaxed with a small liqueur—my only vice—and like a firefly on the darkest night, an idea flared in my mind," he paused.

"Man is the central entity in your system. If the vehicle cannot be made for man, then man must be made for the vehicle. Very simply put, you need to bring in to play the skills and knowledge of our leading psychologists. Not just educational psychologists! You need people versed in leading edge parapsychology. No, don't laugh. Zen, Yoga, ...—yes, and disciplines you've never dreamed of. They must be applied. You see, changing the ship isn't good enough. It is man who must be modified!"

"I sent a letter to your Secretary. I understand that mere chance resulted in his reading it. Most such letters are filtered out as being produced by quacks and cranks. But as luck would have it, his secretary was ill, he examined the incoming mail, and he read my letter. Sometimes one wonders about the validity of synchronicity. Anyway, he called me, I am here. Where do we go now, ladies and gentlemen?"

"Simplistically, we initiate a program based on the ancient teachings I mentioned, modified by our current knowledge of psychology and psychiatry.

"Currently your man-machine interface is indirect. You are broadcasting to and from the brain shotgun style. It is not good enough. Our neurosurgeons have the skills to provide direct interconnections between man's neural system, and that of the machine. We must implement such an interface.

"Man must be tailored to work with the system."

# Frankenstein

John Holms became the guinea pig for the new approach.

Problems surfaced immediately.

"Pat, this is going to be a little different from anything ever done before." John spoke slowly, selecting his words carefully.

"You see, there is going to be an interface between man and machine. Instead of visual signals being processed and displayed on a screen, the signals will go directly to the pilot's brain. Instead of moving a control stick, he'll 'think' the aircraft through the maneuver."

He paused. Pat was looking at him with concern. "John, you've never bothered to discuss your work with me, except when things were dangerous. What do you mean by 'go directly to the pilot's brain'?"

"Well, what they are thinking of is a minor operation. They'll install a kind of electrical jack at the base of the skull. A plug from a skull cap will transfer signals between man and ship. Not a big deal, but different."

"Not a big deal!"

She stopped, shivered.

"John, I'll not be married to a Frankenstein monster! Nor some other kind of freak! They want to operate on you! They are crazy! It's time you resigned your commission! Get a normal job! Let them carve on someone else!" She broke off and began to cry.

He stood silently, head bowed. Then he put his arms around her, held her close.

"Don't do it! John, if you love me, don't do it! It will destroy us! When it's never been done, why do they choose you? It isn't right! No, they can't! I wont let them!"

Preparations continued. A team of neurosurgeons consulted with the program's medical personnel. "Our initial conclusion is that we lack sufficient knowledge. Mapping of the brain has identified related functions and brain location. The requirement here goes far beyond such mapping. It will take at least two years to gather the kind of information needed."

Jim grunted. "Whoa, we can't delay one year, let alone two. Give me some alternatives."

A crash program was initiated to complete such mapping. Emphasis was on those areas and functions needed to control the aircraft. At first little was accomplished.

Professor Volte reviewed the progress with Jim. "This activity has become the pacer for the program. If it stretches out, so does the program. I suggest we modify our approach."

"Doc, I'll go anything that will help."

"Right now were using yesterday's technology for brain mapping. Insert electrodes, make measurements, remove electrodes. It takes forever. I'd like to combine an already developed mechanical device with some microradio pills. The device is called a micro motor. I think we can produce a combination of the two, in conjunction with micro transducers and signal conditioners. It will allow us to map exact points, and wont introduce interference."

Key engineers involved in micro motor development were inducted. Progress went well. In three months the team introduced micro-motor-powered sensors into the brain. Pre-programmed to burrow to specific locations, they served as data transducers and as transmitters to external instrumentation. The mapping project was completed in record time. No indication of brain damage was noted.

Pat was despondent, John quiet, contemplative. They avoided talking about the implant. When word came Pat drove him to the hospital. She sat in the waiting room quietly, did not cry. Fear had led to numbness.

The operation was completed without complication.

Physically small, but incessantly active, John had literally hated the long sessions of mental training. Initially these were the old familiar techniques, known to the mystics since time long past. Long relegated to the vast dark region of damned knowledge, they had been revived by science when more sophisticated methods failed.

The skull cap was modified to interface with the implant. Each time he donned it John felt a shock. The feeling of an alien presence invading his mind. Gradually he learned to ignore it.

At first the skull cap fed into monitoring instruments only. "We really don't have enough information. We've introduced man into the circuit, and man isn't consistent. So we have to extract from the hodgepodge of signals he generates just those that are valid." The psychologists, physiologists, and bioengineers explained the delays.

"You see, we've got to identify the patterns generated. We are developing filters to block out the garbage. When we get consistent patterns from all this, we have to determine how to convert them. We're gathering data. We've had to develop God knows how many new transducers, signal conditioners, filters. Bioengineering just hasn't reached the stage to provide us all the tools we need. We'll get there, but give us time."

Time was a commodity they lacked.

As they better understood the interface they began to add real subsystems for the subject to manipulate. Instruments at the interface monitored continuously the minute signals transferring over the buss. Patterns were identified, cataloged, provided to the psychologists. They correlated with known activities at the time the data generated, analyzed the combination. Procedures and equipments were modified, re-introduced into the ongoing process.

Once the techniques were well learned pattern recognition became a routine affair. The mental scan recorded them in his mind with picture like resolution. At times he was amazed, for his memory had never been that good before.

The simplistic Alpha waves were quickly brought under control. The muon processes followed rapidly. Even with the bio-amplifier interfaces the integro-dynamics responses came slowly. There were limits beyond which physiology could not go.

Essentially the activity was empirical. As each result was analyzed any slight improvement triggered a positive stroke. Of course, any regression resulted in punitive stimuli. The feedback, almost instantaneous, did not always elicit the expected result. John tried to think, and the responses had to be autonomous in nature. Punitive feedbacks were increased, as were rewards.

John noted the infrequent but recurrent anomalous signals. At first he reported them, but they were dismissed as either noise—or unconscious mental inputs from his own mind.

"Doc, I seem to generate these arbitrary signals. It seems like my mind wanders, and then they get triggered. Sometimes I don't notice what's going on, just note it after the fact."

"It can happen, John. We attempt to filter out all irrelevant patterns, but there's overlap between them and the patterns we need. As long as you are alert to the conditions, you can compensate for these perturbations."

He admitted that the explanation made sense, yet doubted the explanation. Still, he discontinued his reports. Any reference to them was lost in the extensive paperwork.

As was his nature, he did not report the pain. Each episode began with the ignored signals. Each episode ended with a pounding headache. He concluded, reluctantly, that it went with the territory.

John had been assigned to the project early. He had followed the black magic of the sensor development, had volunteered for the initial flights. He had been rejected, retained in the lab work as too brilliant a mind to risk. But after frantic effort he had convinced the Program Manager that just such a mind was needed to master the ship. Undoubtedly, he was right. But the circumstances were not.

Each of the selected pilots was given a specific vehicle. They would live with the engineers, the designers, the integrators, the assemblers. Each would follow his aircraft from drawing board to roll out. Fred had Dream Ship One, then was replaced by Andy; Jerry, Dream Ship Two; and John, Dream Ship Three.

Dream Ship 3 was to be the culmination of extensive technical effort. Here, for the first time, a full suite of avionics would be installed. Here, for the first time, control would be entirely through the mental interface.

Mechanically, she was to be state of the art. The electronic sensors, however, were the product of blue sky research that had surpassed all expectations. But even these advances had been inadequate to date.

The physical linkage between man and ship had not existed for the prior aircraft. Earlier signal transfer had been through differential amplifiers on both the sending and receiving apparatus. The minute brain signals were sufficiently amplified to provide adequate input to the communication drivers.

Time and frequency multiplexing were combined to segregate the different brain signals. Unfortunately the existence of external noise often distorted the resultant output.

The physical linkage helped overcome the noise problem. It also added to the discomfort of the pilot, but that was a secondary consideration. Eventually John was unable to determine what was a reasonable pain to expect, and what was one about which the doctors should be informed. Eventually he reported neither.

Patricia noted his frequent moments of despondency. At first she didn't think of it in terms of a problem. Rather, it was a quirk he had developed, merely annoying.

"Johnny, it's a beautiful day. Smile for me."

He looked at her, force a "Smiling Jack" smile on his face. His eyes didn't smile.

"Is it the ship, John?"

"You know, at times, I think you are more concerned with her than with me. My goodness, even I am calling it 'her'. Does it worry you that much?" Her voice was half teasing, half resentful.

He glanced at her, frowned. "Yes, I guess Dream Ship 3 and I are married in a strange sort of way. Together we are a team—no, not a team, but an entity. It is a relationship that is very close. A form of extreme symbiosis, I suppose. We are totally dependent on each other for survival."

He grinned. "Does she make you jealous, Pat?"

"Yes!, it shares your mind. Closer than I do, really. Yes, I'm jealous. And I'm so very afraid."

At night, while he sat in the den reviewing the progress and problems of the day, she lay wide-eyed in their bed. At times she sobbed incoherently. At other times she merely starred at the ceiling, invisible in the dark.

Outwardly, there was little to indicate the existence of a problem. Increased irritability, anger, even fits of sulking—but everyone was on edge. The program was behind schedule, over cost, and under surveillance and pressure. Three Congressional committees this quarter. John's conduct or attitude were not at all out of step. Rather, they were representative.

The behavioral theorists analyzed, concluded a normal learning plateau existed, and opted for continued training, at a reduced pace. Progress did not improve, but emotional outbursts decreased in intensity and frequency. Concurrently John tended to become more withdrawn, more contemplative. This tic was ignored.

"John, we're committed!" Jim Braddock smiled, clapped his broad hand on John's shoulder. He didn't notice, and would not have understood, the sensitive shrug that caused his hand to fall.

"The President's Scientific Advisor says go, the Counsel says go, the President says go…".

"And, most important," He stopped, smiled. "And, most important, Congress appropriated the funds."

Rubbing his hands together he pranced down the hall, a heavy-set, aging child, slightly ridiculous in his exuberance.

John grinned. With a start he realized that he couldn't recall the last time he'd grinned about anything. "Strange."

Dream Ship 3 was go!

Her predecessors, possessing all that Dream Ship 3 possessed, had been built, had operated at low levels of efficiency, had ended in tragedies. The basic concept was wrong, something was missing. Engineers had analyzed, prototyped, modified—all to no avail. Between the massive, impassive creature of the air and the sensitive, live director in the cockpit existed an impenetrable barrier.

Attempts to penetrate that barrier had resulted in 3 deaths. And for John Holms what lay ahead might well be worse than death.

Schedules were revised. Training sessions became nightmares as the pressure for progress became unbearable. The onus fell on John Holms. His was the duty, the responsibility. When progress was lacking he left the Quiet Room head bowed, eyes averted. His empathy with the project made any failure a personal problem. He worked in the Quiet Room by day. By night he lived in it, either in dreams or half awake repetitive analysis of the never-ending problems.

"Joe, the thresholds are set to high, damn it! I can't trigger a response consistently with these levels!"

Joe Sampson nodded briefly. "It's bad, but if we cut it lower noise is going to play hell with us and trigger the sensors. You'll be bombarded with unintegrated data. It can't be lowered.

The solution came from a non-engineering type, Ralph Adams. Ralph was the documentation guru. A quiet, withdrawn introvert he rarely spoke at the meetings. But he read of the problems while editing documents, reflected on other material he had read that had a bearing, and queried John Holms.

"John, suppose they made the sensors both time and voltage responsive. Can you hold a signal at a low level, long enough so that it would not be possible for it to have been noise generated?"

John looked at him, headed cocked to the side. He stood up, grinned. "You are going to get a promotion or I'm quitting this outfit. Let's talk to old Joseph and see what can be slapped together."

"Joe, hey!, Joe! Wakeup and get over here, will you."

They talked, quarreled, worked, tested. Yes, it could be done. Some latching circuits, comparison circuits, juggling a few parameters, maybe an ASIC chip or two.

In three days they were sure. The concept worked. Ralph Adams got his promotion, the system was back on schedule, John Holms was operating at a qualifying level. The monkey was on the back of the Production Shop and they responded with skill and dedication.

John Holms suffered increasingly severe headaches. He lived on aspirin and coffee. He didn't mention the problem to the Flight Surgeon. "After all," he thought, "I've had headaches before. It'll clear. It's just pressure."

"Jim, do you talk to John very often?"

"Very often. Well, everyday. Why, Pat?"

"No, not just good morning, how are you. Do you really talk with each other?"

Jim frowned. Actually, any in-depth conversations were rare. "I guess we've been pretty busy. No, I haven't had any heart-to-heart let-it-all-hang-out talks with John since he knocked over the oscilloscope and kicked it." Jim grinned.

John Holms was rarely angry, rarely showed emotion. But there had been an occasion.

"We were out in the back yard Sunday. He looked up and saw a raven high above. Strangest thing! 'You blind bitch! You'll not win!' he said. It was though he forgotten I was there. I asked him what he meant. He just grinned, said 'I was thinking out loud.', and wouldn't talk about it any more."

She paused, collected her thoughts.

"At night, he dreams a lot. And sometimes, when he's dreaming, I hear the same words. I think this airplane is getting to him. Talk to him, Jim. Help him!"

He looked carefully at her. Her hands were trembling, and there had been almost a sob in her last words.

"Pat, thank you. Of course I'll talk to him. Maybe you and John need to get away a while. You let me know how he's doing. He is under a lot of pressure."

# Roll Out

The iron bird, possessing the control surfaces and landing gear assembly of the final ship, quickly became the scene of action. An unimpressive, rectangular mass of framing, black boxes, fiber optic paths, laser signals, it had little of the appearance of the final product.

To minimize time a decision was made to run fiber optic signal paths between the Quiet Room and the iron bird. John would exercise the controls from his position in the Quiet Room. The ships control surfaces, dummy maneuvering jets, and landing gear could be evaluated even as the control system itself was exercised.

"John, you ain't triggering laser 3. "

"John, why don't you respond to the blockage signal?"

"John...!"

He lay quietly in the mummy shaped confines of the cockpit mockup in the Quiet Room. Because the control was centered here it was often called the executive room. John swore the latter name was appropriate. The body-fitting cockpit, the skull cap, the body sensors, all suggested a modernized version of an electric chair.

The rising pressure to get the job done; the desire to complete this, the almost final phase, brought him often to a level of desperation. But progress was made, the iron bird mastered. The next phase would be familiarization on the Motion Base Simulator.

The first runs on the Motion Base were non-productive. The hydraulic system sprang leaks, the limit switches were out of tolerance, and one leg of the "Four-legged Walking Box" was damaged when g forces were exceeded. The delay for replacement was only 24 hours, but every hour was important. In two weeks dry runs were scheduled on the ship.

Flying the box became the primary activity. For simple maneuvers the response seemed adequate. But when turns, banks, and changes in velocity occurred simultaneously the lag time became significant.

Landings were quickly recognized as major problems. The lag time between application of control signals and response of the physical activators had a limit due to the physical makeup of the aircraft. Added to these was processing time of the simulators computers. The total time approached a full quarter of a minute. At the sink rate of the aircraft such lag could easily be deadly.

Quickly it became evident that the flight control laws on the Motion Base were either inconsistent with those of the aircraft, or that major problems lay ahead. Contributing to the problem was excessive lag time in various signal paths. Of more importance, the number of polygons required for an adequate visual frame could not be consistently generated in the time allotted. And, finally, it was evident that the computer system, using only 10 parallel CPUs, could never provide timely response for all the concurrent functions.

The motion base activity was scaled back, and the dry runs on the aircraft expanded. Multiple ground crews and multiple shifts would permit maintaining schedule. The increased costs of using the aircraft instead of the simulator would be significant.

The possible impact on John Holms, the key participant, were casually ignored. "Hell, Iron John can handle it."

Iron John wondered.

The decision was made to ship the aircraft piecemeal from Georgia to Palmdale plant 42, re-assemble and complete outfitting at those facilities. With the ship finally assembled they would have rollout, then fly the bird to Edwards for ongoing flight tests.

Major assemblies were shipped by train. Lesser assemblies were crated, hauled by truck cross country. The activity paralleled on a lesser scale that of the original move.

For a change, plans worked well. The Fuselage required a special car be developed. They started with a flatbed, extended it in length, and built in side supports. The wings had to be shipped in a vertical position, rising high in the air. The train was rerouted to bypass tunnels, overhead wires or cables.

Special vehicles were assembled to complete the final move to the plant. Unfortunately, even these were not adequate for the job. As it became apparent that major assemblies could not be transported to the plant by available means other techniques had to be developed.

"Maybe we can break 'em into smaller elements."

"It's too late for that. We have no facilities available here."

"You know, I once saw some blimps carrying some heavy loads," John mused.

"Blimps. Yeh, it might work. Or, maybe, helicopters. The big ones. They use 'em for moving out timber. Check it out. I think that's the answer."

Finally, after much head scratching, helicopters were leased from logging firms. These systems had been used in lifting huge logs from the backwoods, moving them to sawmills. The same basic technique proved fruitful here, and in due time the final move was under way.

In the interest of security and to minimize interference with the local economy, the move was made at night. Again, fortunately, there were no mishaps, only minor incidents, such as removing, temporarily, overhead power lines.

The move was largely completed, the major assemblies in place for mating.

Re-mating the major components proceeded quickly. The needed jigs and fixtures had been shipped and put in place well ahead of shipping the aircraft. Key personnel were on hand to oversee and participate in the actual reassembly. Minor delays occurred, chiefly over misrouted assemblies. These were rapidly located, brought on board.

Close tolerances required some minor rework of a few parts. Liquid nitrogen shrank pins sufficiently to allow passage through otherwise impenetrable openings. Jim was sure barbed wire and tape were used somewhere, but no evidence was found.

"Davidson, no one could put that mess together so quickly. Where'd you hide the superglue? Security tells me two-thirds of their barbwire has disappeared since we got here."

Davidson grinned. "Hell, we ran out of both of those. Thank God for Scotch Tape and chewing gum!"

In three days dry runs would be conducted on the ship. Training was now limited to problem areas only. Final Assembly was swearing by their schedule. The grueling drive to be ready had paid off.

The dry runs were being conducted even as last minute work continued on the ship. Only after conclusion of the dry runs would they have roll out. And only a limited number of people would be present, or even know about, roll out.

The paint shop wouldn't be used for this bird. The materials used, and the flight envelope contemplated, insured that paint would be useless.

---

John Holms was hospitalized on January 12.

His wife brought him to the base hospital, driving through a rare but severe snowstorm to reach the Emergency Room. He was quickly examined, and diagnosed as having pneumonia. His wife Pat stayed with him through the night, wiped blood from his lips, when he coughed.

Not noted was the complete ennui, lethargy, depression that accompanied his physical problem. The conditions established a resonant pattern, each reinforcing the worst symptoms of the other.

He stayed in the hospital for a week. At the end of the week he sat on the edge of his bed, watched the brown wind-driven clouds from the hospital window. An RPV arched through the clouds in mankilling high-g maneuvers. He grinned at its slick beauty, turned to summon the nurse.

"Bring me my clothes."

The nurse stood open-mouthed. Without speaking, she left the room. Hastily she talked to her supervisor, who called the doctor.

Some hasty conferences followed. First between the medical staff, then between Program Control and the hospital commander. Finally a decision was made.

"Give him his clothes."

He ignored the pelting, wintry-cold drops as he left the building, climbed into the staff car they had dispatched for him.

"I'd have rotted away if I stayed there any longer." His voice was weak, but calm. "Let's get on with it."

---

Roll out didn't come until early in February. A sudden winter storm, in addition to John's bad health, precluded holding it earlier. When it came there was no fanfare. The program team, the base commander, the Air Force Chief of Staff, a representative from DARPA, and the President stood silently by.

As Dream Ship 3 was slowly tractored to the external test site Program Manager Braddock told the President grimly. "She's good, sir. The problems of DS1 and 2 have been corrected. DS3 will meet specs."

The President smiled, shook Braddock's hand. "You've done well, all of you. Your dedication will not go unrecognized."

The ceremony, if ceremony it was, thus concluded. Days of hard work followed. The integrated system was tested, analyzed, tested, peaked, and retested. The avionics suite failed to interface properly. Finally the multiplexed signal lines were found to have reflected waves,

the result of a terminator of the wrong impedance. With resolution of
that problem the Open Item Status Report was almost clean. After some
arm wrestling among the engineering groups and the assigned pilots
the remaining entries were waived. They would be cleared after completion of high speed ground test runs. A date was set for initial fire-up
of the engines, with low speed run tests to follow.

---

"Mr. Braddock, General Hayley called. Flight Test will not be able to
support tomorrow's flight." Ilene closed the steno pad, put it in the desk
drawer. "And I, sir, am going home."

She smiled as she closed the office door.

He turned away with a nod, thinking of a steak dinner, a stiff drink,
and the warm jacuzzi. Then the meaning struck him!

"Not support tomorrow's flight! What the hell does he mean, not
support tomorrow's flight!"

"Ilene, call him back. This is ridiculous."

He frowned, walked over to her desk, and took out the steno pad.
The notes were not shorthand, thank goodness, he thought. Flight Test
having an organization reunion. All pilots will stand down. General
Hayley leaving for home. Will call on Monday.

Slowly he sat down, starred out the window at the flat brown desert
stretching to the far Tehachapis. Why didn't people do their jobs?
Organization reunion! So you cancel a quarter million dollar mission!

The situation didn't meet all the criteria, but he decided it was time
to call the boys in the basement.

The communication setup, superficially, seemed to be jerry-rigged.
He opened the door to the inconspicuous closet, stepped in, and sat on
the small stool. Pressing an area on the wall opened a panel, and a dial-
less phone was at hand.

"Braddock on, and I've got a problem."

"Roger, Mr. Braddock. you are confirmed. What is your problem?"

He quickly informed the Basement that he had no chase plane for the flight.

"Roger, Mr. Braddock. You will call Washington and inform the director. You may tell him that the boys know the situation. Will that be all Mr. Braddock?"

"Eh, yeh. That'll do it. Thanks."

He closed the panel, once more hiding the phone. He laughed as he left the closet. Just call me Maxwell Smart, the thought crossed his mind. Undoubtedly the closet constituted a safe room, as they were now tagged. Faraday shields, sound proofing, signal monitors to detect stray emanations, scramblers—the works. How they really did it he didn't know, nor did he want to know.

He started to speak to Ilene again, then picked up the phone. There was little choice but to call the Director at home.

It was a bad move, but a necessary one. tomorrow's flight must be made, the schedule met. If the pressure had to come from the top, so be it.

"Sir, we have a problem with Flight Test. The old boy's gone wacky. He's having all pilots stand down tomorrow. An organization reunion. And we can't wait! The boys in the basement are up to speed, and told me to call you."

There was silence at the other end of the line. Then, "Jim, I'll call you back in half an hour." The phone was hung up before he could reply. With a shrug he leaned back in his chair, took his pipe from his jacket

The phone rang, and he waited for Ilene to answer, forgetting that she had left for the day. At the third ring he picked it up. "DS3 Program, Braddock on."

"Jim," the voice was calm but overly soothing. He felt his stomach muscles tightening. "I think we had better walk soft on this one. Let's delay tomorrow's flight for now. We'll make up the time later."

"Delay it! Do you know what you're saying? The conditions are right tomorrow. It may not work out this way again for another month. We can't accept the delay!"

"Look, Jim, I know how you feel. But think of it this way. He's buddy buddy with the oval office. Close. Now we can lean on him, but he can hurt us. Which is better, a few days' delay, or possible loss of the program? We don't really have a choice. I'm sorry. Goodnight, Jim." The telephone was dead.

Cowards! Politicians and cowards! But even worse, he knew they were right. They could easily lose the program. What now?

Thumbing through his list of key phone numbers he selected that of Colonel Dawson.

"Colonel Dawson, Jim Braddock on. I need your help."

"Colonel Dawson? Damn, Jim, when have you ever been so blasted formal? What's going on?"

"I don't have a wing man for tomorrow's flight. How'd you like to do some proficiency flying tomorrow. Right along with us, you understand?"

"No wing man? You mean chase plane, right? I'm getting bad vibes here, Jimmy boy. Of course, I'll do what's needed. If anyone looks at this setup close, though, we may both be handing out resumes damn fast."

"Not to worry, old son! If things go well, they wouldn't dare touch us. and if things don't go well I got this great little place down in Brazil— no extradition, you know." He grinned at the telephone.

"Colonel, you are one hell of a man, and I badly need you on this one. And, seriously, you're clean. You'll just be getting some flying time in. I'll cover for anything else. Now go home and get some sleep. Take off is at 3 in the morning."

"Take-off at 3 in the morning! The damn world doesn't even exist at 3 in the morning. Have them get my bird ready, will you? Nothing but God Damn slave drivers around this place!"

Colonel Dawson was a little old, one of the oldest active pilots. But a good man trying to do a job. They were few and far between anymore. Thank God that he knew those few.

---

The bright desert sun sank slowly behind the Tehachapis. The warm spring air, already cooling as the sun began to disappear, gently fluttered the leaves. Pat slipped her skirt well above her knees to expose them to the last warm rays of the sun.

Coquettishly, she smiled.

"John, it is nice just to relax. It's so seldom."

He nodded.

The pressure of the job, and the long hours of training combined to deprive them of such quiet times together.

"After this one, honey, I'll take a desk job. I'm really worn down. Hell, 45 is too damn old for this test pilot."

She held his hand, leaned her head on his shoulder. They sat thus through an hour, his arm holding her close.

A breeze, softly insistent, fluttered her skirt as the sun disappeared. Reluctantly they arose, walked hand in hand to the car. They felt a touch of pathos, perhaps premonition. They would not again stroll along the lookout above the quiet lake. He squeezed her hand more tightly. A tear formed at the edge of his eye.

"Damn it!"

She looked at him, startled. Then she smiled, "It's all right, John. Tomorrow we'll come again. After the flight."

They sat in the car for a few additional moments. From Vista Point Palmdale Lake lay below, and the panorama of the entire valley stretched out before them. Looking westward the Tehachapis, touched with snow, was the horizon. North and east a jet climbed toward the setting sun from Edwards Air Force Base.

He held her hand, smiled. "Time to go home, baby."

He started the engine for the drive home. Quickly, smoothly, they accelerated down the grade on highway 14. Already they could feel the coolness of the night moving in. High above a contrail glowed, a path of pink and white, in the last light of the setting sun. He turned on the radio, caught the evening weather report, "high of 75 today, falling to 45 tonight, with winds gusting to 30 miles per hour."

The radio continued with news of the day. The Chinese leader was visiting Canada, where the Treaty of Mutual Dependency was being signed. Other world leaders were present, oddly excluding those of the United States.

She rode silently by his side, looking unseeingly at the Joshua trees, their branches beseeching moisture from the dry desert air. The only thought in her mind, repeating insistently over and over, "Tomorrow is first flight."

She was surprised when he stopped at the neon lit bar. It was a week night, and they had it almost to themselves. They cheek danced to the slow music at the Nostalgia, oblivious to everything but each other. The music stopped, and still they held each other until a titter caught their ears. John grinned, led her to their booth.

To them both, these few hours seemed terribly important. Perhaps, unconsciously, they knew the future. Perhaps they didn't know, but even lack of knowledge drove them together. Yesterday is gone, tomorrow is dreams. Today, only today, is real. Like frightened children they clung closely together.

# First flight of Three

The worst would soon be over—that ominous first time. The huge ship would lumber down the runway, leap free of the earth into its own domain, eventually to return and land. Or so John always told her. And, of course, so it went—sometimes.

Thereafter it would be routine. Gradually the flight envelope would be widened, carefully and methodically—a procedure well known to test pilots. But the testing of the new envelope, reconstituted man, had never been so well thought out. John Holms was merely the pilot. And a chain is only as strong as its weakest link.

Mercifully, perhaps, he didn't break while in the air.

Engine runs had been successfully accomplished. Slow speed runs were complete. High speed runs were scheduled. But mother nature, faithful to her reputation, decided to intervene.

The hot dusty winds were reminiscent of summer, whipping across the dry lake bed. The shrimp, not yet dug into the soil below, waited the rains of spring, only to be surprised by the drying lash of the gusts. The aircraft and crew stood by.

But even mother nature at times softened her attitude. A break in the sequence of windy days occurred. The aircraft rolled out, rev'd up, and the high speed runs were quickly and successfully completed.

Fortunately.

For hardly had the last run been accomplished than a rolling cloud of sand and dust arose. Dark red and ominous it hugged the ground, a massive wall. It came from the west, from the open fields once green with alfalfa, now dry and sear.

The craft was quickly hangared, equipment moved off the flight line. Testing would proceed on another day.

A restless crew, with the aircraft grounded, waited for the winds to cease, the visibility to reach VFR levels. Dust clouds obliterated even the tower light, peppered the hangar door with gritty sand.

Dust insinuated itself through zippers, through button holes, through what appeared to be the tightest of seams. Closed doors and windows did not keep it out, nor did filters and tightly closed containers.

Linda sighed. "Jim, the constant wind, moaning and whistling, bothers me. But what I really can't stand is the dust. I close the windows, wipe everything clean. And within hours it's covered again. Look at my furniture. I can even feel the grains between my teeth!"

He nodded. "It's unusual for it to be this bad for so long. And you're right. Get's through every crack, no matter how small. Messing up our flight schedule badly."

Housewives found their clean china coated; clean clothes liberally peppered; and a dust layer, like an enveloping shroud, seemed to place a cover of gloom on the program.

Day after day the gusty winds prevailed. Day after day the crew turned out, stood by, waiting. Short tempers and irritation were the order of the day.

Recognizing the schedule slippage rapidly building up Jim Braddock made the extraordinary decision to widen the envelope two steps at a time in all non-critical regions. There was some consternation among the team. Nevertheless a new set of flight test cards were generated, and additional dry runs accomplished on the ground.

The risks were increased, certainly, but not substantially. And they would be back on schedule by the end of the first 3 months of flight test.

The engineers objected, the test pilots growled but indicated they could fly it anyway but loose. Management was adamant, and the decision held.

Dawn comes quickly on the high desert. At first a band of light touches the horizon. Then, in unbelievable blinding splendor the sun leaps skyward. Small cumulus clouds gleam in the rays of the newborn day. The winds are calm, and the desert basks in the growing warmth. It is a pleasant interlude between cold night and searing heat of day.

The fire trucks stood by, as did a rescue team. Loudspeakers blared for all non-participants to clear the area. John Holms grinned as he walked to the ship, climbed the ladder, and eased into the mummy-shaped cockpit. With assistance from the ground crew he donned his skull cap, snapped the connectors to the various sensors scattered (scientifically, he hoped) over his body.

Cables and hoses, like various sized snakes, coiled strategically around the ship. They carried electricity, fuel, cooling air to the systems.

In the control trailer Program Manager Braddock read each item on his check list.

"Power System?"

"Go."

"Instruments?"

"Go."

And on through the long list, each discipline affirming that their systems were ready.

"John, all systems go. You ready?"

Holms smiled. "What if he said no?" "Pilot is go, sir.", he responded.

"Initiate start sequence."

The hectic scene that precedes first flight generates a picture of incipient disaster in the minds of onlookers. Yet the reality is that all practical measures have been taken to insure safe accomplishment.

So it went with Dream Ship 3, and the flight itself was almost an anticlimax.

Firetrucks, ambulances, and assorted crews were strategically placed. The ship was fueled, inspections completed, walk-arounds accomplished. The pre-flight briefings had been quickly completed.

The engines started with a typical whine, and the power carts were disconnected. Slowly the manta-like monster trundled to the runway. Instrument readings were good, control was being successfully maintained, communications was good.

On the apron at the end of the runway final run-up was smoothly completed. "Tower, Dream Ship 3, ready for take off."

"You are clear for take off, Dream Ship 3. Notify the tower on lift off."

The start of the run was almost imperceptible, but by the time the ship was one third down the runway she rotated, and quickly left the ground. There was no attempt to raise the landing gear, so vibration readings were high, but not excessively so.

The flight lasted an hour. In that time she climbed to 30,000 feet, performed shallow turns, demonstrated her airworthiness, then returned to base.

"Dream Ship 3 on downwind leg. I'll be pulling a touch and go, followed by a full landing."

"Affirmative Dream Ship 3. You have the space. Notify me when you go final."

The touch and go went smoothly, except for some wonderment on the faces of a few ground personnel who had expected a full stop. The aircraft this time rose more authoritatively into the air than on the first liftoff.

Without incident John lined up for final, brought her in smoothly on the long runway, then pulled off onto the apron, cut the engines. Powerless, the ship yet seemed poised to once more return to the air, rather than sit quietly for the ground personnel and the waiting towtractor.

He completed his post flight, filled in the Form 1, and shook hands with the ground crew. Finally he entered the staff car, now with a rare smile lighting his face. "She's one good bird, gentlemen. I think we've got a winner."

The first flight was a success. It established that, systemwise, everything worked at least nominally. The basis for on-going testing was established, the schedule was met—and the glaring discrepancies so carefully hidden away could now be resolved in privacy.

Jim watched as the ship was towed to the hangar. Two ships lost. This one had to continue to fly, had to prove the Dreamship series was feasible. And enough men had died.

As he watched the huge body disappear into the hangar a premonition came. Enough men had not died.

The post flight party was noisy, exciting, and finally raucous as liquor flowed freely. "Jim, I'm so glad it went well. And everyone here is enjoying themselves.

John Holms, usually quiet and inconspicuous, had downed too many cocktails. It was evident from the careful manner in which he placed one foot ahead of the other as he walked across the room. He stood in front of the newcomer, a slight smile on his face.

"Welcome, Major Nestor, to the puppet show. We are the puppets… And she, and I drink to the damnation of her soul!" He lifted his glass on high, quickly finished off the contents.

"And she, that huge black witch in the hangar, is the puppet master." He laughed, looking around to see the others join in the laughter. There was only silence.

Major Nestor laughed. "Well, I hope I make an excellent puppet then. But I suspect I'll pull my own strings."

The Major circulated, politely danced with each of the wives who were of such a mind, and carried on light conversation, spiced occasionally with a joke or bit of Washington gossip. He plainly fitted in well with the crowd.

"You know, I really liked the major who just danced with me, Major Nestor. Will he fly Dream Ship 3?" Linda queried.

"He's backup to John Holms. Yes, he is very personable. But he worries me."

"Oh, why is that," she seemed perplexed.

"He reminds me of a kid who has always had his way. He's been successful in everything he's done. If a prize didn't fall in his lap, I'm not sure how he would react. And, in this business, prizes don't often fall in your lap."

"Well, anyway," she smiled, "he's and excellent dancer. Look at him and Pat. Don't they make perfect partners?"

Jim Braddock frowned. Major Nestor was a hit with everyone. An excellent pilot, though daredevilish. Knowledgeable, a good conversationalist. Why the feeling of uncertainty about him. He smiled. Perhaps a bit of jealousy in me.

The Major was an accomplished dancer, and he was an exuberant one. When he made a rare mistake he was the first to laugh at it, and his partners were quick to forgive. Even now his face was red from his exertions as he and Pat danced to the quick beat of the polka. They left the dance floor, both laughing.

The party began to fizzle out by midnight. John Holms was conducted out by Jim Braddock and Pat Holms, who drove them away.

"Whooee! I'll bet she makes him live hard for a while.", Jim grinned.

"Well, he was plastered. Strange! I've never known him to drink much, nor talk like he did tonight. Poor John!"

Linda smiled. "And how are you holding your liquor, Mr. Braddock."

He went through a brief rendition of a staggering inebriate.

"All right, you! Knock it off, or you'll be sleeping on the sofa."

---

Unquestionably, he had failed to follow protocol in authorizing the flight. If the flight had failed there is little doubt that he would have been swiftly canned. With the success of the flight, however, that was improbable. Nevertheless, he felt sure there would be repercussions.

He wasn't far wrong.

He braced himself for the inevitable phone calls. He had bypassed procedures, violated a number of regulations. Edwards, ASD, Systems Command, and probably the Pentagon were undoubtedly boiling.

"Well," he said aloud, "I was looking for a job when I came here."

"Braddock, this is General Hayley!" The voice was threatening, cold. It stopped momentarily, waiting for recognition. He didn't answer.

"Mr. Braddock, do you hear me!" This time the anger read through, the voice rising in pitch.

"Yes, General, I hear you very well."

"Who the hell authorized you to fly without a chase plane Friday?"

He leaned back, relaxed, pulled out his pipe. Slowly he half-filled the bowl, tamped it down. Then he lit it, took a long puff.

"Mr. Braddock, are you there?"

"Yes, General, I'm here. Just took a moment to light my pipe." He smiled, waiting for the reaction.

"Pipe… Light your pipe!" The General lapsed into silence for a moment. "I…I…", and again he paused.

"Mr. Braddock, you are not competent to manage the DS3 program. I am requesting the Secretary of the Air Force to take steps to have you replaced. Do you understand me!"

He puffed at the old pipe, lay it on its side in the ash tray. "Why, yes, General, I understand you perfectly. However, I think you need to get your facts straight. There was chaseplane on Friday's flight. And, in fact, even if there weren't, that is strictly my concern. I could, and would have, waived the requirement. In fact, General, if it takes it to get this job done, I'll waive every damn requirement on the books!"

"You will not waive a damn thing, Mr. Braddock. You will be hearing from the Air Force Chief of Staff today! And I assure you, you won't like what you hear!"

He smiled. "General, it just so happens the Secretary of the Air Force is the office right now. Congratulating us on the excellent flight achieved Friday. And he wants to talk to you. Oh, yes, he wants to talk to you."

With a smile he passed the phone to the Secretary, puffed slowly on his pipe.

Some days were better than others.

"NASA is up in arms. They want to know why they haven't been involved. A bunch of chief honchos are at Air Force Headquarters today, looking for answers. Gonna be a hell of a briefing."

"They have a liaison man here. They chose not to get involved. Now things are coming to a head, and they want some of the glory."

"When DARPA unloaded this on us NASA was locked up with other programs. Now she's beginning to realize this is the future. Yeh, this is the future, and we've gotten in right at the start. Now we've got to keep up the momentum. It's our program, and we'll carry it out to the finish.

"Klooster wants the program."

"Sure? You know, he had first chance at it. Turned it down. Of course, the risks are substantially less now. He could step in and end up being the successful manager of an important program. That would suit old Tab well!"

"He and Mahaney at Headquarters are damn close. And Mahaney and the Chief of Staff are real cozy. Then there's Hayley. He has little love for you. I'm not saying that anything is going to happen, but watch yourself."

It made sense. Every program manager of a major program had to guard against competitors. There were several who would like to have the job—and others who would willingly see him fail. He and Klooster were hardly bosom buddies.

Thoughts such as these, perhaps, made him drive the team harder. Fear, ambition, conscientiousness—all spurs to enhanced effort.

For several weeks now he had felt strangely elated. The dreams were no longer occurring. His headaches had disappeared.

Looking back over the past months he recognized the change that had occurred in his attitude, even his personality. He had lived under a pall, and now it seemed to be over.

I've got to make it up to Linda. My God, how has she put up with me. And Ilene. Hell, the Colonel, too.

It is strange. Thank God, it's over.

Or so he thought.

The worst lay ahead.

# Bill and Pat

In Washington activity is a sign of importance. If you are not conducting a presentation, you should be attending one. Of course, if you conduct one, the audience must consist of sufficiently prestigious individuals. And if there is one you attend, the presenter must be of similar vintage.

Tab Klooster was well acquainted with the rules. If the President's staff could be cajoled into attending a meeting there was rarely a problem with getting other important individuals to attend.

Should the President's staff not be available, a Senator or Congressman heading a significant committee could be equally useful.

Worst case, if none of these were to be on hand, at least a General should be in the audience.

Tab Klooster placed his viewgraphs neatly beside the projector. He nodded to the assembled brass, turned toward the screen and repositioned the first viewgraph.

"General," he paused, "Gentlemen, the charts I am showing are essentially self explanatory. I will expand on some of the entries. Also, if there are questions at any time, hit me with them."

"Chart one reflects the slippage in the Dream Ship Program. Chart two, the management decisions that have contributed to that slippage. Chart three treats the deaths that have occurred, and the contribution of mismanagement to those deaths. Chart four projects the result if current management practices are continued. And chart five summarizes the material. A short briefing, gentlemen, but an important one.

Each chart was examined with interest. No questions were asked, however, until the last chart was removed and the projector turned off.

General Hayley looked at some notes he had jotted. "Tab, what is your opinion of Braddock as a manager."

"He has a good record. But largely through luck. He's managed to pick up programs that were already well along, already well run, and a shoo-in to complete successfully. And even then he's come close to busting them. But you don't know this unless you do some careful detective work. No, old Braddock is smooth."

General Hayley, nodded, smiling.

The Undersecretary frowned. "He has had five major programs, brought all of them in under cost, within schedule. His records were reviewed extensively before he was given the Dream Ship program. Mr Klooster, I have no information that would corroborate your statements."

"Of course not! As I said, he's a smooth operator."

"Also, we have reason to believe that he may not be able to handle the pressure."

The Undersecretary said nothing, waited.

"He's had several quarrels with his people, has threatened to fire his secretary, and his wife has told friends that he's threatening to divorce her. Admittedly, the program has not yet been impacted. But I know Jim Braddock, and these actions are not characteristic of him."

"If we decided to make a change, General Hayley, who would you recommend for the position." The Undersecretary plainly was nervous, uncertain, was looking for safe alternatives.

"You have the man right here. Tab Klooster. Excellent record. I personally vouch for his skill and integrity. And he probably knows more about the Dream Ship technology than any other man. Tab Klooster—

you can't go wrong" General Hayley smiled. This had been a good meeting. A very good meeting.

Four projects of significance—in each case, prior to project completion, Major Nestor had transferred to a new task. Within 6 to 8 months after his transfer the project would terminate—unsuccessfully.

"Well," Jim Braddock mused, "One thing is for sure!" He paused, a grin on his face. "If he asks for a transfer, we know we're in trouble."

———

It had always been this way. He was handsome, and was pleased with the fact. Women rarely failed to take a second glance when he was near. It wasn't a matter of conceit to him, but an important fact in his life, a pleasant fact.

A combination of circumstances led to his friendship with Pat. She had been drawn to him even when introduced at the party following first flight. By coincidence they met at the BX, and she enjoyed exchanging pleasantries with him.

He had not planned to hit the bars tonight, but on a whim had driven to Lancaster.

She, likewise, had merely been in town shopping, stopped to relax for a few moments over a cool drink.

"Major Nestor, how nice! Are you meeting someone here?"

"Please, it's Bill. No, no one. Mind if join you?"

"Of course, Bill. I'm on my way home. I suppose I shouldn't reveal my dark secret, but I stopped for a margarita. Hopefully you won't tell John?"

He laughed. "I suspect he knows well your many vices."

"Oh no, margaritas are my only one."

"Eh, well, I'm not much for margaritas. But I have vices of my own."

"How interesting! Let's talk about those."

He grinned. "Too rough for your tender ears, young lady."

"Hey, I like that." He was listening to the music coming from the coin machine. "Dance with me?"

And now they were dancing in the clear space at the end of the bar. "A strange sequence of events!" she thought. "You are a good dancer, Bill. I'm sure you've practiced with many of the ladies."

"Whenever I can. Whenever I can. Only, of course, to perfect my steps."

"Of course."

He held her closer than he should, pressing against her as they danced. But he was young, so it was understandable. She watched his face, occasionally in a teasing way thrust herself at him. He responded with an eager smile. Plainly he found her attractive.

"Oh, look at that clock! I've got to run."

"Pat, come to happy hour Friday."

"Well…, oh, I suppose I can do that. I'll see you Friday."

John, when not at the plant, still spent his time analyzing the program problems, working the problems. He had no time for her.

This boy, in contrast, saw her as a desirable woman. He had time to talk to her, to dance with her, to play, even to innocently flirt.

There was no conscious intent by either to let it go beyond that. Plans and emotions don't always go in stride.

As time passed he became more attentive, made passes that she only half-heartedly resisted, then resisted not at all.

They danced during happy hour, danced out the door beside the lighted pool. The music stopped, but he still held her, kissed her lips gently.

"No, don't." She whispered the words, but her eyes belied them. And then she kissed him, laughed. "What will people think. Come on, let's go back inside. And you behave yourself."

Quickly she became infatuated with him. She excused herself. He was attentive, and she was only being kind. At first she limited her kindness to an appreciative touch of her hand. Then to a friendly hug.

He first kissed her passionately at the drive-in. She was passive. But when he stopped she looked at him carefully, sighed. She put her arms around his neck, pressed her lips to his, kissed him soulfully.

His hands wandered, and she responded. Like teenagers exploring the excitement of the forbidden world of sex, they touched each other, petted, and gave themselves over to their emotions.

When he was unable to undo her blouse she quickly loosed it for him, welcomed his hands and lips. At first she tried to restrict it to that, but her own desires were strong, and she soon realized she had lost control.

"You smell like lilacs. I love that smell." He breathed deeply, his face pressed to her bosom. "And you taste like honey." He kissed her smooth skin, letting his lips explore, his arms tight around her.

He held her gently in his arms when he had satisfied his needs, brushing her cheek with his lips. "Pat, Pat, I can't stay away from you."

It was their first time together. It would not be their last.

Pat smiled. Watching him unbutton his shirt, his quick fingers moving dexterously, unthinkingly as he looked at her. How many times had she seen this activity? Yes, it happened before so many times, always in her fantasies. Now it was real. Fearful yet eager she waited.

She reached out, touched his hand. "Please, let me do it."

She undid the buttons, one by one, slowly, looking into his eyes as she did so.

He looked down at her dark hair, her sparkling eyes. She is so eager for this! The smile on his lips was almost a smirk. Funny! It really isn't me. It's her thoughts, her day dreams, fantasies. I'm just an outlet. But, God, it's good!

He put his arms around her, held her close. She struggled slightly, laughed, and relaxed.

"If you don't quit playing we'll never get to bed," her voice held eagerness.

He released her, brushed his hand across her dress, letting it linger over her breast.

"Then I'll be very good."

"You're bragging!"

They both laughed.

"Look, Pat, some of the boys are flying up to Nellis Friday evening. Going to hit the town. Why don't you arrange to visit some friends up there for the weekend. We could have a hell of a good time, take in a show, dinner, and then…"

"Uh-huh, and then what, mister!"

"Well, we could get a nice room, have a real wild party for two whole days."

"God, you horny bastard. This Friday? It's awful short notice. I'll try. Look, I'll let you know. Bye, baby."

It wasn't difficult. Colonel Wheeler had transferred to Nellis three months earlier. Pat had been a close friend with Susan, his wife.

"John, I got a call from Susan today. She wants us to come up and spend the weekend with her, see the bright lights in Las Vegas. Why don't we fly up there. You'd enjoy the time off."

"I can't do it. We're running more tests Saturday morning. Look, call Sue and tell her you're coming. It'll be good for you to get away from this crabby old man. Lord knows, I sure haven't taken you anywhere for a while. After the next flight we'll go somewhere and have a real blast. Promise."

Pat smiled, almost sadly. "All right, I'll call her. You sure you wont change your mind?"

"Can't do it, honey. But we'll sure go another time."

Bill was less reluctant. "God, baby, you do look good."

His eyes followed every curve, then he licked his lips, once more scanned her from head to toe.

She blushed, squirmed under his surveillance. She twisted awkwardly. Almost she wished she hadn't worn the skin-tight dress, so revealing of the naked body beneath. She felt her nipples harden under his gaze. I'm acting like a school girl, the thought crossed her mind.

Bill had come to the airport to pick her up, drive to the Hilton. "Like the room?"

She smiled, hugged him. "Sure I do. So where do we go from here."

"Well, just a little problem. I promised the gang I'd go with them to a show. Want to come along."

"No, I can't do that. Some of them know me. When will you be back? What kind of show?"

"I'll be in before midnight. It's a strip joint. Get me all primed for this weekend."

"You are a bastard. You better be back by midnight, or someone else may be sleeping in the bed."

He laughed, kissed her.

She glared at him angrily as he left the room.

He was indeed well primed when he returned. They spent the remainder of the night and much of the next day in the hotel room.

"Tell me about it. Where did you go, and what kind of show did they have?"

"Hey, come on! It was just a strip show. The girls took off their clothes and shook themselves a little. This is Vegas."

"Just look, no touch?"

"Mostly."

"Hmm, mostly..."

She removed her gown, stood at the foot of the bed. "Okey, look, but no touch!"

"Wait a minute!"

"Well, mostly..."

They laughed as he chased her across the room, caught her in his arms.

"Okey, mostly, then." he growled. They didn't talk much after that.

Saturday night they attended a supper show. Suddenly Bill coughed on his food.

"Are you all right?"

"Yes, Just, well, ...She is, eh, well endowed."

His eyes were following hungrily the young dancer on the stage. Topless, she moved in a pattern designed to give maximum movement to her ample breasts.

Pat shook her head. "Bill, you act like a teenager looking at a girlie book. You make me think of a boy I used to know. But he grew up." Her voice was a little bitter.

"And I didn't. Yeh, I guess you are right. But, God, she is sexy!"

The night and next day were spent in bedroom games. She participated wholeheartedly, enjoyed his manhood. But in her mind the thought wouldn't leave. "If I were the stripper, it would be all the same to him."

She tried to drive the thought away by teasing him, arousing him further. But, reluctantly, she had to admit that it was true.

He drove her back to the airport to catch the three o'clock flight, waved as she boarded the airplane.

# Madness

"Pat, I'm bringing Bill Nestor home with me for supper. You remember, the Major you met at the flight party. He's my backup on Dream Ship 3, and we have some work to do. Be there around 6:00."

She sat the phone down, stared at it for a moment as though it were some dangerous snake. Major Bill Nestor. My God, is he crazy. How dare he come in my house while my husband is here! This is crazy!

She sat on the sofa, starred at the wall wide-eyed. Damn, damn, damn! Men are stupid bastards! Why did I ever let him make love to me? How can he be so brash as to come here? Six o'clock—that's hardly an hour. I better have something for them to eat. Oh, how shall I act…

John was commenting on something humorous, and both men laughed as they came through the door. "Hi, baby. You remember Major Nestor." John hugged her and kissed her cheek. She returned his hug, her eyes on Bill Nestor.

"Why of course I remember your wife. Pat, isn't it?" He smiled. "It's nice to see you again. I recall you were a wonderful dancer."

She took a deep breath, looked at him in disbelief. "Yes, Pat. Dinner will be ready in half an hour. Would either of you like a cocktail?"

Bill Nestor refused, although John had a martini. She is flustered, Bill thought. But she hides it reasonably well. Anyway, it wasn't my idea to come here. John nearly dragged me.

They watched TV until dinner was ready, and engaged in small talk during the meal.

"Pat, this is good dressing. Do you make your own? I don't think I've had this before."

"Actually, I do. It's supposed to taste like Thousand Island, but I know it doesn't. Are you also a chef, Major?"

He almost grinned at the "also a chef" query.

He paid the usual compliments on the appearance of the home, the delicious food, and the after-dinner liqueur. Then John and Bill settled in the study to discuss program problems. She brought them coffee around 10:00, then excused herself as she readied for bed.

She stretched under the covers. My God, what if he knew! That will never happen again. Poor John, I was so stupid. My God, what would he do!

"I'll have to tell Bill it's over. My God, what a mess. What got into me? He's just another man!"

She sobbed softly. Then laughed in a low voice. "But it was fun. God, I'll never do it again, but it was fun!"

The next day she talked to Bill Nestor on the phone.

"Bill, I'm sorry. It's over. I like you, but I'm not going to ruin my marriage. I don't want to see you any more. Don't call me, don't come to see me. Don't you see, it has to be this way."

"Pat, whatever you want is what I want. I only care for your happiness. But we need to talk. Friday night. Come to the Barn around seven. We'll talk, just talk."

Early morning John made office coffee. "How goes it, John? Hey, I saw Pat at the Barn Friday night. You lucky bastard, you sure married one good looking gal. You better watch the Major there. He can dance up a storm. Seen Jim? He has to sign this order for me."

"Jim? Down at the hangar."

The remark had been casual. He responded, unthinkingly, with a grin, sipped at his coffee cup. Suddenly, the drink was tasteless. A bitter seed had been planted. Pat had visited her sister Friday night. All night. They hadn't gone to the Barn. The impact of what he had heard struck him!

With an effort he turned his thoughts to today's flight. But the poison was working in him. Why hadn't she told him? Who had she been with? He said the Major. Major Nestor? Why had she lied about her sister?

In his mind he feared he knew the answer—yet he dared not believe.

---

The most significant advance to be found in the Dreamship series was the man-machine interface. Until now feedback to the pilot had come by way of instruments, through the window visual feedback, kinesthetics, even sound to an extent.

Control had been maintained through physical motion by the pilot. Feet worked the rudder/brake pedals. Hands and arms moved the stick fore and aft, from side to side. Fingers activated switches. In some limited instances voice and eye motion provided control.

The basic problem was simple to understand. As the speed of the aircraft increased the more important became response time of the pilot. But the path from eye to brain to arm was essentially fixed. Even with the most skilled pilot there was a lower limit to response time, established by that path.

The Dreamships changed this.

In both Dreamship One and Dreamship Two the response time had been decreased significantly. Using sensors that responded to the pilots thought processes the advanced devices eliminated the physical movement of hand or foot. By thought alone the mental stick was moved. By thought alone the mental rudder pedals were pressed.

Feedback was provided to the brain from sensors throughout the aircraft. Even the visual was no longer obtained through the eyes, but was fed in to the optic nerves through a form of pseudo-inductance.

But even these advances were insufficient. The external apparatus coupling signals to and from the brain introduced its own processing delay time. Of greater importance was the susceptibility of the equipment to external noise. Even cosmic rays striking the nanochips could trigger incoherent patterns.

Dreamship Three eliminated the external black boxes. The brain was now physically tied to the ship through an interface connection at the base of the pilot's skull. The signal strength was maintained high enough to insure differentiation between noise and valid input. Response time was now very close to the theoretical minimum.

John described the actual operation of the airplane as well as words make possible. He was most impressed with the visual inputs his mind received. With ordinary eyescan the scene was observed, certain elements stood out, and subsequent scans filled in the detail. With the aircraft sensors feeding the optical nerves the complete view was comprehensive and instantaneous. Every detail was etched firmly and clearly. In John's parlance, "This is what seeing really is. There are colors I've never seen with my eyes alone. And patterns I couldn't distinguish. It really isn't just seeing. It's expanded and amplified vision."

He described the control process in the same manner. "I visualize the ship rolling, climbing, diving, cruising—and immediately, or nearly so, it is. At first I visualized control stick and rudder movement. But it isn't necessary. Merely visualizing the ship in the desired mode and attitude is adequate. God, it's smooth!"

As John Holms phrased it, "Yea, verily, the Millennia has come!"

Not that he believed it.

The club was serving two'fers, and a special happy hour was in full swing. Successful first flight this Thursday for the F-35, and a full turnout of the test organization. A group of test pilots sat at a center table, hands busily twisting and turning as they demonstrated the day's flights. Vernon, the bartender, grinned.

The actors might change, but the same show, time after time. "Kate, give those hi-flier's a round on the house."

Bill Nestor sat at the bar, a scowl on his face. He nursed his drink, sipping at the martini with little relish. The TV was on, but with the sound muted. The news program showed the World Oil Congress in session, chaired by the leader of Greater Iran. Apparently the organization title had just been changed to World Energy Congress, as the major sources of uranium were now participants.

Not much of real interest on the tube. Taking a sip from his glass, he took a deep breath, placed the glass on the bar, and started to rise. Just then he noticed in the mirror a new arrival.

He sat down quickly, bent over his drink.

It was unusual for John Holms to be at the bar. In fact, he hadn't seen him here before.

John stood in the doorway, glanced carefully around the room. He looked in Major Nestor's direction, continued to look around the room, then suddenly looked once more at the Major. He walked toward the bar.

"Evening, Major. How's the drink?"

"Fine, fine."

Major Nestor set up, glanced questioningly at John.

"I'd like to talk to you, Major."

He paused, ordered a drink from the barmaid.

Picking up his glass he motioned toward the rear of the room. "Let's sit down at the table over there."

Major Nestor followed him toward the table, biting his lip. "What can I do for you, John?"

"When did you last talk to Pat?"

Major Nestor picked up his martini glass, twirled it gently. "Oh, I suppose a few days ago? Why do you ask?"

"A few days ago," John's spoke slowly, in a low voice. "Friday evening, maybe. At the Barn?"

"Well, yes, I did run into her there. In fact, she danced with me."

"Yes, Major, I know. She spent the night with you, too, didn't she?"

Major Nestor's face whitened. "Now, look, John. If you aren't man enough to keep your woman happy, don't place the blame on me. All right, we stayed in a motel. She got me worked up; and , hell, she already had the room rented. I'm only human and she's a damn good-looking woman."

"You filthy son-of-a-bitch!"

His hand whitened as it curled around his drink. The glass cracked in John's hand, and whisky and blood mixed on the table. He didn't notice.

John stood up, finally noted the blood dripping from his hand. He took out a handkerchief from his right rear pocket, carefully wrapped it around the hand.

"If you come near her again—If I even hear that you've been seen with her, by God, I'll kill you. Do you understand me? I'll rip you open from hip to shoulder, and I'll laugh as you bleed."

He struck out with the wounded hand, smashing it into Major Nestor's lips, the force of the blow knocking him backward, tipping over the chair. John stepped over him without looking, stalked through the door.

He drove recklessly on the way home, braked suddenly to avoid a coyote crossing the asphalt.

As he arrived home he noted the flock of ravens circling, their black wings barely flexing as they rode the updrafts. On the electric pole by the house a white one perched, an albino. He stopped for a moment to look. He'd heard her mentioned, but had never seen the bird. In a moment he walked stolidly into the house, shutting the door quietly.

Pat served New York cuts for supper, one of John's favorites. He dallied with his food, ate silently. She talked about the success of the F-35 flight.

"Why don't we go by the club, John. They're throwing a party. You look like you need some relaxation. Come on, it'll be fun. I love to dance."

He looked at her strangely.

"No, not tonight. Yes, I think you love to…, dance."

He stood up, walked slowly to his study, in deep thought. His dish was only half empty. She carried the dishes to the kitchen, wrapped the remainder of his steak in Saran Wrap, and placed it in the refrigerator.

He came out, stood in the hallway looking at her. Turning away he stumbled back into his study, started to set down. He abruptly rose, again entered the hall. At 19:00 hours, John Holms went out to the garage. In a moment he called his wife.

"Just a minute, honey, let me finish this dish."

She wiped the dish, placed it carefully on the stack in the cupboard. Taking off her apron she unthinkingly brushed a crumb from the table as she left the kitchen.

"Tomorrow night I think we'll have fish, John. Some red snapper, and some slaw. Would you like that?" she asked, opening the garage door.

As she stepped through the door the axe he held came down with such force that the handle cracked, even as the blade cleft her head.

Iron John had broken.

Afterward he strolled around the outside, a red gasoline can in his hands, dowsing the liquid at the base of the house. He laughed, talked to himself, whistled.

Capt. Lamar nodded, "What's up, John? You got wasps around the place?"

Vapid-eyed John stared at him in surprise.

"Oh, no! I'm going to burn it down. Burn it to the ground!"

Don laughed at the humor. "Sure you are. Collect the insurance and retire to the South Seas. Hey, a good basketball game's on. About the last one for the season. Drop by and watch it with me. Got some cold beer in the frig."

He strolled across the lawn, waved as he entered his front door. Perhaps five minutes passed before he noticed the smell of burning wood. At first he didn't interpret the significance.

The ball had just been passed down the court. Phillips was dribbling down the right hand side of he court. He whirled, fed the ball to

Makrowski. Makrowski dribbled around the outside, made a wide sweep around right end. He twirled, warding off two would-be guards, then shot the ball almost daintily, pushing it up into the air, down the court. It swished through the basket, not touching the rim.

With a start Captain Lamar rose from his sofa, opened the curtain on the small window facing the Holms'. The fiery light cast brilliant reds and yellows toward the window, erratic shadows on the wall.

He called the fire department, ran out and turned on his garden hose. John Holms was sitting on the front lawn, pulling at blades of grass, tears streaming down his cheeks.

While driving to the grocery store Jim Braddock heard the fire reported on the radio, and recognized the address. He quickly changed destination, headed for John's place. The firemen were already there when he arrived. They told him of their grim discovery inside the garage.

Holms still sat on the front lawn, rocking back and forth.

"The damn witch! She doesn't move! She doesn't move!", he muttered in the voice of a frightened child.

The firemen looked at him, with mixed feelings of pity and loathing. They thought he spoke of his wife.

The Program Manager knew better.

The doctors spoke quietly together, with much authoritative head nodding, bandying of medical jargon. The inquiry ended with the only possible conclusion. John Holms was insane.

John Holms condition threw a pall over the entire program. In many ways he had carried the brunt of solving the many problems that surfaced. No one had the level of expertise, the grasp of the ship, the confidence needed to master her.

Jim recognized the questions raised by John Holms' insanity. Was the ship at fault, were all who participated going to be victims in the same manner? Who would dare risk, not his life, but his sanity, for the program!

And, of course, Congress was doubly disturbed. The cost of the program, the loss of the first two ships, and the destruction of the mental capacity of key pilot weighed heavy on their minds.

Several hypotheses were advanced. The chemical action between the interface adaptor and the pilots' body chemicals might well have triggered the abrupt plunge into madness.

"I want every lead followed. Check for any reaction between the adaptor and his body. Check for any possibility of pick up of stray signals. Whatever idea you have, let's talk about it and pursue it. If our system did this to John, we must know how."

A thorough analysis of the components of the interface adaptor revealed the materials to be inert, non-reactive with any recognized elements normally found in the body.

Another hypothesis was that, when there was no physical connection between the ship and the man, the interface adaptor could pick up airborne inputs from any generators in the environment.

Further study revealed that, with the interface adaptor in normal closed position, a veritable Faraday shield existed, blocking either transmission or receipt of signals.

John's medical history was reviewed and re-reviewed. There were no indications of abnormality. His family's records were examined for hereditary traits that might have contributed to the problem. None were found.

Physical examination of John reviewed no indications of tumors, no unusual blood contents, nothing that helped isolate the mechanism triggering his lapse into madness.

Initially the psychiatrists held forth some hope that he might return to normalcy, be able to answer questions that would resolve the issues. As each treatment failed, time after time, they eventually conceded recovery was improbable.

With all factors considered Jim elected to stand down until practical alternatives had been examined.

# The Dragon Lady

"Hey, Security, got some action for you!"

Captain Millan glanced at the man in the door. "Well, Jim, you are a rarity in our area. What's happening? Oops!, Security shouldn't ask, they should know, right?"

"A lady checked into the Inn last night. Name of Janice Maldon. A pretty little thing. She's been inquiring about the Dream Ship series. Probably a nosy newsy—but check it out."

As security officer he found chores such as this not too infrequent. Generally the 'spy' was a curios bird watcher. Occasionally a fruitcake. But he had never caught a real, live, bonafide spy. Nor did he really expect to.

Nevertheless he and Sergeant Gilford, dressed in civvies, visited the Inn that evening. They sat at a table near the bar, sipping their drinks and talking a little too loudly about the Dream Ships.

"It will fly to the moon, Goddamn it. Not yet, but by the time the last one is built. There isn't anything on God's earth like it, and never will be."

"Hey, take it easy. Yeh, it's a great bird." Sergeant Gilfords concern was evident. "But we better knock it off for tonight. A long day, tomorrow. The flight briefing is at 3 in the morning."

"They pick the lousiest hours. You go ahead. I'm gonna have another drink."

Sergeant Gilford reluctantly rose, once more encouraged his companion to leave with him. Finally he shrugged and walked away.

The young lady at the bar rose and walked directly to the table. "Hi, I'm Janice Maldon. I heard you talking about the Dream Ship. I'm a Russian military spy, and would like to know more about it."

He stared at her in wide-eyed disbelief. Then when she laughed with a self-deprecating look on her face he grinned also.

She continued. "Actually, I lied a little bit. It's not Russian, but Chinese. I'm known," and she lowered her voice, "as the Dragon Lady. However, I'm traveling under a cover, as a mildmannered reporter, called," she leaned forward and whispered in his ear, "Clark Kent."

Having recovered from her first comment he accepted the latter one in stride. "Sit down, Dragon Lady. My name's Terry. You may have heard of me in the comic strips."

It was her turn to laugh, and she did so very pleasantly.

"Now, as to all those secrets! Do you really know about the Dream Ships? Or are you only repeating the rumors?"

"If I say I'm only repeating the rumors you'll find a more knowledgeable man to talk to."

"Well, yes. But I'm sure he wont be as handsome."

"Some consolation. Actually, I know a little. What would you like to know?"

"Last night I was talking to a man in the bar. Everyone called him Slouch. Do you know him?"

"Sure. Slouch is the janitor here. He usually comes in late and cleans up the place."

"He saw something that frightened him. Something big, and black, and quiet that swooped down from the heavens. Something very different from anything he'd seen flying here."

"I seen it. Twice I seen it. It came down like a bat, a huge bat. I mean it was bigger'n any airplane. And it made hardly a sound." Slouch paused, looked around the room to see the effect of his words.

Everyone was listening.

"That was the first time. The second time was way out to the east side. I'd cleaned up the bar out at the Well, and was heading home when I saw something cross in front of the moon. Only it almost blotted the moon right out of the sky."

He sipped at the drink a listener had ordered for him.

"I stopped my pickup and got out and tried to see where it was going. It was black and hard to see, but it got in the way of th' stars, so I could follow along. It went east a ways, then it turned and came back toward me. Lordy, I was scared. I thought it was after me, so I climbed under the pickup and stayed there 'til it went by."

He smiled, took a deep drink. "Hey, this is good!"

"Anyway, it went right over my pickup, right out into a long stretch of desert, and it came down like a big hawk—right out there in the middle of nowhere. And then I really got scared."

Once more he paused, took another drink as he looked at his audience. "What happened, Slouch?", a pretty girl asked, wide-eyed.

"The earth opened up and swallowed it down. Just like that. It was setting there, a huge black mass on the desert. And then it disappeared, and nothing was there but the desert. Nothing." He shivered, took another drink.

"I talked to the preacher about that. He said it was a demon. He said there used to be one of them things out ta Elizabeth Lake, 'cept it wasn't called by that name then. And he says the preachers all got together and preached and had gospel singing and prayer meetings and drove that devil away. He says it was in the papers, but they didn't give the preachers any credit. But he thinks maybe that demon's done come back. He thinks it don't matter, flesh or metal, the demon's done come back. Anyway, I ain't working out the Wells no more."

He had recited the same story to Reverend Samuels earlier. In fact, he recited it to any audience he could acquire.

Reverend Samuels listened quietly. It was indeed a strange apparition. "Mr. Breton, have you seen it since then? It sounds very strange."

"No Sir, Preacher, I've seen nary a sight of it since then. But I know it's flying up there. Always at night. And, God—excuse me, Preacher, it is big. Man never built 'ary thing that big what would fly. No Sir!" Slouch waited for the preachers response.

"There is evil loose in this valley, Mr. Breton. Sodom and Gomorrah are revived right here. Men frequent the bars, and not the churches. We had only a dozen at Sunday's service. Harlot's walk the streets. The Lord has sent AIDS as a scourge to mankind. But still they ignore his message. Perhaps now he is releasing demons from hell to bring them to their senses." Preacher Samuels smiled, looked upward, closed his eyes.

Slouch glanced around the sparse office. Bibles, choir books, religious tracts were stuffed haphazardly in cubbyholes, lay on shelves, and even covered a portion of the floor.

His eye was attracted by an object that seemed out of place. Nailed to the wall below the single cross in the room, it became a magnet to the roving eye.

"Preacher, what is that black piece there. It looks like an oversize cougar claw."

"Eh, yes, Mr. Breton. You are very observant. It is indeed a claw. But no claw that size ever came from a cougar. No, No!

"A number of years ago my father—he, too, was a man of the cloth— rode from community to community here in the valley, saving souls. May the Good Lord bless him!"

"It was at Devil's Lake, as it was called then. They had gathered to preach the gospel, to sing the praises of the lord—and to drive that creature from its abode."

"Clouds were forming, dark, blotting out the sun. The wind was rising, but he preached to them the evil of their ways, and prayed for the Lord's forgiveness."

Preacher Samuels rubbed his hands together, then reached over and let his fingers caress the object that had started the conversation.

"Then he prayed, and they all prayed, that the demon of the lake would come forth, would depart never to return."

His eyes gleamed, and his voice grew louder and more excited.

"There was a clap of thunder, a blinding bolt of lightning. Ah, how many times did he tell me! His flock fell to their knees. And suddenly the smell of brimstone filled the air, the surface of the lake became roiled, and it came forth."

The preacher strode back and forth, his face wet with perspiration. "It flew down as though to strike the congregation, and my father reached up with his Bible. The claw of the creature struck this very Bible," he held the tattered volume aloft, "and was ripped from its flesh."

"Yes, this very Bible. Look where the claw ripped the back cover!"

He admired the torn cover, flipped through the pages of the Bible, then completed his story.

"He nailed that terrible claw here, beneath the cross. And he said to me—'Let it stay there, protected by the cross, forever. The demon, in good time, will return for what is its own. As long as it remains beneath the cross, it shall not be moved!' His very words."

"Doubters have claimed it is but the claw of condor, that lost its way and was attracted by the sound of the crowd. Look at it! Have you heard of any condor that might have claws of this size?"

"There are strange creatures on this world, and beneath it, Brother Breton. Beware you run not afoul of them."

"Does that answer you? Let us pray together."

"Lord, if this be a new warning to the people, let it rend and destroy! Let blood flow, and the creature of darkness drink its fill. Bring man to his senses, and to his knees. Amen"

Slouch nodded. "Amen, Preacher, Amen!"

He glanced back at the claw before he left the room. What manner of creature had hooked talons longer than the fingers of man?

The visitor was unexpected. "Come in, Reverend. Here, take this chair. What can I do for you?"

"Ah, Professor Wilcoxson, perhaps it is I who can do for you. I have attended your lecture on the myths and legends of the Valley. I find them interesting, quite interesting."

Reverend Samuels smiled in as kindly a manner as his disposition allowed.

"Thank you, Reverend. I've done rather extensive research on the subject. It is strange, how the mind of man conceives and accepts such strange beliefs. Don't you agree?"

"Conceives and Accepts?" Reverend Samuels frowned. "My dear sir, there is little question about it. The history you relate is not a matter of human conception. No indeed! You have surfaced facts, facts that are confirmed by my own father's research. And that is why I am here."

Professor Wilcoxson looked more closely at his visitor.

"Your father was an historian, then?"

"No, sir. A preacher. He saved souls throughout this Valley before you were born. And he wrote of many things, of the Demon of Devil's Lake, of the blind witch—those stories you call myths and legends!"

"Well, I should like to read some of that material. I didn't know it existed. How kind of you to come here! Would you care for some coffee, Reverend. I want to hear more of this."

"No, no coffee. And I am here to tell you more. I am here to testify to the evil that encompasses this valley. The evil of man's ways. The evil that Satan has loosed upon us. But first, Professor Wilcoxson, let us pray."

Somewhat embarrassed, Professor Wilcoxson bowed his head while glancing, eyes partially closed, at his visitor.

"O Lord, bless this good doctor, for he shall bring thy word to the people. Through him we shall awaken the lost sheep, bring them to their senses, and lead them home. Through him the blind witch shall be put to rest, and the demon forever entombed. Amen!"

"You must explain to your listeners that nothing has changed. Nothing! The ravens still fly, the giant still sleeps, and it has returned to its hellish cavern beneath the dank waters. You must lead them back to the church. To my father's church. On our knees we shall drive the evil from our midst."

Reverend Samuels' face gleamed from an inner fire.

"Those who come, those who no longer stray, will be blessed. All others shall be the victims. They shall be devoured by Satan's servants, carried into the depths of the lake. Ah, it will be a great day for true believers. A great day!"

"Yes, Reverend, I see. You must bring me your father's diary. I can see, plainly, I have a great deal of work to do. A great deal of work to do. Ah, and I do have a meeting in five minutes. I apologize for being so abrupt. Mary, will you see the Reverend out. And thank, thank you again, Reverend Samuels."

"Mary…"

"Yes, sir?"

"If we hear from him again, I'm indisposed, on a trip to South Africa, or whatever fancy comes to mind. You understand?"

Mary smiled. "Was it that bad?"

"No, but he does have decided beliefs. And he expresses them emphatically. A strange man. Possibly a dangerous man."

---

Jim listened intently. Not that he expected anything of significance, but there was always the possibility.

"We checked out—Hmm, maybe that's the wrong term—your Dragon Lady. No spy. Freelance writer. No connections with Russians or Chinese; or any other possible group of that type."

"Good. But it doesn't pay to take chances."

"Right you are. Actually, she is a front, but for big drugs."

"Damn! Are our people clean?"

"Sure. The last user we found was old Malcom. Remember him. He almost snuck through. They snipped some hair to test. Turned out he was wearing a toupee. Unfortunately for him, whoever provided the hair was in deep. The tests we used showed the drugs. When we called him back he explained that it was a toupee. So we took a test on his hair. He's in bad shape. That stuff he's on will turn his brain to mush within the year. Nobody else, though."

"So what about the Dragon Lady. You gonna have her put away?"

"Hell no! I doubt that she even knows what's happening. She's just a deal maker. She works with our politicians. Maybe pays a mayor $5,000 for an interview. Or pays a Congressman $10,000 for an article on passing laws. What's illegal about that."

Jim nodded doubtfully.

"Remember prohibition days. They weren't smart, and the Internal Revenue got all over them. Well, they are smarter now. The politicians get paid of for legitimate products. They dutifully report their income. Big Bill wrote 10 articles last year. Got $150,000 for them. Actually, two of them were published. But that's not his concern. He wrote them, submitted them, and declared his pay as income."

"So what do the pushers get out of this?"

"Well, Big Bill supported three anti-drug bills last year. Even wrote part of the provisions. Started out they were all written to zap hard drug traffic. Ended up 90% of the funds is going to catch kids using marijuana. It's easier for the narcotics agents to pick up on them. And less dangerous, too. Now isn't that odd? But no criminal activity."

"And the mayor—he's really out there campaigning to control drugs. Any kid caught smoking pot should pull a minimum of one year, he says. Flat out anti-drug."

"How do you know all this?"

"Easy. Spot a couple of kids to go out and make a buy. Put a tag on the pushers. Just keep climbing the ladder. Top guys laugh. They'll talk to you one on one. They say the price of a politician is much less than it was in prohibition days. Just so they pay for a legitimate product, through a legitimate business. No criminal acts involved."

"As for her being one of them, I know the magazine. They have no more than 20000 subscribers. The rewrite editor is a full time writer, and just about everything published is essentially his product. But they pay top dollar. The only reason they haven't been closed down is that their author list provides an excellent lineup of who in the political world is getting paid off. It can be useful information! But she's just a working stiff, like the rest of us, I suppose."

"Actually, I suspect she doesn't realize that she's a pawn. And she is a good writer. I've read some her articles. Too bad she's in with that crowd."

They sat silently for a moment.

Finally Jim spoke. "Hell, I gotta get an airplane into the air. That's easy compared to chasing drug lords."

"By the way, what's new on the software problem?"

"No hit. But we'll find him!"

"But there is another problem. While checking out—damn, there I go again—while investigating Dragon Lady I got some feedback about what a man called Slouch had seen. I don't know how much anyone is going to believe, but he's pretty well described the backdoor—and in the local bar, where he had plenty of listeners."

"Damn! Just what did he say?"

"Well, he tied down the location. He saw the ship coming in, kind of saw it land, and knew that it had disappeared. He was out at the Well, cleaning up after hours. He's got some kind of idea it's a demon come back to the valley."

"Well, as you know, we only use the backdoor under emergency conditions. It's pretty well fenced and posted. I suggest we ignore it, let his demon theory kill any credibility he might have had."

"You're the boss. But keep it in mind. I suspect there'll be some people watching the sky out around the Well. Sooner or later they may get an eyeful."

"Understand, spy-guy. Not really much we can do, actually. Slouch didn't commit a crime, and his story is out anyway. We'll just ride with the punches. Now get your bottom off that chair and go catch me some spies."

Captain Millan grinned. "Okay, I'm off to round up some spies. Like right away, chief. Any particular flavor you'd like?"

# Handsome Stranger

"Well, I've seen you before."

The pleasant voice came from over his left shoulder. Turning quickly Captain Millan almost bumped into his erstwhile spy, the Dragon Lady. "Miss Maldon, and how are you?" He smiled. "Here's an empty seat, and I'm buying."

"Thank you. No one talks about Slouch's demon anymore. Do you think he made it up?"

"No games, young lady. We both know better than that. Are you back in our area for long?"

"Permanent assignment. I'm to interview local politicians, keep an eye on the sky, gather gossip—whatever might sell our magazine. Sounds like a cush assignment, but it's so general I'm never sure I'm doing my job."

"Look, do you like Mexican food?"

"I like all kind of food. That's why I weigh 500 pounds."

He looked judiciously at her trim figure. "Eh, 499 maybe, but not 500."

She laughed. "Yes, I'm fond of Mexican—don't like it too spicy, though."

"There's a little restaurant over on 20th. Good food. Margaritas are devastating. I'd like some company."

"You're on. But I pay. I'm on expenses, so it's covered. I'll interview you to make it legal."

For a moment he frowned. "On the other hand there's this very high-priced restaurant out on the edge of town…"

Actually, he interviewed her.

"I've been writing for the past 5 years. Freelancing for the first 3. Then I hired on with this outfit. Nice to have a steady income. Do you have a steady income?"

He smiled. "Sure do. I work for Chippendales as a dancer. The work isn't too hard, but I catch a lot of colds. They won't let me dress warm."

"I'm sure! Hazards of the job, you know. Are you ever serious?"

For a moment he didn't answer. "Yes, sometimes. Like right now. Janice, I like you. I'd like to spend more time with you. You're… Well, you're a very pleasant person to be around. I'd like to know you better."

"You are right, these margaritas are devastating." She sipped slowly.

They both laughed, and he liked the way her eyes reflected her pleasure. Then she reached across the table, took his hand. "I'd like that too, Bill."

He drove her to her apartment, walked her to the door. "When do I see you again? Is tomorrow too soon?"

"Tomorrow night. At six, here. And I'll cook supper."

She put her arms around his neck and he kissed her softly. She returned his kiss eagerly, and he hugged her close to him. Then, taking a deep breath he released her, smiled. "At six?"

"At six."

Fate intervened. "Captain Millan, get your backside out of that easy chair and come up here." Jim's voice was cheerful but serious.

When he arrived he found two officers from AFSC talking earnestly, with Jim voicing an occasional "understand". Major Kock he had met, but not Major Wheeling. Introductions completed he asked to be brought up to speed.

"Big meeting in Washington. You'll need to take the afternoon flight. They'll give you the details. Suspect you'll be there from two weeks to a month. Plan on a month. Who can cover for you while your gone?"

"The Sergeant has all the info, he can step in. Just give him the backing he'll need." He spoke quickly, but his mind was on six o'clock. Six o'clock when he wouldn't show. A whole month. How bad can timing be?

"Ilene has picked up the tickets and made arrangements for your quarters. Gentlemen, Captain Millan will show you his office and you can go into details. Bill, keep me posted."

The meeting broke up at one. He quickly telephoned her. No one answered.

He left the office, hurried to his quarters to pack. He was to ride to the airport with the AFSC visitors, but he asked them to pick him up at her apartment. There were some knowing grins, but that was the least concern he had.

He drove down Sierra Highway, hoping that the law was busy monitoring Highway 14. Pulling into Lancaster he slowed from 80 to a more acceptable 40. Her car was parked in the carport, he noted thankfully.

He knocked and as the door opened he started to explain. His mouth shut suddenly. A tall, graying man had opened the door. "Is Jan... Miss Maldon here?"

"Sure. Hey, Janice honey, you're wanted."

She came to the door, stepped out and closed it behind her. There was a surprised look on her face, quickly replaced by a smile.

He told her about the trip, excused himself for missing their six o'clock date, and explained that he had to leave to catch a plane.

He glanced at the closed motel door, frowned.

She flushed, for she knew what his thoughts must be. "Bill, please, call me. Please, Bill."

She kissed him. He responded almost reluctantly. "Goodbye, Janice," he hurried to the roadway where his companions waited.

She waved as they drove away.

Janice honey? Who is that son-of-a-bitch?

———

A vast upland desert, marred by occasional low mounds, the Mojave stretches east and west for nearly 250 miles at its widest point. From the upper reaches of Owens Lake to the Mexican border, running northwest to southeast, it extends for some 300 miles. The Sierra Nevada Mountains form the northwestern border. The Tehachapis form a border southwestward from the Sierra Nevadas. To the south of these rise the Transverse Ranges, a group of smaller mountain ranges tending east and west. On the south the San Bernardino Mountains rise, extending southeasterly and adjoining the Chocolate Mountains. To the east stretches the Colorado River, the eastern boundary. A vast desert region, 25,000 square miles in area, dotted by infrequent settlements.

A westerly spur, lying south of the Tehachapis, is the Antelope Valley. A rough triangle, extending from Red Rock Canyon on the east to the vicinity of Llano to the southwest; thence to near Quail Lake; and finally returning to Red Rock Canyon. An area endowed with extensive dry lake beds, it forms an ideal location for flight testing. The Air Force established Muroc (later renamed Edwards) Air Force Base as an aircraft test center. The smooth sands of the dry lakes provide mile after mile of flat landing surface.

Washington, a vast plain of some 70 square miles, marred by occasional public buildings, stretches along the Potomac River. The river lies to the southwest. Other natural elements do not form a meaningful border. Here the wisdom of a President, Congressmen, and Senators come together to provide leadership to the nation.

And from the Mojave to Washington Jim Braddock found himself once more flying. Jim Braddock preferred flying in to Dulles, even though National was in Washington's center. Actually, he preferred to stay away from Washington. A typical emergency required his presence.

# Pulling Rank

"Jim, the Senate is politicking again." Colonel Goetler's voice expressed deep concern. "And we are sure as hell vulnerable."

"The Big Committee is hot to cut funding, stretch out the program. And the House will jump on it with spurs slashing. You better get back there and calm some nerves."

"Who's pushing the action."

"Remember General Hayley. He's back there with Systems Command. And he is hitting all the right cocktail hours. Right now he has the ears of just about every defense committee chairman. But Senator Grubbing is his big gun."

"It figures. Well, he has no reason to love me, that's for sure. Can we count on the Whitehouse?"

"To a point. He's not up for election this year, but the party is running behind. He doesn't want to back anything that will lose him supporters in the Congress or Senate."

"Right. I'll touch base with the Scientific Adviser and find out whether they are hitting us from a technical or an emotional position. The loss of two airplanes hurts badly. We really need some PR to explain why Dream Ship 3 is essential. And we can't use a thing, because it's so damn classified. You ever read Catch 22?"

"Understand. But get that rump in gear and talk to some of those people. The dollars are classified, but let 'em know how much of the pie their local economy is going to lose if they can us."

"And see if you can get a good analyst to brief them on the dangers from the USSR's military dissidents. Those bastards have pretty well carried all the Soviet offensive weapons with them to North China. And their leader is flat crazy. The least thing could set him off."

"Hell, they know it. And still they are playing politics. God knows how these mental misfits get elected, but they do. They'll adhere to the party line no matter what the damage to the country. And the voters send them right back to office."

"Well, I know we aren't going to solve that problem today. I'll catch the redeye out tonight, and hit our Washington office tomorrow morning. Thanks for the call... I guess."

Jim arranged an audience with Senator Peters, one of the few active supporters of the program.

"Another significant problem, Jim, and we're going to lose the program. There are too many in the House and Senate who believe the millennium has come. And there is a great deal of outside money being spent to foster this belief. I've been contacted myself, and the kind of money they are talking is obscene." Senator Peters shook his head.

"If I were a younger man, well... I might just go along. Hell, no way! Guess it just ain't my style. I'll tell you, Jim, If you have any ethics or morality, Washington will make you regret it."

"Jim, I'm 71, my doctor tells me I have an inoperable cancer, maybe 6 months to a year to live. Now what the hell do I need money for? I admit, they could bribe me with a cure for this monster inside me, but that's not going to happen."

"Senator, I'm sorry. I didn't know."

"It's on the quiet between me and the doc. And I'm not down and out. I'll keep plugging away. But we need some new blood, or this thing is going to die—and our country with it. I've asked Senator Hawkins to come over. We don't have many patriots anymore, but he comes close."

Senator Hawkins was a short, heavyset man in his fifties. He shook hands with Jim rather cursorily, listened to Senator Peters' spiel without immediate comment.

Senator Peters emphasized the need for the program.

"We have problems, as all programs do, but none seem insurmountable. And there is nothing, even on the drawing boards, that could act as a countermeasure to the Dreamships."

Jim finished his speech, waited for comments.

He and Senator Peters glanced at Senator Hawkins, waited.

"You know, old colleague, what my feelings are. But I'm a pragmatist. I don't think the program has a chance. Maybe we can stretch it out for a while, but the opposition has the money, media support, the peace-at-any-price mentality. Even the President is having second thoughts, and he knows full well the inevitable result."

"Senator Hawkins, have we any support from the House?"

"A few of the older Congressmen. The new breed has been pretty thoroughly brainwashed. They've listened to the media so long they actually believe the fairy tales they are being told. No one reads history anymore, and when they do they misinterpret it."

"Have you any suggestions on drumming up support?"

"The Hawaii issue might result in some changes, come election. But it's being sugar-coated by the media, and the people may just buy their version. At best, we wouldn't gain more than 2 or 3 supporters, far from enough."

Jim returned from Washington, gloomy and dejected. Little to do but plug away, complete the program as quickly as practical. Hopefully, quickly enough.

Major Nestor was an excellent pilot. He was a hard-driving team member. Though he lacked John Holms' brilliance, he successfully substituted dogged perseverance.

No one could really fill John Holms' place.

Major Nestor would try. The decision had not been an easy one. The idea of the required operation was itself distasteful. With the knowledge of John Holms catastrophe the distaste blended with fear. What influenced the final decision is uncertain.

The operation was performed. There were no complications. The patient rapidly adjusted to the idea of physical interface with the aircraft. The first step was done.

We are verbal thinkers. returning to an earlier, visual, form of thought is unnatural. For DS3, it had to be done. The role of the psychologist became paramount.

"We could use words, but you'll visualize the object quickly from a picture. Words get in the way sometimes."

They worked up standardized icons of the controls, of the displays, of the sensors. With training and practice the Major was able to associate with each icon his appropriate response. The electronic engineers worked extensively to insure that the ship recognized that response, controls reacted accordingly.

The initial training was surprising effective. Man became the transducer, a filter between voiced instruction and machine response.

"Activate valve three."

Relaxed, confident, Bill Nestor visualized the responding valve. And, in a seemingly miraculous response of cold metal to human imagery, the valve responded. A sputter of applause greeted the feat.

Transition between the laboratory and the outer world surfaced myriad problems. Perhaps the major one was in the pilot himself. When thought patterns did not operate the refrigerator door, or the tv control, or the ship's vectoring jets Bill Nestor became confused—even frightened.

Training continued.

There were times, riding smoothly above the darkened earth, that he felt as though he were but another sensor, a small element in the system. At times frightening, the thought. But as flights passed by he accepted the concept, identified more and more closely with the ship.

His imagination, perhaps. The great ship selectively fed him data not required. At first he tolerated the thought as an amusing idea, existing only in his mind. Then, musing as they cleft the heights, he checked the value of a remote sensor. The result corresponded with the half-intuitive value he seemed to have received from the vehicle. He frowned, contemplated the incident. After landing he discussed it with the debriefing crew.

"No way," big and brusk, sensor engineer Clinton snorted. "There just isn't any way it could possibly happen."

Ferguson, the psychologist assigned to the program, didn't comment. Nor did the programmer. Later they discussed with him the problem.

"Major, are you sure? Could you have come up with this after getting the input?"

His answer was, repeatedly, no. There was no question in his own mind. If nothing else he was methodical in his flying, and his thinking. Inwardly he was amused by all the furor he had wrought. Yet a touch of concern remained with him.

"It isn't a heuristic program, you know!" George commented for the third time. I programmed it to meet the spec. I coded it myself. I debugged it. And the test people went through it completely. It couldn't have happened. It's something your mind's added. It didn't come from the software!"

He stood up, looked at them defensively. Plainly he felt his work was being questioned. Finally, he stomped indignantly toward the door.

"Sergeant! I want to talk to you!" Major Nestor's voice was loud and angry.

"Don't ever call me a liar. And when you talk to me I want to hear Sir, loud and clear. And I suggest you stand at attention until told otherwise!"

Sergeant Broderick's face turned red, and his teeth clicked together. With an effort he stood at attention. "Yes, Sir! Will that be all, Sir?"

"Hell no, Sergeant! Like I said, I don't care to be called a liar."

"Yes, Sir! I understand. There was no intent to call you a liar, Sir. I apologize for the misunderstanding."

Major Nestor smiled. "That's much better Sergeant. I suggest you pay more attention to military courtesy in the future. That will be all."

Sergeant Broderick started to turn, but halted momentarily and saluted. Major Nestor returned a sloppy salute, grinning.

Ferguson frowned as the sergeant left the room. "We don't go in for much formality here, Major. We try to treat everyone as a professional."

"Well, he was getting too damn informal. Don't let it worry you, Fergy. NCO's have thick skins."

Ferguson stood up, began talking slowly, as Jim entered.

"There are two aspects that concern me. The first is the safety issue. If feedback is being inadvertently triggered, why not commands also? You can visualize the result, can you not?"

"The second concern is with the mechanism. The pilot, at the conscious level, can direct the system. It begins to appear that, at the unconscious level, he also triggers responses. Fortunately, the unconscious requests have been for data, not for control response. But that may not be the condition on the next flight. Plainly, we need to examine the situation, look for ways to inhibit subconscious stimuli."

"Fergy, follow up on that. In the meantime, what is the risk if we continue to fly?" Jim queried.

"I believe there is real risk of inadvertently triggering control response. On the other hand, so long as the pilot is alert I believe he can maintain control. I would continue flying, but alert the pilot to the possibility of such an anomaly."

Bill Nestor sat silently through the discussion. Actually, looking back on those moments in the aircraft, he found it a little frightening. He shrugged off his concerns, headed for the steam room. A steam bath, a massage, and a good nights' sleep. Cure for almost any problem.

Sergeant Broderick returned to his barrack, his anger growing each time he recalled the incident. Damn that pompous bastard! All right, he's going to fly the beast! I oughta make it interesting for him.

He didn't sleep well that night. Instead he thought carefully about the dressing down he had received, and about a proper response. Near midnight he dressed, drove back to the center, went to the hangar.

She perched there like a bird of prey. The shadows cast by the hangar lights exaggerated her size. For a minute after minute he stood starring, and finally smiled. "Goodnight, bitch! And thanks for the idea!"

"Hold it! Oh, Sarg', didn't recognize you. The damn dog is finicky as hell. Just doesn't like this hangar, this plane. Listen to that whine." The security guard held the leash loosely in one hand.

The dog stood stiffly, its tail between its legs, its eyes on the ship. It whined softly, then growled deep in its throat. "Okey, okey, we'll move on. Goodnight Sarg. See you at the club tomorrow night?"

"You bet. I'm going to win the drawing. Bottle of Jack Daniels, right? Black label too."

.

# Pressure Grows

"Doc, I've got the willies. I can't sleep, I'm having a weird nightmare night after night. Look at this hand. I used to be steady as a rock."

"How long this been going on, Jim."

"Well, six months or more. It stopped for a while. But it's back even stronger. Messing me up. I'm not getting along with my people, it's causing trouble between me and Linda, and...," he paused, thought for a moment.

"Doc, it's scaring the hell out of me!"

"We'll run some tests, see whether there's a physical problem. Let me feel out these lab forms. How many hours do you work a day?"

"Hey, I've got a program to run! Ten to twelve hours. That's normal for me."

"Your blood pressure is normal, temperature normal, pulse okey. Jim, you drink much?"

"More than I used to. A few glasses of wine before bed. Helps me sleep—well, it used to."

"Okey, we're going to run you through a thorough examination. It'll take about three days. No wine until the tests are done. Get this prescription filled, and take one tablet before you go to bed. Oh, don't eat any supper. Be here at eight tomorrow. We'll get it straightened out, Jim."

"Sure, Doc. See you tomorrow."

The examinations were indeed thorough. The x-rays, upper GI, lower GI, urinalysis, blood tests—they knew more about him than he would ever care to know.

"Jim, you don't have any diseases, but you are physically run down. I'd recommend a long vacation, but I know you wont take it. I'm going to prescribe a new drug that we've recently begun to use. Basically it's a relaxant. It's not habit forming, and there are no side effects. It'll help you quit worrying, but shouldn't impact your work." He scratched out the technical name on the prescription form.

"I'll want to see you once a week for the next month, until we are sure everything is squared away. Oh, sorry, but alcohol doesn't mix with this. Leave the wine alone."

"It figures. Okey, thank you, Doctor."

---

"Jim, I need to talk to you."

Major Nestor stood in the doorway. His hands were clinching and unclenching, and his voice was agitated.

"Sure, Bill, come on in. Pull up and look homely. What's on your mind?"

"I want out. That damn ship is driving me up the wall! Every flight it's the same thing. It's as though she had a will of her own. Every flight!" He pressed his fists on the desk, and his eyes kept moving erratically from side to side.

Jim leaned back in his chair, looked carefully at the man in front of him. This was not the same Major Bill Nestor who had joined them months earlier.

He was thinner now, almost haggard. The aura of self-confidence no longer existed. Rather, a sense of dread seemed to envelope him.

The thought of John's unfortunate crisis came to mind.

"Billy, how long since you had a good vacation?"

"No, it isn't that! Jim, she's a devil! She's killed some of your best pilots, she drove John insane, and sure as God she's going to kill me!"

"I'm putting in for a transfer, Jim. When I first got here I thought this was the best of all assignments. You, Ilene, Pat, ..." He hesitated, looked down, perhaps guiltily.

"Jim, I'm a good pilot. I've flown just about every kind of aircraft. Hell, I've been scared at times. But I've handled it. This is different. I'm not afraid of the airplane. But I'm afraid of her! I know, that doesn't make sense. Anyway, that's it. Tomorrow's flight is my last. If I can't get a transfer I'll resign my commission."

He stood up. The fear in his eyes was evident. He took a deep breath. "Look, I'm sorry. But she's beat me. I want out."

He hesitated for a moment. "There's something else. Something you should know. It's happened not to just me, but to all the pilots. I've talked to them. We've all experienced it. And probably the worst of it is the dreaming. Every night I sleep with that monster. And so did Andy, and Jerry, and—God help him—John. It's tunneled into our minds somehow, and it can't be evicted." He swallowed, stared at Jim, waiting for disbelieving laughter.

"All right, Bill. I could lean on you, but we both know that's no good. Cover me for tomorrow's flight, and I'll get the backup squared away by next week. And, Bill, tomorrow's is supposed to be a four hour flight. Cut it back to two hours, and keep it routine. Now you get out of here. Have a drink, take a hot bath, whatever relaxes you." He paused, rhythmically thumped the desk with his fingers.

"There's no hard feelings, Bill. You've done a fine job for us, and the reports will reflect that. After tomorrow's flight you'll stand down. Look around and decide where you want to go. Or, if you want to stay here, I'm sure we can use your expertise on the ground."

For a moment Major Nestor said nothing. Then he stared hard at Jim, his eyes expressing anger, hate. "You knew, didn't you Jim. Andy told you. So did Jerry and John. You've known all along!"

"Knew what, Bill? I don't understand."

"The blind witch! She's been our co-pilot on every flight. You knew, and you did nothing. What kind of inhuman bastard are you! Couldn't you see what it did to them, what it was doing to me? Damn you and her. May your souls rot in hell!"

He stood up, staggered blindly toward the door.

"Wait! Wait a minute, Bill."

"Yes, I knew what Andy thought he saw. I know what Jerry and John claimed. But it can't be. Bill, it's something in the system. It's triggering the same pattern, the same superstitions. That's all it is. I thought you could handle it. You've a different background, a different attitude."

"Jim, she's with me. On every flight. Imagination? Superstition? Whatever name you give it, she's real to me. And I'll fly with her no more!"

He turned, left the room, head lowered.

Jim sat quietly, slowly pulled his pipe from his pocket, tamped it half full of tobacco. Why? What is causing it? It affects them all in the same way. And my own dreams!

I wonder what it is? The ship is well designed. Mental control! We are using it, yet we know so little about it. He picked up the phone. "Dr. Volte, can you come by the office. There are problems."

"Doc, there is a strange coincidence. They all suffer the dreams. And you know, I haven't flown the bird—but I have them too."

"Pressure, the environment, the fact that we are all slaves to that big, black monster. We humans have so many common thoughts, have heard the same stories of the bogey man, read the same fiction—the similarity of the dreams is the result of the like culture we have lived in. They will fade away once this program is complete."

Doc Volte smiled. "We are all the same children, you know. We have our nightmares, even now."

For a moment Jim was silent, thinking. "Doc, Hiroshi comes from an entirely different culture, yet he speaks of the same dreams?"

For a moment Doc Volte frowned. "You make an interesting argument, Jim. Let me talk to the pilots. By the way, write me out a scenario of this recurrent dream. It will be of value when I talk to the others. Have you swapped dreams with them? If so, that may be the basis of it all?"

"No, I've kept quiet about my problems. I didn't want to fuel the fire as it were. But it is strange, and I am concerned. Of course, since Matt had that accident years ago there has been a groundswell of superstitious stories. And some of the airmen, if they don't believe, certainly don't entirely disbelieve. Several of the maintenance troops just wont work second or third shift in the hangar."

"Anyway, get back with me as soon as practical, Doc. And I wouldn't talk about the fact that you are studying the problem. Keep it informal, okey?"

"Sure, Jim. Where'll I find Hiroshi?"

"He'll be at the hangar, nosing around Dream Ship Three. They all live there, seems like." Jim paused. A thought had come to mind.

"You may want to talk to Professor Wilcoxson over at the College. He's an expert on the early history of the Valley."

Dr. Volte nodded.

"I'll look him up. By the way, are the dreams always the same?"

"Always the same, Doc. Always bad!"

---

"Professor Wilcoxson, I read you treatise on the Valley's mythology. I understand you lecture on the same subject?"

"Yes, it's a subject that attracts a considerable audience. Money in the bank. What did you think of the treatise?"

"You've almost convinced me that were living in a land of enchantment, doomed to serve the sleeping giant. Or is it the blind witch we serve?"

"You can read all kind of meanings into words, can't you? Actually, people tend to be very susceptible to this kind of thing. Mr. Braddock, a stolid engineer himself, tells me some of the stories have even bothered his people. Would you believe it!"

"I am afraid I do. You see, that is why I'm here. To get a better feel for what might be bothering them. Do you have any original material to support your stories? I need to do some digging."

Dr. Volte spoke quietly, yet his concern was evident.

"A limited amount. Mostly from interviews. And we all know how easy it is to slant an interview. But I've never intentionally tried to do so. I'll make my library available to you."

---

Bill Millan's flight ran into thunderheads. They bounced the airplane around the sky. Not that he could have slept anyway. He kept hearing 'Janice Honey' ringing in his ears.

Women are all alike. Who cares, anyway.

In spite of these thoughts, his first action when he entered his hotel room was to pick up the telephone.

"Hello."

For a moment he hesitated, but only for a moment. "Janice, this is Bill."

"Oh, God! I'm so glad you called. I know what you must have thought."

"Why, I have no reason to think anything. You have your own life to live."

He heard her sob, then it turned to a laugh. "Bill, I'm sorry. It is so stupid. The man at my apartment. He's…"

"It's all right. You don't owe me any explanations."

"You men! Damn it, you make me so mad. That was my boss. He was here for a meeting on my articles. Bill, he's like a father to me. I should have introduced you. Oh, this is so crazy. Bill I lo…like you. You sound so hurt. Please, I wouldn't hurt you."

"Well, I guess I'm sorry. Yeh, I jumped to the conclusion—well, I'm glad I was wrong. Look, I'm bushed. I'll call you again tomorrow night. And I…I like you too. Goodnight."

She kicked the telephone table, moaned as her toe struck the wooden surface, lay face down on her bed, sobbing. Then she began to laugh. Such a silly situation! Men! Nothing but trouble!

"Oh, Billy, I think I'm in love with you. What a miserable thing to happen!" she moaned to her pillow as she pressed it close.

On his return he rode to her motel in a taxi. He went to his own car, opened the door, sat quietly thinking. At first he was undecided, but finally got out, rang her door bell.

"Bill? Oh, I'm so glad." She threw her arms around him, hugged him close, kissed him repeatedly. "Come in, please."

"I was afraid you might not stop. But I called Mr. Braddock and he said you'd be here tonight. Our six o'clock date we missed, I cooked tonight."

She was so eager to please. Her eyes reflected the happiness she felt in seeing him. His doubts faded quickly, and he took her in his arms once more.

"God knows I've missed you."

"Don't be blasphemous. Oh, Bill, in a way I'm glad you had to take that trip. It made me realize I don't want to be without you." She stopped, took a deep breath, looked into his eyes. "Bill, I love you."

She stepped away from him, waited, a scared look on her face.

"Come here." He led her to the sofa. "Sit down."

He took a package from his pocket. "Here, open this."

The ring was too large, but they just laughed. He dropped to his knees in front of her, his face a little red. "Janice, will you marry me?"

She slid off the sofa, on her knees beside him, her arms around his neck. "I will, you know I will!"

Supper burned.

They didn't care.

# A Hell of a General

"Captain Millan. What did you think of the flight? Did you ever see one go so smoothly? What brings you to these diggings?"

"Jim, we got a problem. You remember the concern about the software? Well, I had my men pull an audit on the software used in the flight. I don't know whether it's a lapse in the configuration control, or an act of sabotage…"

Jim Braddock took a deep breath. "All right, what have you found?"

"The software used to interface the pilot to the ship has been patched. The patching was done at the machine language level. The source code and the patched code are inconsistent. I'm having my men walk through procedures with Configuration Management. They are also trying to identify who did the actual patching."

"What was the impact?"

"Jim, that's what scares us most! We don't see any immediate impact, but it looks like someone may have managed to plant a virus. If they did we may have to scrap the entire package, drop back to an earlier version of assembly code. Hopefully the source code itself is clean. Regardless, we got a chore ahead of us."

"Donaldson is in charge of Software Configuration Control. What does he think?"

"He says he will work with us, but until we tie down the loose ends he doesn't want to comment."

"Damn! How long is it going to take to clean this up? I can't afford to stand down too long. Congress is already riled because first flight was late."

"We are bringing in some software security gurus to help out. At best, I figure two weeks. Maybe longer. It's a scary area. The viruses get sneakier and nastier with each generation. And they aren't in the software for fun anymore. They are pure destructive."

"We have a clue or two, though. Whoever did the patching had a good grasp of neural networks. That's not the most common software skill around. And he knew machine language on our hardware. That's not yet available in the commercial world. I think we'll tag him. But we don't want him to run. We need to know what he's done to us, first."

"Keep me up to speed. And let me know how you and Donaldson decide to keep the software under control. Right now they're cross assembling on the mainframe, then porting the stuff over, right?"

"Yeh, but this was inserted after it had been ported. We're continuing to check the code, and we're re-examining the security checks. I'll get back to you."

Jim growled. "Software! Even when its clean it scares me! Guess I'm too hardware oriented. Kind of date myself, don't I?"

Captain Millan grinned, closed the door.

Jim knocked on Colonel Goetler's door. "Might as well unload on him now," he thought.

Colonel Goetler laid down the newspaper. The headline read, 'Prosperity League', the title of the newly formed coalition between China, Greater Iran, and two lesser partners. Two lesser partners, India and Indonesia were only mentioned in afterthought. Jim shook his head, sat down.

"Another problem, Colonel."

"Good, Jim, I thought you were running out of them," Colonel Goetler commented facetiously.

———

Ilene picked up the phone. In a moment she buzzed him.

"Captain Millan. He wants to come by and talk to you."

"Sure, tell him in about half an hour."

"We've got the bastard!"

"Okey, but ballpark me. Which bastard?"

"The programmer. The guy that planted the virus. And, by the way, he admits it. We'll hang him high."

"Fine. But are we going to be able to back the virus out? I could care less about what's done to him."

The captain stared ruefully at the toe of his shoe. "He says he can't clear it out. The only thing feasible is to do a low level initialization, re-partition, and reboot. Then reload all the software. He says the machine language didn't do a thing. Modifying it was only a ploy to mislead us. The virus was always in the source code. And that's been cleaned up, so we can get on with the job. Configuration Control has modified their approach, and are working with Quality to improve security."

"Who is it?"

"George Broderick. The tall sergeant that answered most of the questions at Technical Interface Meetings. He probably knows that software better than anyone else. You know what the virus was to do? It would have inhibited the sensors from passing back data to the pilot. He'd have had no visibility, no feel for the ships motion—nothing. Eventually he would have driven into the ground."

"Ah! I hope you hang him high. That is attempted murder in my book."

"I've talked to the Legal Beagles. The best we can do is a Courts Martial and drum him out of the corps. And they may even let him apply for a discharge, drop the whole issue!" Captain Millan's voice shook with anger.

"Eh, see that his records reflect what he has done, and what the likely result would have been. I'd hate for a company to hire him as a programmer. He just might come in one day and trigger some catastrophe I'd rather not think of."

———————

"Mr. Braddock, could you come to my office." Colonel Goetler hung up before he could reply.

"Yes, Colonel, I'm on my way," he voiced to himself, half amused, half irritated.

"I've just got a call from General Hayley. He seems to be in a very pleasant mood." Colonel Goetler glanced sideways at Jim. "He tells me that we'll get a twx in the next few minutes. It will tell us to ground Dream Ship 3 until further notice."

"It's long overdue, Colonel. The loss of the first two ships. John Holms condition. The blue funk the pilots all seem to be going through…I'm amazed that they have waited this long. And, of course, General Hayley is undoubtedly in a good mood."

Colonel Goetler frowned. "I suppose we better get all our data together. We'll have our share of investigating committees in here within the week. What's your assessment of the situation?"

"I think it's something the psychologists will have to sort out. Everyone associated with the bird has developed one kind of tic or another. None as badly as John Holms did, but still there. It's outside my area of expertise." Jim shook his head. He pulled out his pipe and slowly charged it. "Exciting times, Colonel."

"Jim, I like the aroma of that tobacco. Kind of a cherry smell, isn't it? Mind if I borrow some?" He pulled a pipe from his desk drawer.

Jim noted that it was almost a replica of his own.

"Anyway, I'll tell you, Jim. I would have made a hell of a General! The Air Force's loss, I'd say." He half filled his pipe, handed back the pouch.

"Colonel, that stuff's been known to cause cancer. Anyway, I reckon you would have made a hell of a General at that."

They both grinned. Colonel Goetler reached out his hand tentatively, and Jim shook it solemnly.

"What say we go take a look at the bird?"

They left the office, walking slowly and puffing contentedly on their pipes.

Black, ominous, even here in the hangar the ship invoked an image of destructive power. Her huge size, strange shape, and the lack of a cockpit all contributed to the mood she aroused.

The airmen worked around her silently. The quiet was broken only occasionally by a shouted command.

Hard to believe that she's grounded, Jim thought. "Damn Black Witch," John Holms had called her. And truly it was the image she projected. He felt a shudder run down his spine. Odd, the emotion she elicited.

"Will she fly again, Jim? Do you think they'll dismantle her, and ship her off to an air museum?" Colonel Goetler seemed to be talking to himself in rhetoric questions, nor expected an answer.

"She'll fly again. She hasn't tasted blood yet." Jim responded, then opened his mouth wide in astonishment. It was not something he had intended to say. Yet the words had formed on his lips almost unthinkingly.

———

"Jim, shouldn't you take your medicine. You haven't been taking it for more than a week. The doctor called. He said you had missed your last appointment."

"God damn it, will you quit nagging! Bring me my wine!"

Reluctantly she brought him his glass, the wine bottle. Morosely he opened it, started to fill the glass, changed his mind. Instead he took a long slug directly from the bottle.

She watched him for a moment, walked slowly down the hallway. In a moment he heard her sobs coming from the bedroom.

The hell with her, he thought. He took another long swig of wine.

He felt her sightless eyes on him. He knew she would be there.

Always, when he was alone. Always, silently watching, waiting.

"Hello, you bitch!"

He could see her, a misty white form standing in the hallway, watching him. Blind though she were, she was always watching him. He picked up the glass and threw it at her. It struck the wall, shattered.

"Linda, get in here and clean up this mess."

He took another drink from the bottle. And another.

He fell asleep in the chair. The last thing he remembered was looking toward the hall.

She was still there, waiting, for what he did not know.

Watching. Waiting.

———————

Dr. Volte sat down, thumbed through the notes he carried. Jim waited patiently.

"I've gonr through Dr. Wilcoxson's material, made some extensive tests."

"And?"

"There is nothing conclusive. These men were normal. They had no previous record of any mental anomalies. They were stable, responsible, rather unimaginative, really. Not the type one would expect to hallucinate. Not the type to have nervous breakdown. Not the type to fly co-pilot with a blind witch!"

"Ah, they told you about that!"

"Bill Nestor—He says, to him, she is as real as you or I. Yet, he will admit, she cannot logically exist."

"A matter of interest, Jim, are some of the stories one hears, documented by Professor Wilcoxson. This valley has its share of legends. Of course, like any other place, there are a few stories of the supernatural. Your blind witch has been part of that folk lore here for many generations.

"The Indians are said to have believed in her. And the Basque shepherds that worked in the valley swore she is real. When Muroc was first opened the airmen referenced the legend in some of their letters.

"Somehow it's associated with that old boulder, on the road between 58 and Cal City. I drove over there and looked at it. You ever see it?"

"No, no, Doc, never have."

"From the right location it looks like the head of a sleeping giant, another legendary figure of the valley. Well, anyway, your blind witch has been a long-time resident of the valley."

"These pilots, one way or the other, may have picked up on it. May have responded much in the same way. We all have our measure of superstitious belief."

"So what do you suggest, Doc?"

"I'm dealing with a qualitative area. Where practical I've made measurements. Brainwaves, nervous system response, hypnosis. There's not too many direct approaches available." He paused, frowned.

"Jim, I'd like to get checked out in the aircraft. Not to fly her, but to sit in the cockpit, receive the signals they have been receiving. It's the only way I'm going to get close to this thing, get a handle on why 'the blind witch' is the common symptom."

"You forget something, Doc. You'd have to have that damn socket installed. It's not something you would want to do casually."

"I've given thought to that. I'm not eager, but since it's necessary I'll accept it."

"Let me think on this one. It's possible we can't do it anyway. Let me make some phone calls, and I'll talk to you tomorrow. But, Doc, think it over!"

"Look, Doc. Let me ask you something personal."

"Well, you can ask," Dr. Volte smiled, "but you may not get an answer."

"Doc, are you superstitious?"

"Probably not in the way you mean, Jim. But I will admit to something that may surprise you. I do believe there exist phenomena for which we lack adequate scientific explanation. Some phenomena, when science can't easily explain them, are swept under the rug. And, although I think that Occam's razor should be used in the majority of the cases, there are times when it leads to error."

"Occam's razor?"

"Yes. The concept that, from all possible explanations of a phenomenon, that which is the least complex is the right explanation. Of course, it generally leads to the right conclusion. But not always. And, for your question, if it is superstitious to believe that many phenomena have yet to be explained, then I am superstitious."

"What about ghosts, demons,..., blind witches?"

Dr. Volte smiled. "As symptoms, as mental interpretations... Yes, I can accept all of these. As explanations, no. The overall phenomenon has been reported too often. And if we include in the phenomenon the individual, the environment, the circumstances, everything that contributes—then I believe that these exist. As to adequate hypotheses, and certainly as to theories, I have none. But I've never, until now, had occasion to study such phenomena. Perhaps, Jim, we shall unravel the problems here, and lay to rest the blind witch."

The operation was performed on Dr. Volte. It did not go as smoothly as on the pilots. The operation itself went well, but subsequent healing was unduly slow.

"I'm still bleeding around that skin flap. Looking at the operation in the mirror it looks like I'm developing an infection. And it hurts like hell. Otherwise, it was a great operation." Dr. Volte's comments weren't bitter. Nevertheless, he was less than happy.

Infection had indeed set in, additional antibiotics were required, and there was question as to whether the interface itself was damaged. After careful physical examination of the man and inspection of the equipment the conclusion was that no critical damage existed. The new antibiotics worked well, and healing proceeded rapidly.

Upon approval by the doctors he began this phase of his study. Repeatedly maintenance powered up the ship, Dr. Volte at the controls. Repeatedly he exercised the controls, tested the sensors, drove signals down the lines, read the instruments. Repeatedly he concluded that everything was normal, no anomalies of any kind existed.

At the end of one such exercise he started the power down sequence, paused.

Images... He was getting images!

# The Reverend's Project

They were not visual feedback reflecting instrument settings. These were vague, objects as though seen through a fog. And sound, dull, low throbbing. A lake, with the moon full above, but obscured by vapor, smoke, he knew not what, rising from the lake itself. And something stirring just below the lake's surface.

He shuddered slightly, thought—Am I hallucinating. Am I seeing this, feeling this, because I want to—or because it's there?

But he had already inhibited the feedback system. No way could he be receiving real data!

Is this how it began with them? I need to review my interview notes. God, my head aches! And nausea! Yes, they had that. But the images faded, and only one remained. Far away, dimly seen. An image in white. Now it too was fading. He did not need to ask. He knew her!

With a frown he continued the power down process. For a long time he lay still. Finally he exited the ship. He stood beside it, wrote half a page of entries in the pad he carried with him. "Strange! How very real are the images in one's mind!"

Two weeks into his research he showed up at Jim Braddock's office.

"Jim, I'm beginning to get some leads. The images they were receiving—I'm beginning to see them. And the voice they heard! But why they are generated, and how—I need more time. One thing I am sure of. The trigger is external to the man, it comes through the ship. But the response comes from the individual."

"Ah, how so?"

"I recorded what each of them purported to see. I've recorded the images I've seen. True, we've all seen the blind witch. But each has seen his own version. Each of us has seen an image different from that seen by others. For example, Hiroshi has seen her—but in garb and appearance from ancient Japan. I have seen her in the garb with which our culture has always dressed her."

He paused for a moment.

"Except," and he frowned, "she is dressed in white, not the traditional black!"

Jim thought for a moment. "Doc, take some time off before you continue your research. To be honest, this thing scares hell out of me!"

"Perhaps you are right. I've set up an hour of activity tomorrow. I'll complete that, then spend some time on examining the literature on this type of problem. I may even take a short trip to Salem, look through the historical records!"

Dr. Volte's apartment was large. Yet the numerous mounds of books scattered—he like to say, arranged—gave it an appearance of inadequacy. Here he lived with his cat and his studies.

Dr. Volte liked his privacy, rarely had visitors, and rarely visited others. So he was surprised to hear the doorbell late Thursday evening. With a frown he queried at the door. "Who is it?"

"Dr. Volte, I am Kirk Samuels. I'm a preacher here in the valley. I'd like to talk to you for a moment."

Reluctantly he opened the door. He was neither eager to provide a handout nor to have his soul saved.

"All right, Reverend. Come in. And this is…?"

"I'm Slouch, everyone just calls me Slouch."

"This is Mr. Breton, Doctor. But, as he says, everyone calls him Slouch. And I'm not a reverend, just a lay preacher."

"Sit down, gentlemen. Care for a coffee?"

Both visitors declined. "Pardon me, I think I'll have one. It's my only vice, although…."

A hiss interrupted him. The black cat stood in Mr. Samuels way, her back arched, tail stiff.

She hissed angrily.

"Easy! Diablo! Come here, come on." Dr. Volte picked her up, carried her to the bedroom and closed the door. "Strange, she's usually quite friendly. You haven't been petting a dog, have you? Sometimes the smell bugs her. I apologize."

His visitors smiled. "Doctor Volte, you are working on a classified project, an advanced aircraft, are you not?"

"Eh, why do you say that, Reverend?"

"Come, Doctor, I have my sources?", Mr. Samuels smiled. "There have been two mysterious crashes in the valley. You have arrived very recently, the great psychiatrist, from your Washington practice. And by now, I am sure, you are beginning to understand. At least, such is my hope."

"Preacher, I'm really quite busy. Why don't you get to the point?"

"You are a psychiatrist. I am sure you know the tales being passed around among your personnel. The old legends, the giant's curse," he paused for a moment, looked carefully at the doctor, "and the tales of the blind witch."

"I'm familiar with them."

"You are a scientist, doctor. So I'm sure you believe none of this superstitious rot. A scientist believes in measurable quantities. Or so they say. But oftentimes you give a phenomenon a name, then forget about it. Who has measured the will-of-the-wisp, doctor?"

"Burning swamp gas. But the substance of old wives tales."

"Yes, of course. But how hot is it, what is its color? Why does it glow here, but not there? Where are your measurements?"

"What is your point, preacher?"

"My point is simply this. That aircraft is accursed, it will be forever accursed! It is but an extension of the blind witch!"

"And?"

"And it must be destroyed. It will be destroyed. If you do not persuade the Air Force to terminate the program I and my church members will take direct action."

Dr. Volte stood up, walked to the door, and opened it.

"Good evening, gentlemen. I've enjoyed our little talk." His lips smiled.

"Come, Mr. Breton. I see we have wasted our time. Too bad, really. Doctor, we will pray for you. I fear it will not help!"

The next morning Dr. Volte stopped at Jim's office.

"Jim, I guess that's about all I can tell you. I don't know whether they would try something or not. But you might want to alert your security people."

"Doc, the newspapers, radio, and TV have all picked up on it. Samuels may not be a bona fide reverend, but he's a damn good activist. With the news coverage he's getting we'll have kooks from San Francisco to San Diego in here supporting him."

"Besides, we have our share of fanatics in the valley. You name the cause and they come out of the woodwork to carry placards and participate in demonstrations. The worst of it is that the politicians seem to think these jokers represent the people. Anyway, I'll pass this on to Captain Millan. It should make his day!"

"Captain Millan, come in."

"You sent for me, Jim."

"You got it. You haven't flushed out a spy in months. What do you security types do, anyway?"

"Mostly rustle papers, like everyone else. Do you know what's involved in a security check?"

"Thank God, no. And I don't want to. By the way, Major Millan, I expect to be invited to a promotion party."

"Major—ok! When did the word come through?"

"It hasn't officially, but I have my sources. Congratulations. You'll get formal orders eventually. I really don't know how long the list is, or where you are on it, but you're there. That ought to warrant bringing in a spy a day for at least a week."

---

Millan's Chinese

"Jim, you remember the Dragon Lady?"

"Sure, I remember. What happened to her."

Major Millan hesitated. "She's, eh," he paused. "She's out in the hall. I'd like to introduce you."

Jim cocked his head, looker carefully at his security officer. "Yeh, bring her in. What the hell." He shrugged.

"Jim, I'd like you to meet my fiancée, Miss Janice Maldon. Janice, this is Jim Braddock, my boss."

With a start Jim stood up. "Your fiancée, eh? Well, Miss Maldon, I'm pleased to meet you. I've heard a lot about you. But not nearly enough." He gazed at Major Millan, a quizzical look in his eyes.

"Oh, and I've heard so much about you! But you don't look nearly that ferocious!"

"Uh-huh. Thanks, Major Millan." The sarcasm was noted with a grin by the major.

"So what do you think of the Valley?"

"I don't like the heat. I don't like the wind. I don't like the dust. But I like Bill, so it's all right."

Jim looked Major Millan up and down. "God, how women's taste has deteriorated."

"So when's the marriage?"

"Next month. And I'll need some time off."

"Eh, I'll bet you will. Kick in a leave application. You get a promotion, and rush out to get married." He shook his head.

"Seriously, congratulations to both of you. I hope it works out as well as my own marriage has."

"Now, Major, suppose you conduct this young lady around and introduce her to the working types. We do have some folks here working today."

The radios were the first to have an inkling of the Reverend Samuel's project. They weren't overly impressed, gave the news item minor attention.

"Slouch, spread the word. Call the stations, the tv shows, the papers. Ask 'em why they aren't printing my pronouncements. I'm calling on the whole congregation to do the same. We need to get some coverage here. We need support!"

Reverend Samuel's quickly started a call-in campaign to the major TV networks, requesting the status of Reverend Samuel's project. The callers quoted radio reports of hundreds of sympathizers from across the nation converging on the Antelope Valley. Though at first but a gleam in the Reverend's eye, the idea gained media attention—local, then national, notoriety.

The TV networks quickly began dispatching reporters, camera, and supporting paraphernalia, concurrently running teasers to attract the viewers' attention.

Not to be left out, the newspapers sent out reporters to cover the impending event. From a minor incident the activity was now blown up to nationwide news.

Reverend Samuels quickly became a personality, in demand for interviews, commentary, and opinions. His entourage grew rapidly. The phenomenon fed on itself, with each element of the media working to present the true picture of suppression of religious rights by government and military. Each episode of true pictures incorporated greater and greater amounts of propaganda as the reporters found that no meaningful story existed.

Reverend Samuels himself was astounded at the coverage, the impact on the nation, and the legends of demonstrators who were arriving daily to support his "Holy War". But he took it in stride, effectively organizing his new-found followers into a manageable hierarchy.

---

"Jim, a call from Washington. General Mathis."

She looked through the door, "We in trouble?"

He grinned, waved her away. "General, Jim Braddock on. What's happening?"

"The Reverend Samuels ruckus, Jim. There's a lot of money feeding into the media to keep the coverage hot. Money with a Chinese color to it. They've been after the program to shut it down, and they see this as an opportunity. I've talked to the Base Commander, and he's to provide maximum security support. Keep your people on their toes. And call me if I'm needed."

Jim thought for a moment. "Any of their agents directly involved?"

"We don't think so. They believe they can meet their goal, using our own media against us. They could be right. You may recall the frequent successes Goebbels had in his time."

# Placard Carriers

"Major Millan, get over to Base Security. There's something perking, and it involves us. Work with them to keep things under control, and keep me up to speed."

When he reported in to Base Security he found an unusually tense atmosphere. "Joey, what's coming down? You actually look worried?"

"I think we have a nasty one coming up. There's a rabble rouser working up a demonstration for the base. At first we laughed about it. Calls himself Preacher Samuels. Red neck type. Strictly local. But he's got the attention of the media, and they are pumping out the message. Every true believer who can get here is converging on this base."

"Come on, there aren't that many who have faith in the Preacher!"

"Doesn't have anything to do with it, Billy my son. You just don't recognize how these things work. Were dealing with extremists. Doesn't really matter whether they come from the left, the right, or from God know's where. This is an opportunity to stand up and be counted. Ten percent or fewer of the people who turn out for these have any real extreme concerns with the issue. But they are the one's who wont act rationally. And that's dangerous."

"Hey, you sound like my old man. He makes the Birch Society look liberal. You really running scared?"

"I am! I've been through it. Look, the rest are there because it's happening. Hell, they used to advertise at the colleges, 'We need pickets, be at such and such a place at whatever time.' Didn't even tell 'em what's involved. They'd turn out en masse. And that's our supposedly educated citizens. With the media coverage this is getting we'll have students, we'll have kooks—you name it, they'll be here. Hey, I used to go to these things. Thought it was a lark!"

"Are you going to be able to keep things under control?"

"Let's go into the office."

He closed the door behind him. "Not if I have to depend only on the men I have. I've alerted the Base Commander, and he's working a deal to fly in additional personnel. But he wants to keep a low profile, minimum personnel." He paused for a moment, sat down behind the metal issue desk.

"I don't know! I think we should show a massive force right at the start, and try to discourage them from doing anything rash. A limited force may encourage the very thing we are trying to avoid. But I can't convince him. Why don't you give it a try, Major?"

"Are they likely to be armed?:

"Nah, most of them are here for the frolic. But there will be a few, and you can bet on it, who will be here for the kill. They love these demos. They can hide in the crowds, do their dirty work, and kick back and enjoy the results. Yeh, you can bet there will be a few there with weapons, dynamite, what have you."

"Is the FBI doing anything?"

"They're looking for some of the died-in-the-wool terrorists, to cut 'em off at the pass. Hopefully they'll succeed. It's the ones with the screw loose, do-anything-for-the-cause types we need to worry about. Psychos eat this kind of thing up."

"Okey, I'll talk to the Base Commander. I don't think I can convince him, but it's worth a stab. Then I'll alert AFSC to our status. And I'm ready to go on my honeymoon!"

"Tough, old buddy. Maybe you can get someone to go for you. Is she good looking? I've got a little leave time…"

"Eh, thank you, good friend!"

---

Reverend Samuels' Pickets

They arrived at Rosamond at 6:00, riding pick-ups, jeeps, and even a couple on horseback. Some brought placards with them. Others picked theirs up from a van parked beside the road. The first count was less than 20.

The preacher wasn't concerned. "We got the word out in the paper, on TV and radio, and I've called a few people I know. We'll have Rosamond Boulevard full of pickets by week end." He grinned, whistled, "Whistle While You Work".

The count grew slowly during the week. By weekend, however, students poured in from north and south. Few seemed to know why they were carrying the placards, and fewer still to really care. They treated it as an outing, displaying their placards, waving to passing cars, and tossing empty beer cans along the Boulevard.

The preacher decided he needed more media coverage. He called the press, TV, and radio to announce that, Sunday noon, they would march into Edwards Air Force Base to destroy the 'ungodly machine'. The media turned out in mass to support the preachers 'righteous anger'.

Edward's Security maintained a low profile. Until an actual move was made to violate the base security the local authorities had the action. So far there had been nothing more serious than littering, and with the media watching no one was going to arrest a picket for that violation.

Preacher Samuels and Slouch boarded their van at 11:30 and started the march on Edwards. They met a blockade on the roadway shortly after leaving Rosamond.

After ten minutes of talking the crowd suddenly, en mass, left the roadway and moved into the desert, bypassing the roadblock.

A pick-up rolled slowly toward Edwards from Rosamond. As it neared the demonstrators the driver blew his horn repeatedly. At the same time he began to accelerate. The demonstrators quickly spread, clearing the roadway.

The pick-up was traveling at 60 miles an hour, picking up speed, and heading directly toward the blockade. The latter was a simple set of 2 x 4's and stop signs.

"Sarge, watch that bastard!"

Sergeant Matlock glanced toward the approaching vehicle. "Wave that joker down. Can't he read! No, damn it!. Get out of the way, he isn't going to stop!"

The truck smashed into the barricades at 70 miles an hour and wood splinters flew into the air. The pickup swerved slightly, ran across a large piece of wood from the destroyed blockade.

Almost instantly the right front tire blew, the pick-up slewing to the side, raw rubber from the tire tossed into the air.

The driver lost control and the vehicle went sidewards, crashed down and bounced, then rolled. The occupant on the passenger side, a woman, was thrown out as the door swung open.

She screamed.

Her scream was cut short as she hit the asphalt, bounced upward, then landed once more sliding along the hard surface. Blood and flesh spattered the surface.

The driver rode out the trip, as the pick-up rolled over three times. The cab of the car was repeatedly smashed in. To the observers it looked as though the driver were being ping-ponged back and forth within the ever diminishing space. If he screamed it could not be heard over the sound of the disintegrating vehicle.

The Security Police quickly cleared the crowd from the immediate vicinity. As they did so the major portion of the battered vehicle burst into flames. An immediate explosion followed, and the entire vehicle flew apart, scattered widely.

Another explosion occurred quickly.

"My God, the bastard was carrying dynamite!" Sergeant Matlock growled. "Keep everyone back, there may be more."

Even as he spoke another explosion rocked the region where the pick-up's cab had been.

Sirens wailed from the direction of Rosamond and Edwards as firetrucks and emergency vehicles converged on the scene.

Samuels and Slouch were taken into custody. The news spread rapidly among the crowd, and they surrounded the security personnel, who called for reinforcements. Before the reinforcements arrived two shots rang out and two airmen were wounded.

A woman dashed, screaming and waving her arms, toward a network TV camera. "They shooting helpless demonstrators. Somebody stop them. They've killed at least a dozen. Oh, God!" She fell face down in front of the camera, beating the ground with her fists.

The TV cameras zoomed in. Reporters quickly surrounded her, eagerly recording each frenzied word. Now they were getting the good stuff!

A Security Police vehicle pulled up. The officer in charge approached. "What happened? Is she hurt?"

The woman rolled over, saw the uniform, and scrambled to her feet. She started running, screaming, "Don't let them get me. They killed my friends. He did it. He shot three of them down in cold blood, kicked them while they lay on the ground bleeding. Help me! God, help me!"

She fell to her knees, arms upraised in supplication. The crowd closed around her, angry faces directed toward the Security Police.

"Well, if she's hurt, it's from the neck up. Let's get out of here." The officer got into the car, drove once more toward the main base.

A few stones bounced off the back window, but no actual harm was done. The crowd cheered loudly.

The episode was broadcast live by the television stations, the running comments of the reporters describing the action. The terms "brutal military goons," "gestapo," and a few less acceptable words were heard from the crowds.

Major Millan worked closely with Base Security. There was little question that Preacher Samuels wanted a melee for the media. How far he would go to get the coverage was uncertain. They expected the demonstration would be non-violent, and were shocked by the death of one airman and wounding of a second.

"Tear gas. And be quick. We've got to break this up before any more killings occur. Don't worry about stragglers, but move the main body back off Federal property. We've got pictures of the man who fired those shots. Looks like he used a 30-06, Get him if at all possible, but keep in mind that he's armed and dangerous."

"There's a good chance he'll shoot some of the demonstrators." Major Millan spoke the words solemnly.

"Yeh, there is. They'll want some martyrs for the evening news."

"I'd say he'll head for a high spot where he can pick a few off without giving way his position. Better get a 'copter out there and see if we can spot him, before he does too much more damage. "How's the wounded man?"

"Not good. They're giving him blood transfusions at the hospital. Did you hear those bastards out there cheer when the two airmen were shot?"

"When you're dealing with extremists you expect it. Demonstrators hell. These are troublemakers from all over. They care less about Samuels and his campaign to stop the ship. In fact, they probably wouldn't know what you were talking about it you told them. And these are the people we're defending!"

The sniper killed three times before he was spotted. A women and two young men. He had located himself atop a mound, but had dug himself in, so that only his head and shoulders were visible. The 'copter missed him on its first pass, but on the subsequent pass a sharp-eyed observer noted his shadow. Ground personnel moved in swiftly.

Staying outside of gun range they addressed him over a loudspeaker.

"Lay down your weapon, come out with your hands high. You will not be harmed. Lay down your weapon now."

The response was a shot in the general direction of the speaker.

"Damn! Okey, call in that armored vehicle. I don't want anybody hurt taking that looney. And for God's sake, keep these kids back, before they get hurt."

The demonstrators were pressing closer, more in curiosity than to demonstrate. Another shot rang out from the hummock where the rifleman lay, and a demonstrator fell to the ground.

"Get back, get out of rifle range. He is on that sand dune, and he is shooting at you. Get back now!" The command came over the loudspeaker.

The crowd began to fall back, and the Security Police quickly went to the aid of the stricken demonstrator. As they carried him back to their station the rifleman fired again, but his shot went astray.

The armored vehicle pulled up at the station, followed quickly by an ambulance. The wounded boy was placed in the latter and it turned, drove off to the base.

"Sarge, he's up on the other side of that hummock, dug in. Can you ease around behind him. Let him see you up there, and then we'll try to get him to give up. If he doesn't, well, reckon you'll have to take him."

"No problem. What kind of weapon he got?"

"I'd say a 30-06, from the sound of it. Watch yourself. He puts a slug through that slot and it'd get your attention."

The armored vehicle rev'd up, move slowly across the open area to line up behind the hummock. Then it moved slowly toward the rifleman's position.

"Sarge, hold right there and fire a round over his head for effect. Just make sure you're shooting southwesterly. Everything's clear in that direction." The officer directed the action over his communicator.

The rifleman ducked at the shot from behind, looked over his shoulder at the armored vehicle sitting to his rear. He hunched down lower in his dugout.

"You have one minute to lay down your weapon, walk out with your hands high. Otherwise we will take whatever action is necessary."

"You now have thirty seconds."

"You have 15 seconds. Sarge, line up your cannon to blow him to smithereens."

"Hey, lieutenant, are you serious?"

"Hell no. But he doesn't know that."

"Ten seconds, mister."

He started a second-by-second countdown. At the count of three there was a loud scream from the hummock.

"Don't shoot! I'm coming out! For God's sake, don't kill me!"

"Cover him, make sure he doesn't have a weapon."

"Hold your fire. Hold your fire. All right, come out, hands over your head. Walk this way, slowly."

Cameras had captured a portion of the assassin's activity. They now followed his slow trudge to surrender.

Before, the demonstrators were charging the Air Force with random killings. Now they were in disarray, seeing the man who they were sure had shot at them taken prisoner. After it became known that pictures had been taken of his shooting spree the story changed. The assassin was only trying to defend himself from the kill-crazy military. The networks played it up, as did the radio.

---

Sondra, Milly, and Nathan worked their way down by the firing range, then along the roadway toward the flightline. They had discarded their placards. The only object they carried was a large bolt cutter. Their immediate intent—get on the flight line.

"Look, most of the action is on Rosamond Boulevard. Stay away from it, cut across Lancaster Boulevard, then straight out to the flight line. It's gonna' be easy!" Milly grinned.

"Sure! They won't expect anyone out in this area. Just watch for the Security pukes!" To them it was a lark.

It was less difficult than even they expected. The large turnout of demonstrators caused security to dispatch most of their troops to the scene of action. Those remaining were scattered, watching extensive areas. At the right moment the bolt cutter cut through the fence. They dashed for the flight line. At least they would interrupt air traffic!

Sensors along the fence line signaled Security of the breakthrough. A security vehicle roared down the perimeter road, then onto the runway in pursuit of the three figures.

"Hit him, Nate, hit him!" Milly shrilled as the Security personnel surrounded them. Nate lifted the bolt cutter to strike the nearest airman.

The sound of a rifle bolt's mechanism penetrated Milly's eager encouragement, and Nate chose to drop the bolt cutter.

Air Traffic was non-existent, as flights had been canceled during the demonstrations. The interlopers were soon driven to a holding area. Glumly they sat among others who had preceded them.

The mass of demonstrators grew ever larger. Late in the day several large pick-ups rolled on to the scene. The demonstrators leaped out, grinning, unloaded their placards. They grouped across the road from the main group. At first they seemed to plan to merge with the existing group. Then some one noted the signs.

"Preacher, Back to the Pulpit"

"Go Home, Hippie! You Ain't no Local Yokel!"

A few signs carried similar ideas in less sympathetic terms.

"Don't shove me, runt!"

"But I didn't…." His voice cut off as the big newcomer pushed him backward.

In a few minutes shoving started for real. Signs were dashed to the ground. The rednecks, though badly outnumbered, charged into the mass of demonstrators. The latter fell back then rallied and held their ground. However the relish for Reverend Samuel's cause seemed to disappear quickly, and small groups splintered from main body. The late arrivals pressed their attack. Their opponents gradually, then quickly, withdrew from the battle. Their taste wasn't for contact sports.

The number of demonstrators exploded as militant groups from across the country headed toward the Valley. There were other killings and attempted killings during the week. The Governor declared an emergency on Thursday, moved in the National Guard.

A light rain had begun to fall around Wednesday midnight. As time passed the fall became more severe, the temperature dropped, and the winds began to pick up. Soon the winds were gusting to 50 knots, and the demonstrators began seeking the shelter of their vehicles. Those who had been dispatched in special buses plodded toward Rosamond and whatever shelter they could find.

A few fires were lit, placards and supporting lumber providing the fuel. The fires burned out rapidly.

"Hey, how long's this stuff gonna' last?"

"I hear 4-5 days. Maybe a week."

"Didn't anybody say there'd be blizzards."

Grumbling and curses greeted each gust of wind, each spat of rainfall.

Heavy rains followed on Thursday morning. The demonstrators took shelter inside vehicles and under their placards. Staying power was lacking and their ranks thinned even more rapidly. By noon the National Guard was arriving, but Rosamond Boulevard was already largely clear. The guards took up positions along the route to the base, but had little to do. Nevertheless the Governor was castigated for unleashing the military on a small group of peaceful demonstrators. The politicians throughout the nation lashed out in anger at his 'dictatorial' imposition on the people's right to demonstrate.

Two of the wounded died on Friday. Another on Saturday.

One broadcast group reported the facts.

"Some members of the demonstration fired weapons. Not at the military, but at others in the group. Only the quick response of the Security Personnel prevented further bloodshed."

"Coverup!"

"Plant!"

The screams were immediate. But as people listened and compared notes a swell of anger rose. The politicians who had attacked the governor and castigated the Air Force found themselves on the defensive. The extremists who whined for 'justice' and court martial of the base commander found themselves without media coverage.

A few well-known Senators attempted to make political hay from the demonstration, but even they had softened their remarks.

Facts have an amazing ability to silence bombast.

Preacher Samuels' demonstration was over.

Nevertheless, some damage had been done. Power lines leading to the base had been cut, portions of the roadway dynamited. Airman Carter, who had taken the first shot, would never walk again.

The only charge pressed against the preacher was leading an unlawful assembly. He was convicted, given a sentence of three years in prison. A review by higher court did not reject the conviction, but ruled that the sentence was excessive. It was modified to require six months of public service.

Slouch gazed silently at the hospital ceiling. Struck down by the first round from the sniper's gun, early in the demonstrations, he had remained hospitalized for three day. At first there had been little hope. The bullet had entered the upper back, been deflected downward by a rib, and exited in a massive wound of the stomach. The ugly mix of yellow fat, red blood, and torn flesh horrified Slouch even more than did the pain. He had been taken quickly to the base hospital emergency room, then quickly to the operating room.

They were able to sew up portions of the wound, but the damage caused by the exiting bullet was too great. They kept the wound clean, but left it to heal from the inside. Slouch shuddered whenever the bandage was removed. Yet he could not help but look.

"It ain't right! I weren't bothering no one. And now look at me! How could the Good Lord do this. It just ain't right."

The fourth day the nurse found him, lying on the floor. He spoke some incoherent words before he died. They sounded like, "It just ain't right!"

The nurse wasn't sure.

Preacher Samuels conducted the funeral rites. "He lies low now. But he shall stand tall before the Lord. And those who brought him to this state shall face retribution." Tears ran down his cheek as he extolled his dead companion. "A good man, a peaceful man, he was here but to express his feelings. The uncalled for, murderous attack by the military took him from us."

He reiterated his theme. Media coverage this time was limited. Slouch didn't care.

Between Rosamond and Edwards the scars of war remained. Vehicles that had barely reached the area had been deserted where they stopped. Discarded placards, blown across the desert floor, stood out in sharp contrast to the brown surroundings. Hitchhikers lined the on-ramp at highway 14, heading home to await the next demonstration.

The local jails gradually disgorged their occupants as parents reluctantly provided bail or fines for their offspring.

Preacher Samuels extorted his followers to continue their efforts, and expounded on the evils of the government, the military, and anyone who wasn't present in his church.

"They shot our people, they beat us with clubs—only God knows how many lie dead out there on the desert!" He shook his head sadly.

"Brethren, there is evil loose in our land. Satan and his minions have prevailed. But our time will come."

"Yea, verily, I tell you—These evil-doers shall feel the wrath of the Lord. He shall bring his might against them, and they will fall and die and suffer in the depths of hell. Amen!"

"Let us now pray."

A congressional investigation was called for, and several congressmen arrived at the base, the press well-alerted to capture their arrival. They implied that the base commander would, at a minimum, be subject to courts martial. They abhorred the arrest of the alleged gunman, a man merely trying to defend himself from the "military gestapo".

After being shown videos of the riot, of the gunman methodically killing his victims, and of his capture the group left quietly. They had received the desired media exposure. None bothered to retract earlier statements. It would not have been politically wise.

# Dr. Volte's Flight

Dr. Volte was now convinced that he was closing in on an explanation to the Dreamship syndrome, as he aptly named it. Hopefully, with this morning's session, he would be able to tie down the remaining loose ends.

As usual, when first plugging in the skull cap, he felt confused, bewildered. Fortunately, with each additional session, the duration became shorter.

He was used to the routines now. Almost casually he went through power on. All systems were coming in nominal, all controls accepted his input, kicked back normal feedback. He relaxed, waiting, knowing that momentarily the images would return.

Suddenly his eyes widened. He was not following the power down routine! He had waited for ten minutes, but no images had appeared. It was unexpected, and strangely irritating. "Stood up," he thought! "And by a blind witch!"

He had started the power down, ready to conclude the session. Everything went smoothly, and then his mind had wandered. For whatever reason it was driving the system back to normal operations, not power off. With a silent curse he started the sequence once more. But no, it was not power down. A chill centered in his back, spread up and down, and he took in a deep breath. A feeling of dread encompassed him. Damn it, he was cutting power!

The images were starting to form. This time they were different. There was an animal—perhaps a rabbit. And the birds were tearing at it, tearing off slivers of meat. Ravens, black ravens—except one. They moved aside as she approached.

He shook his head. She was looking at him, the raw meat in her bill with blood dripping from its ragged surface. Her eyes were bright, too bright. And glowing. The vision shimmered, disappeared, yet stayed with him.

Damn it, he was re-initiating the power on sequence. The sensors were re-activated. Signals were being fed in. The control lines were now active. His distraction with the images! He had to power down! He activated the comm system. "Open the hangar doors."

The voice was his. The words were not.

He attempted once more to pursue the power down sequence. He was confused, tired. She was there, lying beside him. She would run the ship. Now he could rest. She would run the ship…?

"No, God, no!"

He moved his hand to actuate the emergency power off. He felt the arm rise, the fingers seize the switch. He flicked it. Nothing! His arm was numb, useless. He again visualized the sequence. Again his arm did not respond. He felt cold, yet sweat dripped from his forehead, into his eyes, over his lips.

Chief Master Sergeant Howard heard the direction, and his eyes widened. "Doc, we got no authority to do that. You are to be allowed to make run-ups here. That's all!"

"Sergeant, you'll open the damn doors, or I'll plow through them!" The voice was strange, emotionless, that of an Automaton. "And patch me into all conversations."

"Get Jim on the phone. Tell him it's an emergency!"

"Doc, listen, it's going to take a few minutes. The hydraulic pressure is low, the pumps have been turned off. For God's sake, give me a little time!"

"You have three minutes, sergeant. Then I'm rolling. Do you understand? Three minutes!" He ended with a snarl.

"Jim, it's Doc Volte. He wants to taxi out of the hangar. I have no authority to allow it. He swears he'll smash through the doors!"

"Keep talking to him! I'm on my way. But don't let him smash the airplane. Even if you have to let him taxi, do it. He's no pilot. He can't get her off the ground."

As the hangar doors opened he goosed the throttle, rolled smoothly out on the tarmac. Without stopping he moved toward the apron, ran through the checklist on the way.

Jim Braddock was talking on the comm line. He sounded frightened. Dr. Volte smiled. Well might he be frightened. This plane belongs to me. To me and the blind witch!

"Dr. Volte, power down. You don't know how to fly it. Get out of there now, Doc. Whatever it is, it's got a hold on you. Damn it, power down and get out!"

Dr Volte was silent. The ship was lined up with the runway. Mentally he gave her full throttle. The engines roared. All sensors were go. Swiftly, smoothly she rolled down the runway, rotated, climbed gently into the air.

Faster now and faster she drove the ship. Nosing it upward she climbed for the stars. How quickly she reached the limits of her low level mode, and how smoothly she switched to scramjet. How beautiful was the world seen through her sensors. It had been so long since she had seen light, seen colors—ah, how beautiful.

She could fly now without help of the obedient flock. Faster and higher than she had ever flown. Like a dream, to escape from that tired, blind body and live. The master would wait! For now she was free. Soon she would return, once more maintain her vigil. But for now, freedom she had never known!

Dr. Volte moaned. Power down, I must power down. Again he projected the orders. This time the system responded. But the sensors! My God! I'm at altitude! Quickly, frenziedly, he began the power up sequence.

She's wobbling. The sensors screamed it in his head. She's loosing altitude, they screamed. She's not responding to power on. She's in a dive! Pull up! Pull up! Help me!

Finally, at the last moment, power returned. Slowly, carefully, he brought the ship to straight and level. The G forces were severe. A little more and the wings would have buckled.

Now! I must finish it now!

But even as the thought went through his mind he felt her presence. He cringed as she enveloped him, took over operation of the aircraft. With an effort he forced her from his mind, drove the ship toward its inevitable target.

Oh, God! The pain! The burning pain. Pressure rose in his temples, his skull. His neck ached in a way he had never known, and each movement of his head caused bones to rub, to grind. She was tearing at his mind, sending pictures of torment, hideous pictures he did not understand, but merely felt.

Then he saw. The sensors fed him the scene far below. The deserted road, the huge stone, the grim visage of the sleeping giant!

He wept. Must it end like this! There must be another way!

Even as the thoughts came to mind she fed him new visions. Visions of sunny fields, of forests and lakes, visions of wide oceans and sandy shores, of beautiful women—of power. Of power over man and world!

He sighed, felt a tear trickle from his eye. Dully, reluctantly, he forced it away. He brought the engines to full power, dropped the nose, and begin the steep descent.

How quickly the target was approaching! Deadly, unswervingly the craft maintained its course. It would soon be over. The curse would be lifted. He would end this for once and all.

A tremendous explosion! And fire! Fire everywhere, enveloping him! Burning hair and flesh and pain beyond comprehension! She fed the picture into his mind. Torments beyond anything he had ever known.

And then it ceased.

The vision of the verdant valley, the forests, the flowing rivers and the placid blue lakes. Oceans and islands—Power! All for the taking!

Turn the ship! Turn the ship now. Choose—the fires for eternity or all the sweets of the world! Turn now! Turn now!

No! He locked the ship on target. The lot indeed was cast. Explosion, fire, pain—but it would end. There would be peace. There had to be peace!

Her face loomed large in his vision, the hate and venom flashing from her eyes.

No peace for you! No peace…No…Ah, peace!

Now! Dead ahead! Looming larger and larger. He swooned even as the ship reached its foreordained target. The sleeping giant!

CMS Howard looked at his watch. He stepped over to the comm line. "Hey, Doc, shut her down. We've got to run through some tests here, and the men are breaking after that."

He frowned when he received no reply. "Doc, your comm line okey? Do you read me?"

Finally he put down the mike, scowled at it, and walked over to the ladder. Climbing, he opened the compartment slot. "Doc, sorry, the comm line's down. You got to shut her down. We…"

He paused, looked carefully at Dr. Volte's wide, unseeing eyes. Then he jerked backed, closed his eyes for a moment, looked cautiously within. He shook his head. Strange! He could have sworn he saw something else in the cockpit, a strange white mist. With a deep breath he slid down the ladder, placed a call to emergency services.

# The Volte Papers

Jim Braddock had impounded Dr. Volte's logs and notes. He decided that Colonel Goetler, as well as himself, should read them. They sat before the fireplace, the cardtable between them. Dr. Volte's notes lay on the table.

"I'll kick off, Colonel. I think we can work this best together."

Colonel Goetler nodded, lit his pipe.

Jim laid aside the title page. It read, whimsically perhaps, "TALES OF THE BLIND WITCH".

Jim read slowly, with each page his uncertainty growing. Either the Doctor was going mad, was on drugs, or—he didn't like to even consider the final alternative.

The initial pages contained routine material. Notes on the various routines common to powering up the dreamship. Notes on physiological and mental exercises necessary to build up the proper mental conditions.

"I really don't see much unusual here, Jim."

"Nor I, Colonel. Let's proceed."

Later pages had short, unconnected comments that presaged other matters. Over time these comments began to dominate the logs.

The initial sections were generalities, grasping after straws. By the third section patterns were beginning to emerge.

Dr. Volte had spent some limited time examining material on the witch phenomenon of Salem. His interest was not on the rather grisly description of the burning of the witches, but on the evidence of their alleged powers. Numerous sources were cited, several annotated with numeric codes. Jim interpreted these as assigning level of validity to the instances.

Three were noted as being highly reliable and validated. He turned to extracts from those citations. A chill touched him as he noted one consistent entry. Of the three whose powers were validated none were burned at the stake. They survived!

Dr. Volte's notes had three capital letters. WHY.

Section 4 addressed the peoples of the valley and their beliefs. Records and viable source data were limited. The key information was from descendants, and from those who had known the ancient ones. The reticent nature, the strange rites, and the belief in a brooding night demon dominated their pagan religion. The myth of the giant and the legend of a one-time green and verdant valley was the earliest account. A vague, uncertain record, passed from generation to generation, of rejection of that myth. A hint of a strange curse, on the valley and its inhabitants. Then an ominous foreboding, a tribal fear. Return of the land to a drear and desolate waste—and the coming of the night demon.

A few pages further treated the night demon. Dr. Volte plainly read some importance into this tale. He had highlighted some of his material. The highlights were on means of appeasing the creature of the night. Ritual dances, gifts from the dying fields—and blood sacrifices—human blood—dominated the entries.

"I hope the old boy didn't believe this gibberish. Of course, the way he ended up, maybe there's a kernel of truth in it."

Section five drew parallels between the ancient night demon and the more recent incidents that he tagged, Tales of the Blind Witch. There were uncomfortable similarities. In both cases the creature was designated 'she'. At first only known through dreams, dreams that began with the creature far away, hidden, foreboding. These dreams became ever more real to the victim, ever more specific in depiction of the fearsome object. And, in both cases, eventually the dreams transcended sleep. The companion became real, even in the desert sun of day—even in the interior of a modern technical masterpiece!

"You talked to him often, Jim. Couldn't you tell this problem was getting to him. I mean, it is pretty evident that he was nearing a breakdown." Colonel Goetler shook his head. "Well, go on."

Section six rambled. Dr. Volte was, for lack of a better term, brainstorming. He surfaced possible approaches to resolving the problem facing the Dreamship program. Acceptance of the blind witch as real, and appeasing her with the tokens practiced by the ancients. Use of mindbending drugs to compensate for the psychotic state of those who saw her. Lobotomy of the brain. Shock therapy to drive out the strange hallucination. Bringing the descendants of the ancients into the program as intermediaries between modern man and these ancient spirits. On and on he pursued concepts that came to mind. They were extensive, filling two dozen pages.

"He gets rather grisly in some of this material. You'd almost think he was ready for blood sacrifices, using the Dreamship as the altar for execution!"

Section seven was incomplete. It began by evaluating each of the concepts in section six. This was dropped in the middle of a statement. On a new page he had written.

I have the answer. I will eliminate the cause, and that will eliminate the phenomenon. The sleeping giant! Tomorrow it will be finished!

That was all. He did not spell out his idea, did not expand on his solution.

The last entry was dated the day before his death.

Jim shook his head.

"Colonel, I do not believe we should release this document."

"No, Jim, there is nothing to be gained. And it would destroy the old boy's reputation. I'd say burn it. Right now."

They crumbled the pages, one by one, fed them to the flames in the fireplace. The title page uncrumbled, burned slowly, as they once more read the words.

---

Jim and Linda sat quietly at the dining room table. Jim took disinterested bites at the chicken, ate a spoonful of mashed potatoes and gravy.

"Where did you learn to cook! You know I can't stand this stuff. Why don't I have some coffee?"

He rose, walked to the front room. "You loaf around this house all day. The least you can do is cook me a decent meal when I get home. I said, where is my coffee!"

He glared at her, and she brought a cup of coffee, setting it on the tray beside his chair.

He picked up the cup, spilled the hot liquid on his pant's leg. "Damn you! Why did you fill it so full! Look at these pants. Get me a towel. Hurry up, will you! My God, and I could have had Teddy!"

"And bring me my wine bottle!"

---

Dismantlement of Dreamship Three proceeded without significant incident. Interfaces were examined, black boxes were tested, fiber optic lines measured and remeasured. Signals were fed through the mux lines. Suspected anomalies were analyzed.

Day after day the tear down continued. Records were kept in detail, as though they were giving thought to reverse engineering the entire aircraft.

The team of engineers, physicists, programmers, and psychologists reviewed the mass of accumulated data. There were no patterns, no indicators. They concluded that operation should have been nominal.

Not satisfied, congress assembled a second team of experts. Few were engineers in a true sense. The Lysenko Science Syndrome, as the older engineers had termed it, had replaced objective methodical engineering work in many of the universities and colleges. Politically correct engineering solutions took precedence over science and objectivity.

In a short time the eager reviewers completed their studies. They, too, returned the verdict. But their view differed. The extensive exposure to environmentally dangerous materials, they explained, were primary contributors to the aircraft's problems. The anomalies were plainly the result of dangerous, outmoded, engineering approaches.

The newspapers found the latter conclusions more to their liking. The report was highlighted, along with the headlines on a more formal formation of the now renamed Greater China Prosperity League, consisting of Red China, Greater Iran, and lesser entities which had eagerly embraced the concept.

---

A lonely road branches off Highway 58, aims generally in the direction of California City. Midway along the road, to the drivers left, is a huge boulder. As one approaches it, at a certain place along the roadway, the structure of a face appears to be chiseled on its surface. It looks as though a giant lay down to sleep, and the desert sands enveloped him, leaving only his head above to rest on earth's bosom.

Of day, a large flock of ravens gather round, foraging for food in the drifting sand. Though they venture near, none perch on that enormous head. When approached they rise quickly into the sky, returning when danger is past.

Of night, they are gone. But perched on a brown branch of a tortured Joshua tree one may see still a raven. Not black, but a rare albino, with the look and awkward movement of age the white specter waits silently. With unseeing eyes she scans the empty desert. She waits for the rumble that tells her the earth is moving, she waits for the release of the lake demon. And when it comes she will arouse her master, and the great battle shall be met.

# On The Drawing Board

Senator Grubbing spoke slowly, weighing each word. "Gentlemen, we've lost three ships in this series. Four men have died because of her, and one has suffered an even worse fate. We have had an elite group of our more respected engineering community examine in detail the third ship. They have concluded that the use of materials and fuels of extremely environmentally dangerous substances has been a primary contributor to the problems incurred by the pilots. I am not superstitious, but there is an aura of evil around this plane. I recommend to this committee that the program be terminated."

The committee members sat silently, each considering the recommendation. Finally Senator Peters rose. "Let's give it a little more thought. Table it until tomorrow, then we can make a decision. There's a lot of money tied up in the program, and a lot more future expenditure. Loss of this program could badly hurt the economy of my state, and of yours."

The morning edition of The Daily Press had two major banners. One treated major world events. The other, on page two, major local events. The inner banner announced the death of Senator Grubbing. In the words of the reporter:

"Senator Grubbing, a youthful 53, died during the night from a massive heart attack. The emergency crew noted that death must not have been instantaneous, as his face held a look of horror—as though he knew full well the nature of his attack."

"No member of his family had a record of heart problems. Nor did he have a record of any related health problems. The family doctor refused to answer questions relating to the sudden deadly attack."

"Senator Grubbing has been the primary opponent of the controversial Dream Ship Program. With his passing the hearings on this activity will be delayed, or terminated."

Both banners combined to create a furor among the members of the committee. The banner reflecting Senator Grubbings death. And the front page banner, reflecting Red China's massing of troops, warships, aircraft, and nuclear weapons on the coast opposite Japan.

Advocates of the Dream Ship cited the implications of the military build up.

"It is evident that, by threat or by violence, the communists intend to seize Japan. We cannot, will not, stand by and countenance such a takeover." Senator Peters voice was angry.

"And we cannot drop development of our most advanced weapons when such potential enemies not only exist, but are rattling arms at the doorsteps of our friends. Dreamship development must be brought to culmination. Failure to continue is, to be blunt, capitulation to our most dangerous adversary."

The immediate response was much the standard line. Senator Bates stood in for his dead colleague. "The communists are being misjudged. The administration has a phobia, and supports dictators throughout the world. The communists are only acting in behalf of the poor, enslaved peoples of the world. The Red Chinese mean no harm to the people of Japan. They merely are pressing to remove their dictatorial leaders."

The meeting was interrupted by a page, who handed the committee chairman a note. He read it carefully, looked around the room, reread the message.

"Gentlemen, two nuclear bombs have been detonated on Japan by Red China. It is estimated that they had the power of 50 of the most potent of the World War II nuclear weapons. Death toll is unknown. The

President has placed the military on alert. He will be making an address to the Joint House in half an hour. Japan, at this point has chosen not to retaliate, as The Greater China Prosperity League has stated that any military response will result in a blitzkrieg of nuclear weapons."

Senator Peters stood up. "As you were saying, Senator Bates?"

The opposition was silent, recognizing themselves the possibility of world events beyond their control. The steady determined fight previously spearheaded by Senator Grubbings was left without a leader. The committee approved quickly continued development of the Dreamship series. The committee broke up to attend the joint session.

Senator Peters quickly navigated a bill through the Senate in support of extending the program. There was no organized resistance.

With the President's announcement that any further attacks on Japan would be interpreted as an attack on the United States the Red Chinese held their position on the mainland. The President interjected at several point in his speech the threat of dispatch of the entire dreamship armada. The cards he held were worthless. Did the enemy know that?

There was rapid movement of the Chinese army. They were scattering their forces to preclude complete destruction by a single strike. The main force was drawn back from the coastline, dispersed inland. For the moment, at least, the President's hand was not being called.

Japan was left to recover as well as it could from the unprovoked attack. The Red Cross called for world wide aid. Red China stated that any craft entering or leaving Japan would be considered hostile, and would be destroyed.

Congress busily rattled dull sabres, promoted build up in defensive forces, and postured for the adulation of their followers.

The thunderclouds built up in the later afternoon. Above the Tehachapis huge lenticulars formed, their size presaging deadly updrafts beneath their lens-shaped mass. At times the larger cumulonimbus buildups would glow as lightning played within them. The thunder was a dull rumble, and no rain fell.

Old timers at The Shed sniffed at the oppressive air. "Too hot, too humid, and too quite. Don't like it! Damn earthquake weather."

The others nodded in silent assent.

After midnight the storm struck. Heavy gusting winds whipped up the sand, and pelting rain drove it back to earth. The lightning marched along the desert's edge. Intermittent thunder wakened man and beast. The very fury of the storm soon used up its store of energy, and only a light but steady rain remained.

The earthquake followed near three o'clock. The first jolt was mild. Houses shook, dishes rattled, and dogs barked grumpily. Those awakened lay quietly, thinking. Should I get up, or is that all!

It wasn't.

The followup was a rolling, undulating wave. It shook the houses from side to side, up and down. It seemed to subside, then a second and stronger wave followed. The third and last wave was mild.

Cracked walls, cracked windows, and crack concrete were the major damage. One man was cut by falling glass. There were no other reported injuries.

Devil's Lake was drained. Only muck and small pools of muddy water remained. An odor of rotting vegetation and burning sulfur combined to discourage any detailed survey. Intermittent clouds of brimstone smelling smoke issued from fissures in the bottom. Miles away, on a lonely desert road, a huge stone had disappeared. Swallowed, perhaps, by the desert sands as the earth shook around it. An ominous silence fell over the valley as the sun rose. The retreating clouds were visible on the horizon. Flocks of raven wheeled high overhead.

Madam Sheba took no customers on this day. "There is something evil loose. I will read no palms this day. Today my doors are locked. Tomorrow, God willing, I will tell your fortune. If tomorrow comes."

Throughout the day the air weighed down. "Hot and humid. That rain shoulda cooled it off. Strange weather for these times."

The thunderheads rose grim and foreboding above Red Rock Canyon. Though the wind blew in strong gusts near the earth, they held their positions. Lightning flashed from cloud to cloud, from cloud to ground.

At times the clouds seemed to reach the ground, and sand and dust reached upward. A roar filled the air, as though a tornado was approaching, then faded away. The desert creatures dug into burrows, hid in their lairs.

The storm burst without warning. Sheets of water fell, and gullies and ravines were rapidly filled with running streams. The roar of the wind, the thunder, and the rushing water united to form a continuous bedlam.

In the midst of a ravine a huge boulder lay, blocking the building stream. Carved by wind and water, a semblance of a face marked its surface.

The clouds formed and reformed, always centered near the blocked ravine. The lightning dashed downward, and the bolts seemed to explode. Within the clouds the form of a winged creature was outlined for a moment, then disappeared.

The unusual weather continued on into the night.

With sunrise the clouds had dissipated. The region was silent, and even the flowing streams from the storm had melted into the earth. The huge boulder, too, was gone.

Preacher Samuels sat in his office, wide-eyed. The earthquake had done no significant damage. His choir books, a few tracts were disturbed. The desk was slightly askew. A crack ran down the length of the window, but the pane remained in place.

The cross had been jolted from the wall. He stood up, picked it up carefully, started to replace it. For a moment he seemed confused. He looked at the nail, still firmly in place, then at the cross, at the hole through which the nail would extend.

The hole was easily wide enough for the shaft of the nail to slip through. But not wide enough for the head to pass through. And the head was still on the nail. He placed the cross on his desk, pulled at the nail. It remained firmly in place.

Again he sat down, stared morosely at the cross. A thought crossed his mind, and his mouth dropped open. He stood up, turned very slowly, looked for something on the wall. Something in the space beneath the cross's position. Breathing slowly, eyes wide, he let his hand brush across the wall. Then he examined the floor in the immediate area. He got down on one knee, ran his hand under the desk.

Wordless he stood up, backed out the door, slammed it behind him.

———————

"Jim, Jim! I'm glad it's over. It's as though the clouds had lifted, the sun broke through. Since we lost Andy…the first flight…I have been so afraid of this program. Senator Grubbings has recommended terminating the program. And I thank God!"

She put her arms around his neck, pressed herself close to him.

"Do you remember the night of the first flight party. When John was introducing Major Nestor to Pat. John was drunk—I had never seen him drunk before. And he said…Oh, how did he say it!"

Jim Braddock looked at her, at the tears trickling down her cheek, and held her close, as they both remembered.

"Welcome, Major Nestor, to the puppet show. We are the puppets…And she, and I drink to the damnation of her soul!" He lifted his glass on high, quickly finished off the contents.

"And she, that huge black witch in the hangar, is the puppet master." He laughed, looking around to see the others join in the laughter. There was only silence.

The wail of the wind, which she normally ignored, now seemed to embrace her. It rose, then fell, only to rise again in a senseless but never ending pattern. In the distance she sensed, rather than heard, the yip-yipping of a coyote. She glanced out the window.

There, on the Joshua tree, the white raven perched, head tilted as though listening. It preened itself, spread its wings, then settled down, as though for a long stay. Its feathers were ruffled by the gusting wind. But above the wind she heard Jim's words—words that seemed, at first, meaningless.

And then their meaning struck her!

She stared at him, wide-eyed, unbelieving of what she heard.

"Linda, Linda, I am sorry."

"This has been a strain on all of us. We need a vacation, you and I. This damn program has been a load on the minds of each of us."

"Senator Grubbings died last night. This morning the committee decided to continue the program."

Her eyes widened, face paled, and she gasped.

"Dream Ship Three is gone," he spoke musingly, then paused.

"But we must bear up. Indeed, Dream Ship Three is gone."

"But, on the drawing boards…"

She noted with mounting fear the fanatic gleam in his eyes, the rising fervor in his voice.

His voice deepened in timbre. At first he had spoken softly, almost reverently. But now his eyes gleamed as though he were seeing an inner vision, and his voice rose in volume.

"Dream Ship Four!"

# About the Author

Adjunct Instructor (Webster University, Communication and Technology), System Engineer, Author of numerous articles and books, both fiction and non-fiction.